Perfe

Jeff Spencer set the mug on the ground and eyed the intruder, listening to Slade's account of how he'd captured this Will Barber riding a sorrel mare toward camp. How the boy was packing a shotgun. How he had asked for Captain Spencer by name.

Jeff had never met Barber before, otherwise, he'd remember. The boy's clear green eyes glistened with excitement, or maybe fear. The kid clutched a floppy slouch hat in both hands. His wavy light brown hair was badly chopped.

"How do you know me, Will?"

"I stopped at a farmhouse for directions." The boy shrugged, nervous, darting his eyes about. "A man there told me which way your troop was headed."

"Randall, I bet. That old drunk. I'm surprised he was sober enough to remember my name." Jeff looked at the picket. "Why is he beat up, Slade? Did he resist arrest?"

"No, sir. He came in that a-way."

"Very well," Jeff said. "Go back to your post."

"Yes sir."

Jeff returned Slade's parting salute, then turned back to the boy. "You been in a scrape?"

"Branch caught me in the dark, sir."

"Must've been some wicked branch. Got in plenty of licks." He lifted an eyebrow. "How come you happened to blunder into our picket line? It's hardly even daylight."

Will looked him in the eye this time, but his fingers picked at the floppy hat-brim. "I want to volunteer, sir. Join the cavalry."

Jeff ran his fingers along his own stubbly jaw line, noting the boy's fine cheeks. "How old are you?"

"Eighteen, sir."

"If you're under sixteen, you better join the home guard instead. They take little boys."

"Sir, I am not a little boy. I'm old enough."

"Your voice hasn't even started to change. If you're eighteen, I'm Abe Lincoln."

Will's jaw tightened. "Then I guess you're Abe Lincoln, sir."

Lydia Hawke has penned another winner with *Perfect Disguise*. Her three dimensional characters, vivid Civil War setting and intricate plot will fill a voracious reader's need for entertainment. The developing romance between Willa and Jeff will tug at your heart strings in hope of the elusive happy ending.

—Carol McPhee-Wings ePress author of *Something About That Lady*, *Undercover Trouble*, *Be Still, My Heart!* and *Means To An End*

Set in Civil War Era Georgia during the Siege of Atlanta, Lydia Hawke's historical romance, *Perfect Disguise*, is a perfect blend of high adventure and tender romance, crammed with authentic historical details that keep the reader steadily involved in the action.

Graphic details of life and death in battle are interspersed with poignant passages that trace the growing love between Willa and Captain Spencer, two wounded people who seem more afraid of getting hurt again than they are of the treacherous Yankees.

So cleverly has Ms. Hawke suspended disbelief that by the end of *Perfect Disguise* the reader will believe that once a young female rode with the Confederate Cavalry because life gave her no other choice, and that she made a contribution to the Cause, while striving to win the heart of her dashing captain. *Perfect Disguise* is a definite Five Star book.

—Dorothy Bodoin, author of *Winter's Tale*, *Shortcut Through the Shadows*, (Wings Press) and *Darkness at Foxglove Corners* (Five Star Press)

Lydia Hawke is at it again. Beware! If you start to read *Perfect Disguise* at bedtime, you will be reading all night. You won't be able to put it down. Perfect Disguise combines the excitement of an action novel with the poignancy of a romance.

Like her previous epic, *Firetrail*, this book plunges you into the latter days of the Civil War. This time Ms. Hawke tosses you right into the desperate Southern attempt to stop Sherman before Atlanta falls. Her characters and plot rival *Gone With the Wind* but there are differences. Willa is not your typical southern belle. Oh, no. No keeping the home fires burning for this gal. She gets right into the heart of the action. She runs away and joins a unit of Wheeler's Calvary. Of course she needs to pass for a boy and endure the rough camp life. That doesn't faze this heroine. What does cause her a lot of grief is that she falls in love with her dashing but already heartbroken captain.

Add to the mix, a vicious killer intent on making Willa his bride no matter who he has to murder to do it, a group of unique Rebel soldiers, one fighting rooster, a spirited horse and enough Yankee troops to keep everyone on the edge of their seats.

Things really heat up when the virile captain begins having romantic thoughts about his new aide, "Will." You can imagine his discomfort. Or maybe you can't. You'll just have to read this one of a kind book.

—Kathleen Walls, author of *Last Step, Georgia's Ghostly Getaways, Kudzu, Man Hunt - The Eric Rudolph Story* and *Finding Florida's Phantoms* (all Global Authors Publications)

Perfect Disguise

Julian

Enjoy the
adventure!

Lydia Hanke

Perfect Disguise
©Lydia Filzen 2005

ISBN: 0-9766449-0-8
Library of Congress Control Number: 2005921899

Published by

Global Authors Publications

Filling the GAP in publishing

Edited by Kathleen Walls
Cover Design by Christine Poe
Interior Design by Kathleen Walls

Printed in USA for Global Authors Publications

Perfect Disguise

Lydia Hawke

DEDICATION:

To my patient husband Larry,
my supportive mother Marilyn King,
my encouraging daughter Jennifer,

and critique partners
Judy Dobrie, Ted Stetson, Carol McPhee,
Carla Hughes, Mary Veele, Tim Conroy,
and the late Clyde Rogers.

Chapter One

Southeast of Atlanta and South of Covington, Georgia
July 29, 1864, during Siege of Atlanta

Protected by darkness, Willa Randall knelt by the stream and washed the dried blood and tears off her face. The hem of her skirt trailed in the water but that didn't matter because she had to discard the dress anyway. She rinsed the taste of blood out of her mouth; even the silt-laden water was an improvement. Feeling cleaner, she blotted her split lips and wiped her hands with a dry patch of skirt, blew her nose, then stood and picked her way through the underbrush to where she had tethered her mare.

She ran her hand down the saddle, reassuring herself that the shotgun was still strapped on. Past the weapon, close to Annie Laurie's rump, she found the hastily tied sewing kit. It was one of the few possessions she had managed to snatch as she fled. She whispered gentling talk to Annie and thrust her hand inside the bag, gripped the scissors and pulled them out.

She'd often trimmed her own hair but had never cut it short, certainly not in the dark without a looking glass. But it had to be done, and done immediately, so she would be prepared when she caught up with the soldiers. Although she had left Pa and Edgar senseless, she still feared they would come looking for her. Telling herself they couldn't possibly follow her so soon, she nonetheless peered into the dark to make sure she really was alone. She took off the slouch hat and let her hair fall about her shoulders. Her scissor hand trembled as she lifted up each lock and cut it close to her head, trying to shape it in a neat boyish pattern. She dropped the clumps of hair to the ground and kicked leaves and dirt over them. She must make sure that come daylight, the sun wouldn't shine on the evidence of her plan. Freed from the bulk of her hair, the hat fit looser on her head.

She located the shirt, trousers, old chemise and boots she had tied onto the saddle. Quickly she stripped off her dress and arranged the chemise in a tight fit around her chest, flattening her breasts. She threw on her brother's clothes and inhaled deeply, wishing she could catch his scent or something of his being within the hug of denim and homespun, but the only place he still existed for her was in her memory. She didn't fill his clothes, but she figured that wouldn't matter because most people wore what they could get their hands on these days, whether it fit or not.

She needed a man's name. It occurred to her that "Will" ought to be familiar enough for her ears to lend a quick response. Barber seemed fitting for a last name, the one that had occurred to her as she cut her hair. She said her man's name out loud. "Will Barber." It sounded all right, a name she could live with. She repeated it louder, trying to deepen her voice, and that took some of the shakiness out of it. Her natural voice didn't sound masculine enough, another worry.

Willa rolled the dress into a bundle and mashed it down as small as she could. She hid it under a bush, praying her hand didn't scare up a snake. She traded her shoes for the boots Bobby had grown out of and hid hers. She listened again for sounds of pursuit.

The woods were quiet except for small hushed noises and the occasional night bird. Willa untied Annie from the branch, mounted, and continued her own pursuit of the soldiers who had come foraging to her home that afternoon.

***

The blow came out of nowhere. The next thing she knew Willa was lying on her back staring at pinpoint colors of pain. The bright flashes faded and her vision slowly cleared. She looked through the leaves at the moon-bright sky, and spotted the low-hanging limb that had clobbered her. The roaring in her ears gradually subsided, and she heard a hoot owl calling from deep in the woods.

She nerved herself up to touch the hurt place on her forehead. It felt damp, barked, and raw, another hurt added to the ones Edgar Dodds had given her. She ran her fingers down her battered cheek to her mouth and found the earlier injuries numb and puffy.

But the deepest pain throbbed in her heart. How could Pa give her away to that vile man? Her own father cared more for his whiskey than for his daughter, and nothing Edgar did to her would have changed that. Had she been unable to leave, and once Pa found out what had happened while he lay in his drunken stupor, he'd treat her like he usually did. He'd tell her to wash her face and quit complaining, wouldn't see a thing wrong with hitting a woman or trying to force himself on her. Bobby wasn't around to defend her any more since the Yankees had killed him, and she realized nobody else was willing to side with her against her own Pa. What choice did she have but to run away?

Even her horse had deserted her, leaving her stuck in these woods.

Lord, it was lonesome out here. It seemed no longer a refuge but a menacing dark place where evil seemed to lurk in every shadow. Still, home wasn't any safer, not with Edgar waiting there. What would he do next? Kill her for fighting him off and knocking him out with a whiskey jug?

She shuddered, then shook off the terror. *Don't panic*. Which way did Annie go? *Think.* It wasn't easy. Her thoughts were a sticky mess of cobwebs. Perhaps she should try to consider one problem at a time. First, find the mare.

Willa elbowed herself up, got to her feet and stood swaying, dizzy and sick to her stomach. "Annie," she whispered, afraid as ever to raise her voice in case Edgar was chasing her, wanting to finish what he'd started. The moonlight let her make out the dirt trail. But it was torn up from many hooves. Which set belonged to Annie? It was impossible to tell.

She blinked back tears and rubbed the new sore place where her hip had struck the ground. She hurt all over and it didn't matter which bruises resulted from the beating or from the fall. At least she hadn't broken any bones. She started walking, stiffly at first, following the trail nearest the west bank of the river. She hoped the kinks would work out after awhile.

Fortunately the cavalry troop was easy to track by the violence it had done the road. How far could the soldiers have gone since they left her place? Probably miles and miles, if they were in a big hurry to catch those Yankees. Surely they'd had to stop for the night to rest themselves and their horses. She despaired to think that losing herself among strangers was preferable to staying with her own blood. She hoped they didn't turn out to be as mean and low as Edgar.

Instead of dwelling on such grim possibilities, she recalled the troop's captain. The fine looking man showed restraint, refusing to get riled even when Pa as much as called him a horse thief. True enough, the troopers did help themselves to provisions, and probably would have taken the Randall horses had they not been hidden in a paddock away from the house. But she didn't begrudge the soldiers a little corn. They and their skinny horses looked hungry.

The captain didn't see Willa because she was hiding in the house at Pa's insistence. Wasn't it just like Pa, to protect her from a decent man so he could throw her to a mean and low creature like Edgar? She'd so wanted to meet the captain, but had to content herself with peeking through the curtains at him. He reminded her of her brother Bobby, not in looks but in some other way she couldn't name. Maybe it was how he disregarded Pa and his drunken threats with a kind of wry humor that showed him to be the better man.

She would get to meet him after all, provided she could find her horse and catch up. It was a good thing the soldiers hadn't seen her in the house. Captain Spencer would be less likely to recognize her as a girl, though she feared he'd see through her disguise.

Bobby's boots were meant for riding, not walking, and they felt awkward on her feet. She raised the hat and fluffed the short hair on the back of her head, missing the weight. The fabric she'd bound around her chest vexed her, but she'd have to get used to it.

Movement and a sound up ahead. *Chuff, chuff, chuff.* She slid behind a tree and stared into the darkness. Who was coming? To stop her trembling, she tucked her hands under her armpits.

A horse plodded toward her along the trail, riderless but saddled. Annie!

Willa let out her breath and laughed, though smiling hurt her face. Of course Annie would wander back to find her way home. Horses always knew how to get back to their own stalls. She slowly stepped out from behind the tree and walked toward Annie, making kissing noises. The mare stopped, head held high, ears pricked.

"Come on, Annie. You know it's me."

Annie snorted and stamped a hoof as though undecided whether to let herself get caught.

Willa paused. "This is no time to play games. Stand still." She started forward again.

Annie turned and sauntered the other way.

Willa grabbed a handful of leaves from a low-hanging branch. "Here, Annie. Don't you want something nice to eat?"

The contrary animal didn't even look at her.

Willa followed Annie a short way, then the horse finally stopped to munch a clump of grass alongside the ditch.

"Got you." Willa grabbed the reins and climbed onto Annie's back quickly, before the mare could take off without her. She settled into the saddle, sighing in relief. She checked and found everything in place, both the saddlebags and the shotgun.

"Now let's go. We have to hurry if we're ever going to find them," she said to the horse. "But let's not find any limbs this time."

Keeping her throbbing head low, she urged Annie into a trot.

Willa pushed on through the night. The horizon lightened as dawn neared, and she welcomed the coming of day. Individual trees stood out plainly. Night mist clung close to the ground, and with it, the scent of wood smoke.

Willa hesitated and peered down the curving road, but couldn't make out a thing. If cavalry campfires were making the smoke, should she just ride boldly among the soldiers and declare herself? What if they mistook her for an enemy and shot at her? What if they were the wrong kind of soldiers, those terrible Yankees? Or renegades. Her throat tightened with fear.

What would Bobby do? She pictured him going forward to face whatever awaited him. If only she could take on Bobby's courage as easily as she could slip on his trousers and shirt.

She shut her eyes and opened them again, then summoned all the nerve she could muster. Wishing she weren't going in blind, she nudged Annie to a walk, right into the bend.

"Halt," a male voice called. "Who's there?"

She stopped, then spotted a shadowy man, blending gray into the brush. He was pointing his rifle right at her.

"Don't shoot!" She called out, remembering to deepen her voice. "I'm a friend."

The rifle didn't waver. "Best go back wherever you came from, kid."

She ran her fingers along the fabric of Bobby's trousers, wishing his spirit could seep in through her pores. "I've come to join up with the cavalry."

A snicker. "Did you, now?"

"I have a horse and a shotgun and I want to fight Yankees."

"Ain't you tough!"

"Let me talk to Captain Spencer."

"How d'you know him?"

She realized she had let on too much and tried a bluff. "That's my business. It's between me and him."

"Dismount and approach. Keep your hands in sight."

She slid off Annie's back then walked forward, leading the mare right up to the picket, who still had his weapon aimed toward her middle. She halted again, staring at the deadly looking carbine.

"I'm Will Barber." She stuck to her bluff. "Where's Captain Spencer?"

"Never mind him. Where's that shotgun?"

"Tied to the saddle."

He ran his gaze over Annie Laurie and back to her, then lowered his rifle. "Let's go."

***

Jeff Spencer lounged back on his saddle he'd been using for a pillow, sipping a mug of the parched okra brew that lately passed for coffee. Already steamy at dawn, the day was going to be another stinker. His shirt, unbuttoned over his chest, was starchy with yesterday's dried sweat and dirt. Gritty-eyed and sleepy, he needed a shave.

They hadn't flushed out any Yankees, not one. Apparently the whole lot had crossed the river at Covington just as he had figured, and Colonel Crews had sent him on a useless chase. Jeff hoped he wasn't delayed so long he missed the fight. Whipping Yankees was about the only thing worth doing any more.

His attention shifted to one of the troopers he'd placed on picket duty. Slade walked toward him, escorting a prisoner. Not a bluecoat, nor a military-looking fellow at all, but a walking disaster. Just a kid, slump-shouldered tired, button-eyed awake. Maybe sixteen, one side of his face purple and swollen. Raspberry colored goose egg on his forehead; nose reddened and puffy as though he had gone down in a brawl. The civilian clothes hung on him as though they belonged to someone bigger. Stolen?

Jeff set the mug on the ground and squinted up at the intruder, listening to Slade's account of how he'd captured this Will Barber riding a sorrel mare toward camp. How he was packing a shotgun. How he had asked for Captain Spencer by name.

Jeff had never met Barber before, otherwise, he'd remember. The boy's clear green eyes glistened with excitement, or maybe fear. The kid clutched a floppy slouch hat in both hands. His wavy light brown hair was badly chopped.

"How do you know me, Will?"

"I stopped at a farmhouse for directions." The boy shrugged, nervous, darting his eyes about. "A man there told me which way your troop was headed."

"Randall, I bet. That old drunk. I'm surprised he was sober enough to remember my name." Jeff looked at the picket. "Why is he beat up, Slade? Did he resist arrest?"

"No, sir. He came in that a-way."

"Very well," Jeff said. "Go back to your post."

"Yes sir."

Jeff returned Slade's parting salute, then turned back to the boy. "You been in a scrape?"

"Branch caught me in the dark, sir."

"Must've been some wicked branch. Got in plenty of licks." He lifted an eyebrow. "How come you happened to blunder into our picket line? It's hardly even daylight."

Will looked him in the eye this time, but his fingers picked at the floppy hat-brim. "I want to volunteer, sir. Join the cavalry."

Jeff ran his fingers along his own stubbly jaw line, noting the boy's fine cheeks. "How old are you?"

"Eighteen, sir."

"If you're under sixteen, you better join the home guard instead. They take little boys."

"Sir, I am not a little boy. I'm old enough."

"Your voice hasn't even started to change. If you're eighteen, I'm

6

Abe Lincoln."

Will's jaw tightened. "Then I guess you're Abe Lincoln, sir."

Jeff maintained a stern expression, suppressing a smile, liking the kid's spirit. "You don't have to "sir" me every time you open your mouth. Where are you from?"

Will hesitated, blinking. "Up near Ringgold Gap." Not a good liar.

"That's way behind Yankee lines now. Since Sherman pushed us south last spring."

"Yes, sir. I slipped through. To get away from them."

"What are you doing in Middle Georgia?"

"Refugeeing."

The boy's eyes wavered under Jeff's scrutiny, convincing him he had plenty to hide. A runaway, for sure. Jeff gave Will Barber time to stew before he slid in the next question. "Mama know you're here?"

His eyes widened, but the boy shook his head. "Got no mama."

"No mama, eh? You got anybody?"

Will shook his head again. "My brother was in the army. Yankees killed him."

"You want the same thing to happen to you?" Jeff leaned forward, studying the boy. "Why'd you run away from home, Will? You in some kind of trouble? Or is it patriotism? Looking for adventure? Revenge? Or do you have a deep longing to become cannon fodder? Maybe join your brother in the sweet by and by?"

Will visibly gulped, then squared his narrow shoulders and said, "Sir, I know how to shoot. I have my own mount and a shotgun. I can hold up my end and I am not afraid."

Just like a kid, thinking himself indestructible. Boys like him either won battles or got themselves killed. Jeff picked up his cup and forced down the last seedy mouthful of okra broth. Runaway or not, now wasn't the time to search out the boy's family. Besides that, volunteers were scarce as real coffee in the Confederacy these days. When he needed more troops how could he turn down a willing one?

"God forgive me," Jeff said. "I'll let you ride with us today. We don't have time to school you properly, but you can watch the others and learn."

"Thank you, sir." Will exhaled.

"See if you're still thanking me by the time this campaign is over." He pointed to the ground. "Sit down. You had breakfast?"

"No, sir." The boy settled on his rump.

Jeff fished inside his saddlebag, found the chunk of cooked bacon, hardtack, and the handful of parched corn he'd saved for later. He pulled out the meat and gave it to the boy. "Here. It's pretty good. Not musty old army issue, homegrown civilian bacon."

Will accepted the food gratefully, cutting his gaze from side to side as he gnawed, clearly wary of whatever might get after him while he was busy eating.

Jeff settled back on his elbows and studied the boy. The unhurt part of his face was smooth, good-looking on the sound side, anyhow. He didn't talk like white trash. Not a clay-eater by any stretch, might even have decent breeding. "Can you read and write?"

Will looked up at him over his bacon and swallowed. "Yes, sir. My mother and brother taught me."

"What have you read?"

"Books we had around the house. *Pilgrim's Progress, The Bible, Macbeth*—"

"Great God, what a high-toned collection. No dime novels?"

Will's brow wrinkled. "Sir? I've read oth—"

"That will do." Jeff allowed a slight smile to show. "You can prove it to me later. Do you write with a neat hand?"

The boy nodded.

"I've been needing a copyist to assist me with paperwork from time to time. Stay close to me, I'll use you as an aide if you work out."

The boy relaxed a little, grinning. "I can do that."

Jeff noted Sergeant Quinn walking up. The noncom looked at Will with open curiosity and gave his commanding officer a slouching salute. "Sir, the men will be ready to ride in fifteen minutes."

"Very good, Sergeant. This is Will Barber, our latest recruit. See if you can find him something to wear that looks halfway military. And when we have a breathing spell, let's get him a proper haircut. Looks like he gave himself his last one." To Will he said, "Somewhere in this army there's bound to be a soldier from up Ringgold way who can vouch for you."

The boy's smile faltered.

Jeff was willing to bet a month's pay he'd never find that soldier.

Chapter Two

"**D**amn you, Dodds, what did you do with my little girl?" Edgar forced open his sticky eyelids and peered up at the enraged face of Jason Randall. The old man grabbed him by the shoulders and shook him. Edgar's skull banged against the headboard.

"Stop that! You're killing me!" Edgar threw off Randall's hands. "Are you crazy? What the hell are you talking about?"

"You're laying on her bed with your pecker hanging out and there's blood on the sheet!" Randall raised his fist. "Tell me what you've done with her, or I'll whup it out of you."

"Wait." Edgar lifted his arm, protecting his face.

Randall hesitated, blowing like a mad bull.

Edgar rubbed his aching temple and felt sticky blood, as though somebody had pelted him. His cods hurt. Then he realized his pants were unbuttoned and around his knees, his drawers, too. He hurried to snatch them up and fasten himself back together.

What did happen last night? He stared at the stained sheets, trying to remember. "That must be my blood. Where'd she go?"

"Hell, I asked you first!"

"Calm down, old man. I don't know where Willa's gone." Edgar sat up, leaned forward, then rested his head in his hands. Lord, he felt awful. He wasn't used to drinking so much whiskey. He'd been stupid to keep up with Randall. "Don't remember a thing but supper, then sitting with you, drinking awhile."

"Your memory better improve quick, neighbor. Appears to me you didn't choose to wait until your wedding night."

Then he recalled kissing Willa, wanting her, and her fighting him like a wildcat. He closed his eyes and groaned. Did the whiskey make him forget to bide his time? He'd often longed to teach her to shut that sassy mouth, but needed full authority to do it properly.

He squinted at the outraged Randall, and knew if he didn't think of a reasonable defense, the marriage would be called off and with it his

9

access to that rich bottomland.

The old man's eyes were thunderous with fury. "You touched her out of turn."

"What difference does a day or two make?"

"I never should of trusted Willa to you. Clouded my judgment with whiskey, you did. Give me that agreement back, so I can rip it up."

Edgar stared at Randall, trying to sort it all out. All he knew was, he'd pretty well incriminated himself. And when she got back, she'd tell her Pa the whole story, then there wouldn't be a shred of doubt. Randall, the weak, miserable drunken fool, would hang his hide on the wall.

Exposure would ruin his social standing, and much, much more. He'd lose his home guard commission, the respect of his peers, maybe he'd even get arrested. Did they hang men who raped white women? Was that what he'd done? He couldn't recall.

How could he head off her accusations before she had a chance to talk? "We'd better find her." Edgar shifted to stand up.

He moved, then grunted as pain stabbed through his bruised testicles. His sore head throbbed and ached from the double misery of injury and hangover. Hell, he didn't even know what he'd done, but she'd sure made him pay. He couldn't let her get away with that. He'd pay her back. Double.

"She ran off," the old man said. "Took her horse, my shotgun, that hat hanging by the door. My boots, too."

"How do you know somebody didn't come in and steal them? A runaway field hand, maybe. Stole them and busted my head."

"Ha. Stole Willa, too?" Randall's gaze was accusing.

Edgar shook his head, at a loss for another alibi, then followed the old man into the parlor.

"You corrupted her." Randall was working himself up into a rage. "You can forget about marrying her. I'll kill you instead."

Edgar tried to swallow, but his mouth was dry. He'd better get ready to defend more than his honor. His life might be at stake. Randall glanced at the gun belt Edgar had hung by the door last night, and Edgar could just about read the old man's mind. He calculated whether he could reach it before Randall and came up short, then he remembered it didn't matter. He flexed his hand and griped the hunting knife he always carried hidden in a sheath in his boot. "You can't shoot me, old man. I've got the caps in my pocket."

Randall turned on him and took a threatening step forward.

Edgar reached into his boot and drew out the knife.

Staring at the blade, Randall paused. Then he lunged for it.

Edgar jabbed forward, slipping it past Randall's groping hands, burying the blade into his gut. Randall's eyes widened. His mouth dropped open. Then he let out an agonized howl and clutched at Edgar's knife-filled fist.

Edgar had to finish the man. Couldn't leave him half done. Couldn't leave those accusing eyes looking at him like that. Grunting with the effort, he dug the blade upward through Randall's belly and jerked it out, his hands drenched with hot blood. The old man tottered, quieter now, but still struggling, hanging onto the knife.

Edgar yanked the knife from Randall's grasp and plunged the blade into his neck. More blood spurted forth. Randall's dying hands weakened, trembled, convulsed, trying to hang on. Like a stomped snake, the old man just wouldn't die. Edgar followed him down to the floor, jerking out the blade and burying it again and again into Randall's body.

Finally Randall let out a sighing gurgle and relaxed, his hands opening, falling away from Edgar's arm. Edgar crouched over him, panting, then wiped the dripping blade clean on Randall's pants leg. He slid the weapon back into its hiding place. He'd never killed a man before, but he could get to liking it. The excitement had pleasured him almost as much as taking a woman.

Randall's blood had spewed everywhere, drenching his body, the chair, the floor. And now his dead eyes stayed wide open, still accusing. Edgar's exhilaration died in a wave of remorse.

"Don't look at me like that, old man." Edgar closed Randall's eyelids.

Looking down at himself, he discovered that he, too, was covered with blood. Randall's blood.

Edgar spat the sour taste out of his mouth. He started to wipe his mouth on his sleeve, then hesitated. Too much blood. He took off his soaked shirt, wiped his hands on it, and threw it aside. He found the jacket he'd shed last night and shrugged into it, hiding the rest of the blood that had spewed onto his clothes.

Edgar had needed to kill Randall. It was self-defense. Hadn't he threatened to kill him? Besides, the old man had figured things out. He didn't even need to hear Willa's testimony to know all about it.

Even if he didn't try to carry out that threat, Randall's change of heart would have messed up things good. He wouldn't have let Edgar have Willa, so she would never warm his bed or bear his children. The Randall land wouldn't fall naturally into his hands.

Still, Edgar was a killer.

But nobody saw him do it. He patted his shirt pocket, heard the satisfying crinkle of paper. This could come out all right after all. The land could be his now, sooner than he'd planned. In truth, he'd hoped Randall would drink himself to death, and was happy to provide the means. He'd blame Randall's death on Yankee stragglers. That would work. Stoneman's raiders had conveniently passed within striking distance, and Yankees made a habit of burning and destroying. Edgar could claim he'd found the house, all burned up, and Randall with it. Who would suspect

Edgar had killed his neighbor, his own future father-in-law?

Edgar closed his eyes, shuddering with relief. It was a good plan. He'd deal with Willa later. When he had a chance to talk to her, he would shame her out of telling anybody about last night, make her believe Yankees had killed her Pa. Failing that, he'd figure out something else. The important thing was to get her under his power as soon as he could.

He ducked back into her room, eyeing the rumpled, bloodstained bed sheets. He found the brown ceramic whiskey jug she'd used to brain him, still intact, upright next to the bed. He turned and looked over the only other stick of furniture in the room, a little chest of drawers, then ran his fingers over the rough surface. He opened the top compartment, thrusting his hand into the soft fabric within. He held up the garment, one of her unmentionables, gray from many washings. He held it to his nose and sniffed, but all he smelled was lye soap. He stuffed the underpants in his pocket.

One by one he rifled through each drawer of the chest, fingering Willa's belongings. He got aroused all over again, just thinking about her.

Enough. He'd better do what he had to do.

He found a match and lit a candle. Walking around the room, he set fire to the curtains and the bed sheets. He hurried into the main room, torching the chair. He found a glass oil lantern, lit it and threw it at the floor next to Randall, smashing the glass and scattering flaming oil all over the wood floor and Randall's shirtsleeve. The cotton material caught fire and flamed, hissing.

Flames licked hungrily at Randall's body. His blood-damp clothes steamed. The smell of searing flesh filled Edgar's nostrils.

Murderer. Murderer. Murderer.

Edgar let out a hoarse groan of self-horror and staggered out of the burning house onto the stoop. He stepped on a loose plank that popped up and hit him on the chin. The bright hot daylight hit him like a blow. He swore and covered his eyes. Sweating, he lifted his hands and looked over his shoulder at the house.

But he didn't see Willa, Randall's ghost, or even a mortal man chasing him.

***

Willa took off the boots, then stripped off her socks and stuffed them inside. She tied the bootlaces together, draped them over her neck, then led Annie toward the stream bank, taking her place among the cavalrymen in line to cross. She was so overheated that she expected to see steam rising from the water around her when she waded into the stream. A cold bath would feel wonderful.

"Hey, kid," a trooper called out. "Ain't you gonna skin off them clothes?"

Willa gave him a tight-lipped smile, wishing he would hush, and shook her head. She averted her gaze and glanced back at the other troopers who must have heard the question. The men were prepared to ford the stream bare-chested, wearing only their union suit drawers. She felt conspicuous, being the only fully clothed individual in their stripped-down company. It was hard not to show her embarrassment. She avoided looking directly at their exposed farmers' tans, but saw enough to notice the tough, wiry condition among the lot.

Captain Spencer took notice of her failure to strip, too. "You won't have any dry clothes to put on after you get those soaked," he pointed out.

"I don't mind, sir," she told him, leading Annie closer to the water.

To her relief, he shrugged and let it go. She sneaked a glance at him, half naked as the rest of them. Something about his flat belly and the ripple of muscle showing under taut skin made her want to stare, but she cut her eyes away from the interesting sight.

She waded into the stream, picking out the sandy area to place her bare feet. She'd been heavy-headed and sleepy all morning, slouched in the saddle. The cold water shocked her to alertness as she walked in deeper. Her bare feet felt along the slick bottom rocks, touched nothingness, and she splashed into depth over her height. She clung to the saddle, swimming alongside Annie Laurie, her clothes hampering her movements.

Then Willa scrambled up on the east bank amidst the wet-dog-stinking soldiers and their dripping mounts. The rough, stony ground pained her feet. She unslung the boots from around the back of her neck, then whoa'ed Annie and steadied herself by leaning on the mare's shoulder. She bent over to squeeze out her trouser cuffs and wiped the water off her feet. She pulled on her socks, then the boots. The swim had relieved some of the stiffness from her bruises. She hoped the coolness stayed with her a while.

She looked around, still self-conscious, but nobody seemed to be taking any more notice of her. Now loaded with muddy water, Bobby's loose trousers threatened to sag down to her ankles. The suspenders dug into her shoulders and the tight bindings over her breasts were soaked. She looked down at herself to make sure her clothes were still intact enough to hide her figure. Thankfully, the wool military jacket Sergeant Quinn had given her was big and unrevealing. It was too heavy to wear on a hot day, but she'd kept it on anyway. At least the soaking had cooled her off.

So far she hadn't seen her first Yankee, just the rear end of the horse in front of her. So far nobody had shot at her, either. She'd kept her mouth shut and studied the men to learn how they moved and talked. Would she have to take up chewing, spitting and smoking to become one of the boys?

She caught a flurry of red-orange motion from the corner of her eye. Private Reynolds' gamecock, General Johnston, shook his tail feathers free of water. The little banty rooster rode on Reynold's shoulder most of the time, but he must have gotten wet crossing the stream. His head was scarred, likely a veteran of many cockfights. Reynolds acted friendly and talkative, which eased her nervousness.

Willa straightened, looked around and spotted Captain Spencer. He had already mounted, fully clothed to the point of buckling his gun belt back on. He cut a bedraggled figure, tiredness lining his face, black hair slick with river water, clothes clinging to his wet body. Nonetheless, he sat tall, watchful, clearly in charge. To her he looked nothing short of heroic.

Her ploy was working so far. Willa had him and the other soldiers fooled into believing she was a boy, despite awkward moments like the one just past. Nobody had questioned her closely about the bruises on her face, though she had received a few curious stares. Captain Spencer was actually letting her tag along with the cavalry, at least for the time being. She was grateful he accepted her, although she realized he suspected she was a runaway. It seemed to help that she was able to read and write, making herself useful. Mama had taught her well, one of the precious few legacies Willa could claim.

She had to perform well as a soldier and gain his respect so he would continue to let her stay. Odd how she felt safer with soldiers on their way to battle than she did at home.

Pa most likely knew she was missing by now. What would Edgar tell him? Whatever the lie, Pa would swallow it. She hoped they would never think of looking for her in the army. That thought gave her comfort.

She climbed onto the mare's back. Captain Spencer ordered the troop forward, and she swung into place next to him. That was where she felt safest of all. In truth, she craved his presence.

He turned to her, arched his right eyebrow and nodded slightly. "A right good day for a swim, isn't it, Will?" His voice was cultured and smooth.

"Yes, sir." She smiled at him, happy she had attracted his notice. "I'm mighty glad to be rid of that dust."

"Oh, don't get used to being clean. There's always more dust."

"I don't mind it so much."

"Neither do I, truth be told. God bless the heat." He shook water off his hat then replaced it on his head. He adjusted the brim, shadowing his gray eyes. "It's hard on us, but it's murder on the Yankees. They aren't used to it and they get worn down even quicker."

Their mounts touched noses, whiffling their lips. Captain Spencer's gaze lowered to observe Annie Laurie. "Nice mare. Too bad you've got to use her as a cavalry horse and risk getting her killed. She'd make a valuable broodmare."

She frowned, disappointed. Were all men like that, rating anything female by its sex and reproductive ability? Good thing he didn't know she was a girl. He'd be looking at her the same way Edgar did. How she'd bear Edgar a litter of brats while she ran his household for him. The thought of that man planting babies inside her made her feel sick.

But then, she wasn't against having children, just not Edgar's children.

"We had a nice string of horses back home," Captain Spencer continued. "But my brother and I have used them up shamefully in this cavalry business. He's in Virginia, Wade Hampton's command. Baron, here, is the last of the lot. The waste is a crime."

"Where's your home, sir?" she asked.

"Richmond County, near Augusta. That's where most of the boys in my troop are from, too." He reached into a saddlebag, withdrew a couple of thick square crackers, and offered her one. "Haven't had a chance to issue you rations yet. Want some hardtack?"

Willa mumbled, "Thanks," and took it. Despite the bacon he had given her for breakfast, she was already so hungry her mouth watered even at the unappealing sight of the hard pale biscuit.

She started to take a bite, but spotted a small black insect clinging to the surface of the hardtack. She stared at the bug, wondering how old the biscuit could be.

Captain Spencer tapped his biscuit against the pommel of his saddle. "First, you knock off the weevils, although some Epicureans prefer to eat hardtack meat and all. They claim it's more nourishing that way."

She flicked off the bug and bit into the hardtack, determined to like it. The stuff was tough and salty, barely edible, but she was too hungry to be choosy.

He handed her his canteen. "We don't have any spare equipment, but we'll capture you some. The Yanks are our favorite ordinance supply."

She realized her commander was taking care of her needs the best way he could by sharing his own rations. She grinned her thanks and took a swig, washing down the dry cracker.

He nodded at the shotgun strapped to her saddle. "You any good with that thing?"

"Yes, sir." She dropped her hand and touched the stock. Should she try to impress him or be truthful? Better level about what she could, fewer stories to keep straight. The one big lie about her gender was enough of a stretch. "I've done some hunting, for food. Squirrel and rabbit. I'm pretty good at shooting vermin, too. Rats."

"Nothing bigger than a rodent?"

She shook her head no.

"The vermin we're hunting shoot back." He smiled grimly. "I haven't sworn you in yet, on purpose. Truly, you don't have to join if you're underage."

She lifted her chin. "I'm not underage, sir."

"It's only fair you know why I was short an aide." His features went stony and his voice flat; his eyes betrayed bitterness. "The last one got shot a couple of days ago. At the Flat Shoals fight. I expect he'll lose the arm."

If he meant to scare her, he succeeded. The same thing could happen to her. Or worse. What had she gotten into? But where else could she go? Besides, it was hard to fear Yankees in the midst of these hardy men, especially Captain Spencer. She stiffened her back, not wanting him to think she was a coward. "It's my fight too, sir."

"Very well." He smiled again, humorlessly. "You'll sure have your chance."

Chapter Three

Just after noon, Jeff led the first ferry load of troopers and horses onto a flat boat to cross the Ocmulgee River. He sat on the deck, bracing himself against the motion, watching the ferryman launch the boat and navigate them across. The latest recruit had stretched out on his back next to him and dropped off to sleep immediately.

The boy's shotgun resembled the one Randall had brandished and possibly was the same one. Had he stolen it along with the ill-fitting clothing? All day Jeff had noticed pain in Will's movements, suggesting his face wasn't the only part of him that had taken a vicious beating. Still, the boy hadn't uttered the first complaint. Whatever he was running away from must be more frightening than the prospect of getting shot at. Will's guileless ignorance of military matters confirmed he wasn't a deserter, jumping from one army unit to another to escape some difficulty.

Perhaps a sheriff was on the lookout for Will, though Jeff would have been surprised if this shy youth had committed a serious crime. He claimed to be eighteen, yet appeared much younger. Jeff studied the sleeping face. Will was softly molded on the unhurt side of his face, too pretty, unusual for a farm boy though he rode well for a city boy. He had good hands and guided his mare with considerable skill. Cavalry life would either toughen him up or kill him. Jeff resolved to protect him from the worst of it until he received the proper training, or until he returned to wherever he belonged. He wished no ill upon the lad.

As the boat scraped onto the east side of the Ocmulgee, Jeff stood up and his veterans prepared to disembark without his having to instruct them. He glanced down at Will, who was still snoozing. He bent down and shook the boy awake. Will's eyes opened wide, scared at first, then as recognition set in rationality took over. "Sir? Are we there?"

"Let's get these horses off. I have a job for you while we're waiting for the others to cross."

Will obeyed eagerly, untying two sets of reins and leading the horses off the boat. Jeff picked a spot in the shade of a sweet gum tree to tether their horses. He dug in his saddlebag and pulled out a pad of paper and a pencil. He handed the writing materials to Will. "I expect we'll be meeting the rest of the brigade soon. I need to file a report when we do. Sit right there and write while I dictate."

His new aide settled with his back against the tree trunk, rested the pad on his thighs and looked up expectantly. Jeff noted Will took the pencil in his right hand with an easy grip as though he were used to writing.

"Date it July 30, '64. Address it to Colonel Crews." He paused, watching Will carefully write the heading in a neat script. "It is my honor to report…" Jeff rattled off the words, pausing often to let Will get it down and to keep track of the ferry's progress on its return trip across the river. The missive was a short one, as his search for the enemy had come up empty.

Will handed him the completed letter and he read it over. It was mistake free and legible. He nodded. "Very good, Will." The boy beamed, pleased as a puppy receiving a scratch behind its ears. Surprised he wouldn't have to copy it over in his own hand and make corrections, Jeff signed the report and handed it back to his new aide. "Make a copy to keep and we'll turn in the original." The boy truly was literate. He hadn't lied about that, at least.

* * *

Edgar rode up the hill toward Randall's hidden paddock. He looked behind, where smoke curled high into the air. He'd destroyed the evidence and had scattered Randall and his house to the winds. Now it was just his word against Willa's.

Calmer, he recalled bits and pieces of last night. How the thought of her lying in bed in the next room had driven him wild. Her jumping up when he came into her room, him remembering the shift flowing over her firm young body, nipples poking out the fabric, eyes widening in fear.

He remembered his need, her fighting him and how it made him even wilder to get into her. He couldn't recall everything. But he must have failed, considering his raw-edged, restless mood and the unsatisfied way his body reacted as he thought about taking her. He wouldn't be able to rest until he had her. He'd teach her the cost of fighting him. He'd make her tame and meek and willing, no matter how much teaching it took. In a way it was a shame he had to break her, because her spirit was one of the things that attracted him.

Wouldn't she need to come home sooner or later? He must find her before she noised it all over the county that he had attacked her.

But if anybody said anything about it, he would be kind, understanding

18

and sorrowful. Explain to whoever would listen that she was beside herself after what the Yankees did. The poor girl was hysterical, and who could blame her? Willa couldn't even tell what was real, judging from the crazy story she dreamed up.

Nobody would disbelieve a man of his stature, a major in the home guard. She was only a young girl, an orphan at that. He'd give her a home, all right, and anybody that paid any mind would be satisfied he was there to take care of her. How could she reject an opportunity like the one he offered? He'd salvage his control over her and his claim to the land at the same time.

The land mattered. Jason Randall reminded him of his own daddy, one rung up from white trash, always blaming bad luck for his sorry lot in life. Edgar didn't believe in luck, except the luck he'd brought himself with his smart dealings. He'd done a good job of acquiring the land and the influence, but he wanted more, and Randall's rich land lay strategically between Edgar's and the river. Even without her lazy father's help Willa had managed to feed the two of them decently from the fruits of that fine bottomland. The efforts of a field crew could multiply that yield many times over.

Most of all, Edgar wanted what had eluded him in his quest for empire. He couldn't found a dynasty without heirs, and he hadn't succeeded in producing any. So far the only woman who'd agreed to marry him had proved unsuitable, a weakling who had died before serving her purpose. Another wife was surprisingly hard to find. He'd meet a woman, talk with her family, but despite his stature in the community, he'd failed to bring a courtship to a satisfactory conclusion. The world was full of women who didn't know a good thing when they saw it.

After a brief search, he found what Randall had told him to be true. The sorrel mare was gone; only the old farm horse and the milk cows grazing and flicking their tails at flies remained.

He followed the hoof prints headed out of the paddock to the road. There he yanked his horse to a stop, tugged his beard and looked around furiously. He'd lost them among the tracks of the cavalry horses. Couldn't even tell which way she had gone in that jumble.

Hell, how was he supposed to think like a girl? Most likely she would have run to the Tate place, or maybe into Covington. Or Atlanta, a big enough place to lose herself for a while.

Wherever she went, he was damn sure going to find her.

***

Later that day scouts sent ahead located the main force. Willa saw the red dust from many riders hanging in the air before they met the cavalry. She was with her captain when he handed the report over to a

19

staff officer. She had passed a test in being able to do what she'd claimed. As long as she proved useful she gave him reason to keep her with him. Sticking with Captain Spencer made her feel safe, and she was happier than she'd been since losing Bobby. The pain and tiredness in her body might slow her down but she would not let it stop her from performing whatever assignment he gave her. While serving in the army wasn't a free existence, at least she was free from Edgar.

Willa knew of just two kinds of men. Most were bossy and mean like Pa and Edgar. Then there was Bobby. Captain Spencer reminded her more of Bobby than the others. She noticed how the men seemed to respect their commander, sharing her good opinion of him. She hadn't met many cavalry officers, but surely Captain Spencer was one she could trust.

Then she remembered what he told her happened to his last aide, and shuddered. Nowhere was she safe.

Nonetheless, the thought of going home, back to Edgar, was too horrible to consider. If he didn't kill her, he'd make her want to die. And she wanted nothing more to do with Pa, who loved his jug more than anything, even her. It grieved her to have to give up on her own flesh and blood, but she had to face the sad fact that he only valued her for the price she could bring. Marrying her off to Edgar was worth a field hand, a cook and a jug of whiskey to Pa. That was the offer he'd accepted from Edgar. She ought to be proud that he figured it would take two workers to replace her.

So far she hadn't seen the first drunken soldier, not even a flask of whiskey. So far not one man had treated her mean, unless she counted a little harmless teasing. Next after Captain Spencer, she liked the easy going Reynolds and his pet rooster. They made her laugh despite the pain it gave her beat-up mouth.

After reuniting with the rest of the brigade, it was clear the Confederates had intercepted the track of the Yankee raiders. The invaders had left a trail any fool could follow, marked by burned-out houses and killed livestock.

She spotted a farm dog lying in the road, headless, caked with its own blood. Flies made a dark cloud around the bloated carcass, and its heavy brown stench filled her nostrils. A stone's throw farther up the road, the dog's head sat on a fencepost, grinning at her.

Her stomach knotted and threatened rebellion. "Yankees did that?" she asked Reynolds, who ranged alongside.

"Their idea of a joke. Watchdog, watching us. Funny, ain't they?" Perched on Reynolds' shoulder, General Johnston spread his red-orange wings like a stubby eagle and cackled.

She wrinkled her nose. "That's pure meanness."

"Sure they're mean." Reynolds spat tobacco juice. "We're mean too. We catch them, all hell's gonna break loose." He offered General Johnston a kernel of parched corn. "Ain't that right, Gen'ral. We gonna whip 'em, too."

Willa stared at the gruesome Yankee handiwork. Sooner or later she would catch up with them and there would be a fight. She wasn't immune to bullets, not any more than the rest of the soldiers. And they would expect her to become a killer, just as they were.

Could she end a man's life, even in self-defense?

She reminded herself whom she was going to be fighting. Yankees had killed her brother, and had come to her homeland to pillage and destroy. She'd always wanted to do her part against them. Even that part promised to be a great adventure, more interesting than watching Pa get drunk.

Seeking a diversion, she dug in her pocket and found a piece of hardtack she had saved. She broke off a bit and offered it to the rooster perched on Reynold's shoulder. The bird reached out and plucked it from her palm, barely brushing her skin with its beak.

"He's an army cock," Reynolds said. "Eats army food."

Stokes, riding behind them, snorted. "I'd rather see him being the food."

"You wouldn't kill him, would you?" Willa said, feeling uneasy for the welfare of her new friend. "Anyway, he's too tough."

"What do you care, kid?" Stokes leered at her. "Ain't you ever eat chicken before?"

"Killed and plucked them, too." Willa groped for a defense of the rooster. "But this one's different."

Reynolds winked at Willa. "Truth is, Stokes is still mad cause General Johnston whipped the dominecker he bet on."

"Only because you cheated," Stokes said. "Clipped back my banty's spurs."

Captain Spencer turned in his saddle, joining the debate. "I'm not betting on that bird any more. He's lost his good luck since General Hood replaced his namesake."

Reynolds shook his head. "Never. My little banty is invincible."

Laughing, Stokes forged alongside Reynolds and made a grab for General Johnston. The rooster flew at his face, squawking, spurs working. Stokes swore, threw up his hand and deflected the bird. It flapped to a nearby bush, still fussing.

Stokes drew his saber and charged toward the bird. "That's it! He's supper!"

Willa reined in between, cutting him off. "No!" Her voice went shrill. "Don't kill him!"

Stokes' horse banged into Annie Laurie, then both animals staggered apart.

"Damn it, sissy-kid, out of the way!" Stokes hollered, a fearsome sight, saber drawn, a drop of blood rolling down his rooster-spurred cheek.

Willa flinched but held Annie steady. She gathered her courage, stuck out her chin and shook her head.

Stokes snatched for her with his free hand. Willa dodged Annie sideways, determined to keep their bodies between Stokes and the bird, leaving him grabbing at air, like she did to Pa when he tried to hit her.

She looked around for help from Reynolds, but he was just sitting on his horse watching, his face twisted in amusement. "Go get him, kid!" he hollered from his safe distance.

She whirled back to Stokes, who was going after General Johnston again, saber upraised. Then the bird flew back up to his perch on Reynolds' shoulder. Stokes hesitated just short of taking a whack at Reynolds.

Captain Spencer had stopped and turned to watch the fracas. "Put that pig-sticker away before you hurt somebody, Stokes."

"Hell, Jefferson, you're no fun." Amazingly, Stokes' voice and manner changed, going good-natured. He hadn't bothered to call Captain Spencer "Sir," something she'd noticed from certain of the men. He sheathed his saber, then wiped the blood off his cheek and examined it. "Damn that bird."

Willa looked back at the rooster. General Johnston spread its wings, settling his glare on Willa. The danger had ended, just like that. Now Reynolds was watching her and laughing. So was Stokes, like she was a joke.

Confused, Willa felt her cheeks heat up. Were they going to gang up on her? She cut her gaze from one face to the next, feeling foolish, cornered, out of balance.

"No hard feelings," Stokes said. "Just wanted to see if the sissy-kid would scare."

"He didn't." Captain Spencer was the only one not laughing. "Leave him be."

"That's the first time General Johnston's had somebody to do his fighting for him. He always takes care of himself," Reynolds said. "You got sand, kid."

Captain Spencer's voice lapsed into a bored drawl. "One of these days I'm going to wring that chicken's neck and put an end to all this nonsense."

"You wouldn't do that, Jefferson." Reynolds stroked General Johnston's wing affectionately. "He's won you a penny or two."

"He's used up his favor by disturbing my peace once too often," Captain Spencer said.

Stokes dismounted and walked to the side of the road, leading his horse. His britches were a patchwork of odd bits of cloth, and saddle-friction had rubbed even his seat-patches thin.

He unbuttoned the front of his trousers and sent a yellow stream arcing onto a pine trunk. Nobody else seemed to pay any mind, but Willa's face went hot again and she averted her eyes. The fountain made a warm hissing sound. She cut her gaze back and slyly watched the procedure. The healthy stream dwindled to a few squirts. Then Stokes buttoned himself back up and mounted his horse.

What would he say if he knew she was a girl, watching him like that? She imagined his mortification and smiled to herself, covering her mouth. She'd just gotten even for her humiliation, although nobody else better find out.

Later that afternoon, Captain Spencer halted the troop for a supper break and a few hours' sleep. Willa dismounted stiffly and leaned against Annie Laurie, flexing one leg, then the other.

Excitement had kept her on edge except when she'd stolen that nap on the ferry, but the lack of rest was telling on her. She considered herself a good rider for a girl, but she'd never before ridden a night and nearly a day straight, mostly at a trot. She felt tired and sore all over, as though she'd been doing the legwork instead of her mare. Determination aside, her abused body was about to give out

Willa wouldn't complain. No one was going to hear a word from her about it. She was a soldier now, expecting hardship. And every mile took her that much farther away from Edgar Dodds.

But she couldn't rest just yet. She had to rub down her tired horse and somehow find food for both of them. The other soldiers were reaching into their saddlebags for rations and unstrapping bags they had filled with corn, taken from her own storage.

She tied the mare and dragged the saddle off, suddenly weak and shaky. Against her will, tears welled up in her stinging eyes. Angrily she wiped her eyes with her sleeve. This wouldn't do. Although her stomach was empty, her bladder was painfully full. She hadn't relieved herself all day because she lacked the equipment to be as casual about it as Stokes.

After making her mare comfortable, she slipped off into the woods, looking around nervously for witnesses. Seeing none, she dropped her trousers and long male underwear, sat on a rough log, and let go. She shut her eyes, enjoying blessed relief.

A footstep crunched on leaves. She whipped off her hat, covering her crotch. Then she swiveled around, spotting Reynolds making his way through the woods, straight toward her.

Partly hidden by underbrush, she remained calm and squeezed out the last few drops. Then, turning her back to him, she snatched up her pants and buttoned them.

"Hey, Willy-boy," Reynolds said.

She let out her breath. "Hey."

He scratched under his waistband. "You join anybody's mess yet?"

"Mess?" What horrible army thing was that? She stared blankly at him. How could she find out what he meant without sounding ignorant?

Reynolds continued, "I take mess with Jefferson—Captain Spencer, that is—Stokes and Quinn. Back home we were neighbors, been sticking together ever since." He looked her up and down. "I guess Jefferson took it for granted you'd join us."

Whatever he was talking about, she wanted in. "Sure," she said. "When do we start?"

"My turn to cook," he said. "Grab up some kindling and haul it along."

So, mess was about eating! She swallowed the saliva that poured into her mouth at the thought of food. Here was a way she could make herself useful. "I can cook. Then you won't have to."

Reynolds laughed. "Your folks raise you up to be a girl?"

Telling herself he was merely joking, she forced herself to laugh back at him. "At my house, if you didn't cook, you didn't eat."

"You better not be lying. Burn my bacon, it's you I'll chew up."

"Just give me the food." For once she felt confident, on solid ground. "I'll cook it all right."

"Ain't you a wonder, Willy-boy."

She gathered an armful of tinder wood on the way back to camp. Other soldiers had already started their cook fires, and she hurried to build her own. Reynolds came up with a slab of bacon, a bag of cornmeal, several ears of corn, and a spider pan.

"Where's Captain Spencer?" she asked him.

Reynolds shrugged. "Off doing officer stuff, most likely. It's a wonderment he still associates with us lowlies."

"He's a fine officer, isn't he?" She expected him to agree with her admiration of their leader.

"Better then most." Reynolds scratched under his waistband thoughtfully. "He does what a captain's supposed to do and makes sure the men are all right. Didn't even get all puffed up when we voted him Captain, like some do. In spite of his being important folks back home."

That didn't surprise her. "What kind of important folks?"

"His daddy was a planter and a judge. Jefferson got the fancy schooling so he could read law too. I guess it didn't hurt him none." Reynolds hunched his shoulders defensively. "I never did learn to read, and that didn't hurt me either."

"Don't you want to learn how?"

"I been getting along all these years without it."

"Oh, but think of the advantages," she said. "I'll be glad to teach you."

"Don't try to improve me. I ain't no school kid."

"Don't get insulted." Willa backed off, fearing the loss of her new friend. "I just said I'd help if you wanted."

"Let it go at that, then." He relaxed a little, coming down off his high horse.

Willa made up corn batter, shucked the corn, and fried the bacon in the spider pan. The aroma of bacon frying even made her eyes water. Famished, she could hardly keep herself from reaching into the pan and sampling her supper ahead of time.

She set the cooked bacon aside on a tin plate and fried corn dodgers and the ear corn in the grease. In another pan she boiled the parched okra that made do for coffee. She didn't think she'd drink any, though.

The rooster, General Johnston, came strutting around and she tossed him a pinch of the corn. He pecked at the food hungrily. She grinned at him, thinking most people made pets out of dogs or cats. Of course, in Reynolds' view, he earned his keep, if his fighting exploits were to be believed.

She divided the food five ways and served her messmates on the tin plates they provided as they straggled in to join her.

"This don't look too bad." Joel Reynolds poked at the meat with his fork, then sampled a chunk of the fried corn bread. "You did all right, boy." He winked at the captain. "Guess we got us a cook, don't we, Jefferson?"

"So far so good." Captain Spencer looked straight at her, a rare half-smile lighting his shadowed features. "Where'd you learn how to cook, Will?"

Careful. Cooking was women's work, even if soldiers did it out of need. And she didn't relish getting more teasing about it, either. "After Mama and the colored people were gone, I had to do the cooking or Pa and I wouldn't get to eat." There. Once again, she didn't even have to lie.

The captain took a swallow of the so-called coffee. "You don't incinerate the food or mess it up, we'll keep you."

"Yes, sir." She licked the grease off her fingers and rested back on her elbows, starting to realize she was having the adventure of her life. This sure was more exciting than picking pole beans, and she was too busy to be homesick.

She could do it. Keep up with the soldiers, do whatever they did. Just because she was a girl didn't mean she was any less brave, or any less enduring than a man. She counted up her assets, as Captain Spencer must view them. She had her own horse and gear. She could read and write. Finally, she could cook, which she assumed the men would just as soon not bother with. She no longer doubted they'd let her stay.

Stokes tossed a stick at General Johnston, who dodged it in a red flurry. "Next time it'll be stewed chicken instead of this endless bacon."

Joel Reynolds snickered. "Over Will's dead body, I wager."

"I believe that." Captain Spencer was watching her, amusement in his eyes. "Tell me, Will. Do you stick up for your friends like you stuck up for that worthless bird?"

She met his gaze, sensing a challenge. "Yes, sir. I sure do."

He seemed to look right through her, and he must have liked what he saw. "Then you'll do."

She went warm all over, pure delight.

Unlike Pa, who always took to drinking after supper, Captain Spencer took a Bible and a tintype out of his saddlebag. He balanced the open book on his thigh and picked up the tintype. He studied it, touched his finger to his lips, then tenderly to the image. From where Willa sat trying not to let on she was watching, she could make out the likeness of a young woman, luxuriant long hair framing her face.

From the reverent way he looked at the picture, Willa concluded he loved the woman very much. She felt an unwanted pang of disappointment, knowing some woman had already staked a claim on him.

Lucky lady.

Chapter Four

A rough hand and a string of curses jarred Willa awake. She mumbled a protest as she slowly took in the smell of wood smoke and moldy earth. She remembered where she was, recognized Sergeant Quinn, and elbowed to a sitting position.

"Saddle up. We're moving on," he hollered as he strode away.

She looked for Captain Spencer, but didn't see him. "Where are we going?" she asked but the sergeant had moved on to the next clump of sleeping soldiers.

What business did he have waking her up, worn out as she was? Upon hearing Sergeant Quinn's repeated shouts and the sleepy growls and seeing moving shadows of stirring men, she realized she wasn't the only one he was picking on. The whole camp was in like straits.

She dug her knuckles into her eyes, then noted the still-light sky to the west. Just sundown, and the cook fire wasn't completely out. Had she even slept as long as an hour? It only felt like a minute or two, not nearly enough.

She didn't need to dress because she hadn't taken anything off before lying down. She heaved to her feet then made her way to the horse picket, setting her blood into motion.

Captain Spencer was already there, saddling his own horse with quick, decisive movements. "We are in for it now," he told her. "Scouts said the Yanks are backtracking. Coming this way. Our troops must have beaten them off Macon, and they're retreating. We're going to move up the road and dig in, dare them to try to get past us."

She blinked at him, trying to comprehend. "What do you want me to do, sir?"

"Just follow orders, Will. That's all." He tightened the cinch, then gave the horse an apologetic pat on the neck. "We're not going very far this time, Baron."

Just follow orders. It sounded simple enough.

After a short ride, Captain Spencer halted the troop then set them to work building breastworks. Willa helped the men carry axes and shovels from the supply wagon. She imitated the others, grabbing branches, stripping rails from a nearby fence, anything that might stop a bullet, dragging them into line at right angles with the road. Horses wheeled a couple of field pieces into position. As she worked at building the barricade, Willa watched the artillerymen unlimber the cannons and aim them right down the road. Who would be dumb enough to run straight at those wicked-looking weapons? Maybe the Yankees were that dumb. Not Bobby. A shell had sought him out, not the other way around.

Finally, weary to the bone, hands torn from splinters and smeared with blood, she was allowed to lie down and rest once again. She chose a place by Captain Spencer, and he let her stay where she dropped.

She curled up on her bed of leaves not quite touching him, but close enough to feel his body heat on her face. She missed her own bed in her own home, but she wasn't a stranger here. This patch of middle Georgia woods was her home for the night. Whatever Captain Spencer couldn't be for her, she could still pretend he was her elder brother.

***

Before dawn, Jeff shook Will awake and sent him off to find them fit drinking water. Then he walked down the line, making sure his men were secure in the fighting positions they had taken during the night. Sergeant Quinn stationed himself at one end of his troop, and he would take the other.

He ran his gaze along breastworks manned by a couple of the regiments that came along with Colonel Crews. They extended in an obtuse "V" a good way from either side of the battery. Shaped like a cattle chute, it would guide anybody who attacked from the south directly into the jaws of the cannons and make them eat canister. To the front, other lines of defense had been set up to retard advancing enemies.

The ground ahead, piney woods and deep ravines, wasn't suited for cavalry fighting. His side held the high ground. Thank God they had enough warning to find good diggings and plan intelligently. And thank God his men weren't going to be the ones trying to breach these defenses.

Reynolds' rooster strutted about, scratching and pecking the earth for bugs. Nearest Jeff's position, four men huddled behind the barricade playing cards, tense faces attending to winning or losing hands, carbines propped within reach. Jeff looked over the weapons, satisfied that no matter how shabby his men looked they kept their steel shiny clean.

"Weapons loaded?" he asked the men.

Nods. "Yes sir. We're ready as we'll ever be," Harris said. "You better keep your head down. Might be sharpshooters about."

Jeff stretched taller, looked past the barricade and lifted his hat into the air. "See, nobody there. No Yankee bullet will take me before my time."

28

Reynolds tossed down a card. "You're making it right tempting for 'em to make it your time. You looking to die?"

Jeff considered, evaluating the depreciated value of his life, then shook his head no. "Not yet. Not until I've driven every last Yankee out of Georgia."

"Then I guess you're planning to be around for a while," Reynolds said. "Want to play a hand?"

"Don't need to clean up on you all."

Jeff turned to watch a courier coming in, galloping through the works. A few gunshots cracked, down the road leading south toward Macon.

Jumpy, Stokes threw down his handful of cards and reached for his carbine.

Reynolds said, "Don't like your hand?"

"I believe you'd gamble in hell," Stokes said.

Reynolds snatched the cards Stokes had dropped, looked them over and laughed. "No wonder you're so hot to quit. Losin' hand. Pay up."

Jeff watched Will return, the canteen slung heavy over his shoulder, his expression eager, green eyes bright, full of life and illusions. "I found a branch, a ways from camp. Water looked nice and clean."

Jeff opened the full canteen and sniffed, then took a swig. It tasted all right. He dug four crackers from the saddlebag and handed Will two. The boy tapped the hardtack against his palm, dislodging the weevils.

Then Jeff found his razor in the saddlebag and set it down on the waterproof next to the two crackers he had kept for himself. "If I don't make it through this day, I might as well get shipped home clean shaven." He glanced at the boy, noting his battered face had gone sober, as though he finally realized what could happen to him. But the boy still lacked understanding. Better try to give him some. "You haven't told us where to ship your remains. Is anybody home to receive you?"

Will paled and shrugged jerkily. "Nobody cares."

"I shouldn't either, but I do. I won't say a word if you clear out while there's still time. You aren't even sworn in yet."

The boy set his chin, stubborn. "No, sir. I'd sooner stay."

Over the murmur of talking soldiers Jeff heard distant snaps, like breaking twigs, or a brushfire.

Will glanced over his shoulder. "What's that noise?" he asked.

"Gunfire. Carbines and revolvers." Jeff lifted his chin and sniffed the air. "The Yankees are exchanging pleasantries with our outpost pickets. Sounds like they're still a ways out yet."

Will did appear spooked. "Are we going to beat them?"

He shrugged, nonchalant, then let himself down next to the boy. "Odds are only three to one against us. Better than usual. And they were considerate enough to give us plenty of time to prepare. That's pretty good too. Anyway, I'm sending you back to mind horses."

The boy's shoulders sagged slightly. Was the youngster foolish enough to be disappointed? "Sir, I am not looking to get out of the fighting."

"Boy, all you've got is that shotgun, and it'll be useless until the Yanks are right up on you. Besides that, you are so green you'd stick your head up and take a bullet through your brain the minute the shooting starts."

Will's cheeks reddened girlishly. He sure did blush a lot.

Jeff continued, "Some have to fight, others have to mind horses. You'll be more useful where you can relieve an experienced soldier who can fight." He upended his canteen to his mouth, chasing the hardtack down with a gulp of water. "Feed up Baron and saddle him, but leave the cinch loose. Get Sergeant Quinn's horse too. I'll send for you if we need them."

He dismissed Will and watched him amble toward the rear. Good. He would be safer there.

Stupid, letting the boy get to him. Next he'd be forced to give him an order that would cause his death. It didn't pay to get attached to people. All that did was shred the heart. He wiped his hand across his chest as if he could rub out his grief. He turned to face his enemies, slamming his fist into his hand. "Come on, you Yankee scum," he told them.

Small arms fire intensified to the front, still out of sight, but closer. He interpreted the sound as advancing troopers engaged with the enemy.

"Prepare to receive," he called out. A bloodthirsty line of carbine muzzles pointed toward the enemy, all along the barricade. He nodded satisfaction. His men were onto the job.

He knelt behind a nice fat log, waiting. He wasn't frightened. Really, he didn't care about dying so long as he found his way to the right place for a joyous reunion. Sometimes he wondered why people who had so much to live for perished and he was still around.

He closed his eyes, remembering what Jeannie said to him the last time he saw her before riding away. Fighting tears, keeping a brave front, she was so worried about him, afraid a Yankee bullet would end his life. She begged him to be careful, not to take chances, to come back to her whole and sound. Their child needed him, she'd said. Needed a father, just as she needed her husband, loved him, and wouldn't feel wholly alive until he returned to her. Did loving him give her enough joy to counteract the pain it brought?

The pain was all he clearly remembered. He'd have been better off never knowing what it was like to lose himself in another. He was finished making that kind of risky investment. From the depths of his pit of despair, living itself seemed too chancy an affair. The alternative would be easy to arrange, because plenty of Yankees would cheerfully oblige. But he wouldn't mind sticking around long enough to see them thrown out of Georgia before they got to his own home back in Richmond County and ruined it.

And this particular band of Yankees was especially virulent, burning and destroying eighty miles behind the lines. He'd even heard that one of their Kentucky regiments was partly composed of galvanized Yankees, men recruited from Confederate deserters. He'd like to catch some of those.

The rifle fire grew louder, closer yet. The Yankees must have broken through the advance breastworks, probably believing the rest of their trip would go just as easy. They were in for an ugly surprise.

"Look sharp, boys. Don't fire until our pickets are clear," he called out. Even if he didn't much care whether he lived or died, he realized that others did.

He shifted onto his side to drag out his revolver, feeling the spare cylinders in his trouser pocket grind together. It was satisfying to know he had 18 more lead balls loaded and ready. He left his saber sheathed. A blade wasn't likely to be worth much in this kind of fight.

A movement ahead caught his attention, a man running from tree to tree toward the barricade, wearing a slouch hat and a butternut jacket. Jeff recognized one of his own men, Canfield. "Hold your fire," Jeff shouted.

The runner wheeled, threw himself behind a pine and reloaded his carbine. He knelt and fired at something behind him. Then he leaped up, sprinted to the barricade, and vaulted over it. Canfield crumpled next to Jeff, blowing and sweating, grimy with gunpowder and grinning with strain. He dug feverishly in his cartridge box for more ammunition

"How many?" Jeff asked him.

"Maybe a regiment, sir." The scout gulped a lungful of air. "Mounted. The woods are slowing them down."

The other outpost men raced in and took refuge at various points behind the barricade. Jeff looked over it and saw blue uniforms on horseback dodging around trees, barreling down the road in front of the battery. He looked toward the center for a signal, then felt the deep boom of the cannon bounce through his chest. He pulled down his pistol on a moving target, yelling, "Fire!"

Gunfire exploded all around him, sending out sheets of fire and thick sulfurous smoke. The men behind the other arm of the barricade opened up at the same time, catching the attackers in a crossfire that hit them up one side and down the other. Bluecoats fell off their horses. Others reined in, running into each other. Horses screamed, stricken and floundered.

Some of the Yankees managed to get off shots that buzzed overhead. A bullet thunked into a nearby log, spraying bark that stung Jeff's cheek. A Yankee officer waved his saber and yelled for his faltering men to charge.

The officer was brave, determined, working hard to gather the survivors and reorganize the assault. Jeff pointed him out to Stokes, who was a crack shot. "Get that officer."

Stokes leveled his carbine and fired. The Yankee officer fell backwards off his horse.

"Fine shooting," Jeff said.

Stokes nodded. "Right under the armpit."

Jeff shook off a touch of regret at having to order the death of a valiant man, enemy or not. He fired again and again and again.

Black powder smoke hung in the air, a stinking acid fog that etched the inside of his throat and made him cough. The hammer clicked empty. He reached into his pocket and fished out a fresh cylinder. He popped out the used one, hot in his hand. Then he caught a swift movement from the corner of his eye and looked toward it.

One of the Yankees drove to the barricade and jumped his horse over it. The Yankee wheeled and rushed at Jeff, saber upraised. Jeff's empty revolver was useless. No time, no maneuvering room. He shifted to roll away from the down-swinging blade.

A gunshot banged next to him. The saber glanced off his back and the heavy, softer impact of a man's body thumped onto him. He shook the Yankee off himself, noting the big bloody hole in the chest. The man groaned and writhed and coughed up torrents of blood, his stricken eyes looking straight ahead at nothing, helpless with shock and agony and the effort of taking a breath.

Unburdened, the horse trotted peaceably away.

Jeff ran his hand up his own back and found a bruised place but no blood of his own. His jacket wasn't even cut. He'd escaped losing his unsatisfactory life one more time.

He looked across the dying man and watched Canfield reload his carbine. "Thanks, soldier," he said.

Canfield touched his hat brim and turned back to shoot another Yankee. The one between them convulsed one last time. Jeff shoved the warm corpse back to make more room.

"Let's throw him on top of the breastworks." Canfield bit a cartridge and spat out paper. "He already proved he's pretty good at stopping bullets."

Jeff scowled, jimmied the loaded cylinder into his revolver, added the caps, then emptied his weapon into the backs of his retreating enemies.

***

Edgar Dodds looked out over the black faces. Most of them stood impassive, stoically waiting to find out what their master wanted. They acted respectful, and they'd better. Some maybe a little scared, and that pleased him. Scared slaves and women were easier to control.

He strolled down the line, riding crop in hand, catching each gaze until it dropped away in submission. He inhaled the musk of sweat, the scent of prosperity. Clavett, his overseer, strode along behind him, heavy tread thumping.

He was in charge. Nobody impudent enough to challenge or thwart him lived there. Nobody like Willa.

He paused, watching Josh, a Negro he had bought from Randall three years ago. Josh watched him back, stony faced. A stubborn black bastard who'd deserved and felt every bite of Clavett's whip. It had taken some work to undo the spoiling he'd been given at the Randall place. Edgar ran his fingers over the riding crop, imagining the give of live flesh quivering under its blows. The memory of killing Randall came to mind, bringing its odd mix of pleasure and revulsion.

Next to Josh stood young Gabe, his housekeeper Daisy's son. Gabe was lighter skinned and stouter-bodied than the older slaves, smarter, too. But the dark half of his inheritance made the white half not worth counting. Or mentioning. Edgar often cursed the bitter irony that his only living heir was a mulatto bastard, conceived during his first experiments with the opposite sex.

Still, Edgar had ordered Clavett to give Gabe less work and more privileges than the rest of them. After all, Gabe was his issue. Edgar would have had real heirs if his first wife had done better by him. But she was a timid, frail creature that wouldn't keep anything of his growing in her. Never a good doer, she'd more or less dried up and blown away.

His mistake, picking a sickly woman. The next one would be strong and robust, fertile ground for his seed. Willa would bear offspring he could proudly acknowledge.

He drew himself tall, letting them know he was about to speak. "Any of y'all heard the news? A terrible tragedy. The devil Yankees murdered old Mr. Randall. Burned him out, too. His girl, Willa, is gone. Disappeared. Not a soul I asked has seen her since."

Daisy cried as though prompted, "Lord help the poor child."

He nodded. "Yes, the poor child."

Gabe perked up, interested. Josh's expression didn't change, like he already knew. Nigras sniffed things in the wind, like hound dogs.

Where was the little witch hiding out? Edgar tried to control the nervous tic under his eye. "Somebody knows. Somebody has to." He searched from face to face to face. "Poor little thing, all alone in the world. No wonder she's scared. Hiding from the murdering Yankee devils.

None of y'all ever seen a Yankee, I'll bet. They've got pitchforks and horns and cleft feet and pointed tails. Carry a soul straight to hell."

He couldn't tell whether they believed that last part. He studied the expressionless faces that gave nothing away, damn them. Nothing but rut and laziness and tomfoolery.

"It's for her own sake I'm looking for her. Willa needs somebody to take care of her, give her a home. I'm willing."

"Bless you, Master Dodds," Daisy wailed.

He gave her a benign look, recalling her keeping him warm during many a cold night. He swept his gaze over the crowd. "Sometimes you folks know a thing or two that's going on. Tell me, or Clavett here, where to find her, and you'll be rewarded. No work for a whole week. Any nigra tells me where she is, gets to loaf for a whole week, right smack dab in the middle of the busy season."

That got their attention. A few whispers, new interest on their faces that they didn't bother to cover up. Gabe looked thoughtful. The word would spread from one plantation to another, and would flush Willa for sure.

He turned to Clavett. "I've got to report to headquarters, back to Atlanta, and I'll look for her there in case she went that way."

"Atlanta? I dunno." Clavett slipped his hand under his belt and scratched his waist. "I hear most folks that can get away are leaving that place."

"Just in case. I got to show my face anyway."

"What if the Yankees carried her off, Major?" Clavett said.

Edgar shifted on his feet. "Lord, I hope not, for her sake. Send word if you hear anything. Get a crew and wagons together and take them over to the Randall place. We'll collect her harvest for her."

"No sense letting perfectly good corn rot where it stands, Major," Clavett agreed.

"Get it all. The garden, smokehouse and livestock, too." He would leave her no place to live and nothing to eat. Then she would have fewer choices. He recalled the black pile of ashes where the cabin used to be, and the charred bones within and hawked his throat clear. "Have them bury what's left of the old man, too. Do it proper, hear?"

* * *

Willa didn't feel so left out after she passed several companies being held in reserve. She saw how many comrades she joined in the horse-holding ranks. Her chicken-loving friend, Reynolds, had drawn the number four and had three horses in tow besides his own. He smiled through his beard at her while he scratched under his waistband, and seemed satisfied with the job. General Johnston dug his spurs into

Reynolds' shoulder, stretched his feathered neck, and crowed.

She'd no sooner fed and saddled the horses before the rifle fire broke loose, echoing through the woods. The two seasoned war-horses merely pricked their ears, watchful, but Annie Laurie started pawing the ground and rolling her eyes.

If the mare bolted, there wasn't any way Willa could hold onto her without being dragged, so she climbed into the saddle, hoping to maintain better control. At least she was less likely to get stomped while astride the horse. She kept a tight rein on Annie's bit, shifted her saddle-sore rump, then wrapped the other two horses' reins around her fist.

She stood up in the stirrups, but couldn't see the battle because the barricades were on the other side of a wooded ridge. She called out to Reynolds, "What's going on?"

He scratched his ribs thoughtfully. "I guess old Stoneman's done found us."

***

Jeff wiped gritty sweat out of his eyes with the back of his hand. The Confederates had absorbed the assault amazingly well, little harm done them. But the Yankees had galloped off, leaving their dead and wounded littering the ground. He didn't mind the view of dead enemies, even the one lying beside him.

A dead Yankee couldn't kill any of his Georgia boys.

Today was going to be another hot one, hell boiling over. Once the sun rose high the corpses would stink just as high. Most weren't corpses yet. The wounded ones bothered him as they writhed in pain, groaned and cried out. A stricken horse trying to rise floundered. Anyone with a soul would be bothered.

He heard one voice praying. Lifting, saying clearly, "Yea, though I walk through the valley of the shadow of death . . ."

The voice trailed off, weak.

"I will fear no evil." Jeff finished the sentence, then let out the breath he'd been holding and reloaded all his cylinders. He looked out over the field but didn't see signs of a renewed attack.

"Harris," he said to the corporal nearest his left. "Lots of good weapons and ammo out there for the claiming. Take a couple of men and bring them in."

Jeff followed his men, walked the ground with them, taking a notion to look for the Yankee officer he had ordered Stokes to shoot. Maybe he was still alive and not beyond saving.

First, he came across the wounded horse. The poor beast had given up trying to rise, lay on its side, its breath coming in groans.

He knelt and stroked the sweaty neck. Blood-matted hair marked the bullet hole in the animal's shoulder. Pink froth dripped from its mouth. It lifted its head, a plea in its pain-stricken eyes, then settled back on the ground and let out a rattling breath.

"Sorry, fellow," he said softly. "There's only one thing I can do for you now." He gave the horse a final pat, then stuck the muzzle of his revolver in front of its ear and squeezed the trigger.

The horse jerked once, then relaxed, relieved of its suffering.

He stood up and turned away. Animals didn't have causes or convictions. They just obeyed their human gods and died for them.

"Though He slay me, yet will I trust in Him," he whispered.

He found the Yankee officer lying on his face next to a maple trunk. He turned him onto his back. The arms, legs and neck flopped lifeless, the handsome face blank of expression. He discovered the blood marked bullet hole under the man's armpit leading into his chest. Right where Stokes said. Flies had found the wound too, wheeling and buzzing around the drying blood.

He probably died before he hit the ground.

Jeff straightened the body, then removed the gun belt and saber belt. He picked up the weapons dead hands had dropped. They'd do fine to outfit his newest recruit. He watched Harris give a canteen to a wounded enemy. The wretch drank thirstily.

"I'll help you bring him in," Jeff told Harris. He collected the Yankee's carbine and ammunition for his own use. Then he helped Harris half carry, half drag the bluecoat off the field. The wounded man struggled on his good left leg, the right flopping useless. He grunted and swore at every step.

He and Harris lifted their prisoner over the barricade and laid him on the ground, where he lay panting. Harris scampered back to the field to glean more weapons.

Jeff ran his gaze over the Yankee, who was sweating and swallowing. Blood oozed from his mangled leg. Jeff said, "I'll have you sent to the field hospital after you answer some questions."

The Yankee nodded, lower lip trembling. "Thank you, sir."

"What outfit you in?"

"Eleventh Kentucky Cavalry."

Jeff frowned. "I've heard of that regiment, you have a rotten reputation. Brigands, vandals and turncoats."

The Yankee went a shade paler, if that was possible. "Not me."

"Fine. Which other regiments, then? How many men you got?"

The prisoner babbled on, happy to betray his comrades. Jeff didn't learn anything surprising, just verification of facts he already knew. His estimate of three times as many Yankees as Confederates still rang true. He wrote the information down and dispatched it to Colonel Crews, along with a request for stretcher-bearers.

Now the Yankee was in a repentant mood, ready to renounce his sins, join the Confederates after he healed up, and help drive out his former comrades.

Jeff snapped, "How many times you going to change colors, you slimy chameleon?"

The prisoner fell silent, blinking, frightened tears in his eyes.

Jeff turned away, resisting an urge to pull his revolver and finish off the faithless turncoat. He busied himself reloading the carbine, and felt much relieved when the medical assistants carried the wretch out of sight.

He heard a sudden boom to his front, and watched a shell plow into the ground, exploding a hundred yards ahead of him. A cloud of red dirt spewed into the air. The Yankees were trying a new tactic. "Good try, but too short," he said under his breath. Another shell screamed overhead and burst somewhere well behind him. He laughed in his throat. "Split the difference and you'll have me."

He glanced around to see how his men were taking the bombardment. Just as he expected, they were staying low, watching the trajectory of incoming fire. No damage so far. He figured two guns at most, not very accurate at that, not enough to unnerve seasoned troops. They'd been through worse.

Nothing much to do but hunker down and wait for the shelling to quit. Then the real fighting would begin.

***

Willa was watching Reynolds demonstrate loading and aiming his revolver when the first cannonball slammed into the ground not a hundred yards away. Annie Laurie screamed and reared. Willa cried out too, but clung like a burr and fought Annie back onto all fours. Fortunately Baron and the sergeant's mount were not so panicked as her civilian mare, but they caught some of the fear and milled, shivering, eyes showing too much white.

Willa glanced at Reynolds, fearing he'd noticed she was having trouble. Amazingly, he had his horses under control. Then he started singing "Home, Sweet Home." He winked at her and kept on singing.

She clenched her jaws and held onto the lead ropes, fingernails digging into her palms. She couldn't help picturing a bomb blowing her out of the saddle, her dead hands still gripping those ropes.

Captain Spencer wouldn't let her into the fight, but he'd given her a job, entrusting her with his horse and the sergeant's as well. She'd already made up her mind. The horses weren't going to get away from her, no matter what happened.

A cannonball waffled overhead and exploded somewhere behind them. Annie startled again, but Willa checked her with a tight bit. She spoke soothingly into the mare's ear, stroking her neck and shoulders to calm her, maybe trying to calm herself as well. "Whoa, baby. Look at the other horses," she whispered. "They know better, they aren't spooky. There's nothing to be afraid of."

She hoped she wasn't struck dead by a cannonball as a punishment for lying.

Another round burst nearby, proving the lie to her words. There was plenty to fear. Annie Laurie dilated her nostrils and gathered her rear legs underneath her haunches to bolt. Willa held the reins with all her strength, barely maintaining her mastery.

She looked around for shelter, then decided to keep the horses out in the open, because the strikes came like lightning and she imagined a tree falling down on her. As far as she could tell, none had hit any of the horses or men at the rear, a miracle. She fought to keep the three horses from fleeing in different directions, then she started singing along with Reynolds. Her voice quavered, but it did seem to soothe Annie anyhow.

To her vast relief, the artillery fire stopped and all she heard was the crack of rifles. The horses settled down, pricking their ears toward the splitting sounds. If it was this bad in the rear, what must it be like where the real fighting was? Where Captain Spencer was?

She tried to swallow past the sulfur-tasting knot in her throat, fearing not only for herself, but for him.

***

Now the Yankees were charging on foot. They burst out of the woods shooting and shouting for Southern blood, a grand, intimidating sight. Watching that mob coming to kill him quickened Jeff's anemic sense of self-preservation, almost made him forget how little he cared for his life. He controlled the sane impulse to cut and run, willing himself to be an intrepid example.

After all, the Yankees weren't so smart, coming in straight like that. The Confederate line was thin and didn't extend very far. If the Yankee officers had enough sense to whip their forces around, find the flank and pour in behind the shields, they would have themselves a fine shooting gallery.

They pull that one, I'm close enough to the flank to die in the first wave.

He emptied the carbine at his enemies first, then resorted to his revolver. His hat tore off. Stokes screamed, spewing blood, then slumped over, clutching his face. Jeff squeezed off one round after another into the bodies of his enemies.

38

Still the Yankees pressed forward, heads averted as though breasting a wind-driven downpour. Those still on their feet ignored the crossfire and their comrades falling out of line.

A clot of them rushed up to the barricade. He stood to meet them, revolver in one hand, saber in the other, flanked by Harris and the vedette. One of the Yankees swung his carbine toward him. Jeff was quicker with his smaller weapon. He blasted a hole through the man's belly. Then he whirled, ready to take on the next, and faced empty air.

The one he had shot drooped over the barricade vomiting blood, and two others had fallen in front of it. The only enemies yet on their feet were moving away, fading into the woods.

Stokes lay where he fell, arms and legs jerking, convulsing his life away. Jeff felt a stab of loss, another hometown man gone. Sorrow exploded into rage. He leaped over the barricade, yelling, "Come on! Don't let the bastards get away!"

He glanced over his shoulder to make sure his men were following, backing him up. Gray soldiers poured over the breastworks, hitting the ground at a run. Behind them, the reserves pushed into the fight. He yelled out the wild desire to smash his enemies and make them sorry they'd ever set foot on Georgia soil uninvited to kill his friends.

Chapter Five

A n officer that Willa didn't recognize rode through the ranks of horse-holders, raging, hollering at them to move forward. "Where's Captain Spencer?" she asked him.

The officer acted as though he hadn't heard her and shouted his order again. "We're going in mounted," he yelled at Reynolds. "We're going to surround them."

She nudged Annie Laurie toward the breastworks, leading the other two horses.

Now that she was in sight of the barricades, the gunfire was sporadic and distant. Nobody appeared to be defending the works, but as she drew near she noticed men lying about, not moving.

She was right about one thing. The fighting had been as deadly as it sounded from where she'd been cowering with the horses. A bluecoat lay across the logs. The face of another on the near side of the barricade was raisin-dark, the sun parching him into jerky. Most likely it was his death she smelled. A Confederate with a bloody place where his nose should have been, stared up at her.

Reynolds hesitated. "Damnation. They got Stokes."

"Stokes?" She stared at the body, suddenly recognizing the patched-up pants. Then she averted her eyes, feeling her stomach knot up on the hardtack she'd eaten for breakfast.

"He ain't going to eat General Johnston now," Reynolds said quietly. "Lord have mercy on his soul."

Willa wasn't sure she'd even liked Stokes. He'd called her a sissy-kid and she suspected he'd made a fool out of her. But she'd ridden beside him, cooked for him and shared a meal with him. He'd been bursting with life. Now he was dead.

She made herself look over the bodies again, but didn't find Captain Spencer's. This was the last place she had seen him. Relief flooded through her. If she found him dead, it would be like hearing about Bobby all over again.

"Where's Captain Spencer?" she asked Reynolds.

"Right out front, most likely. Making the Yankees sorry they ever took him on."

She lifted her gaze toward the sound of battle to their front. "He said the Yankees had three times as many as we do. Didn't seem too worried, though."

"He won't make us do anything he wouldn't do hisself." Reynolds shrugged, his face grim. "Trouble is, he don't mind going straight into hell." He hustled his horses past her, all humor gone. "Hurry up, kid."

She followed him to the low place in the breastworks and watched him cross his horses over. But when it came her turn, Annie Laurie balked and shied.

Willa dismounted, tightened Baron's cinch and climbed onto him. As she expected, the trained cavalry horse was accustomed to the sight and smell of dead men, and moved forward at a touch of her heel. This time Annie followed along.

***

Jeff crouched behind a tree, resting, watching for enemies. The fighting had lulled. Only sporadic shots and a few shouts here and there let him know they were still out there.

He breathed fast, inhaling the reek of burnt gunpowder and the odor of his own sweat. It soaked his shirt and union suit. He had long since emptied his canteen, so he had no water to soothe his parched throat. The fighting rage had burned itself out, leaving him empty and shaky. The sun flared high and broiling hot.

But he sensed the Yankees were far worse off than he was. They seemed to take longer to rally every time they were scattered. The ones he saw up close, prisoners being marched to the rear, looked blown, beat up, and exhausted. A little more pressure, and the holdouts would fall apart. He could smell it.

Lieutenant Graham, a member of Colonel Crew's staff rode up, saluted, and told him to have his men fall back to the barricade.

"You must be mistaken," he said. "We've got the Yanks where we want them. We can smash them."

"Orders, Captain." Graham coughed into his hand and cleared his throat. "Compliments of Colonel Crews. I can't help it if you've got your blood up."

"All right, all right, we're coming." Maybe it would be all right. Colonel Crews was no fool, therefore he must have a better plan.

***

Willa spotted Captain Spencer as he ran up. Although his shirt was dark with sweat and blood, it must not be his blood because he didn't seem hurt. Now everything was going to be all right. She quickly

41

dismounted and handed him his own horse. "An officer said something about surrounding the Yankees," she told him. "He said they wouldn't expect us to attack their rear."

"Now *that* makes sense." His voice sounded hoarse, as though he'd overused it. "Got any water?"

She handed him a canteen she had managed to refill. He took a long drink, wiped his mouth with the back of his hand and gave the canteen back. Then he unbuckled a spare gun belt and a saber belt from his waist and handed them to her. "You know how to use an army Colt?"

"Private Reynolds showed me, sir." She dragged the weapon from its holster and checked the cylinder. Loaded. It lay heavy, cold and deadly in her hand.

"I'm giving it to you in case you need it for self defense," he said in a low, confidential voice. "You have my permission to stay in the rear and help with the wounded. We will have some."

Fear boiled up from her belly, bringing the same sick taste into her throat as when she saw Stokes dead. She tried to choke it down, suspecting Captain Spencer knew every one of her doubts and fears. She feared getting killed, or being hurt so bad she might as well be dead.

Even worse, she feared performing badly, acting like a sissy-kid, being found out, then treated like a faint-hearted girl. All her life she'd been told what girls couldn't do. But Pa didn't know everything. She'd prove she could hold her own.

She set her jaw. "Is that an order, sir?"

"You aren't an official soldier yet. It's a suggestion."

Captain Spencer was showing her a certain respect, not bossing her around, but letting her make her own choice. She must live up to it. "You need every man to fight, sir. I joined up to do my part. I'm not backing out unless you order me to."

He studied her for a moment, then said, "It's your call, Will."

"I have to do this, sir."

He nodded. "So be it."

She felt the warmth of his approval, and her own craving for more.

"God be with you." He checked the cinch, mounted Baron, then rode over to a batch of officers and conferred.

She strained to catch what they said, but could only hear an occasional word. She made out his expression as he turned to look over his troop, resolute and fearless. She wished courage was as contagious as fear.

"Are we all going to fight this time?" Willa asked Reynolds, who sat on his horse nearby.

"That's my guess. Maybe we'll have something to do besides standing around smelling horse shit." Reynolds grabbed General Johnston in both hands and stuffed him into a saddlebag. The rooster didn't resist, as though he was used to that sort of treatment. An orange feather tore loose and floated to the ground.

The officers' counsel didn't last long before they split off and rode in different directions. Captain Spencer came back to where his men waited, a hard smile on his powder-blackened face. "Attention. We ride around to their left and attack the Yanks from the rear. Mounted." The corners of his mouth hardened even more. "Follow me, columns of four. March."

Willa lined up Annie next to Reynolds, keeping her focus on the captain's lean back bobbing just in front of her. The gun belt dragged heavy on her waist and the saber banged next to her thigh.

During the long, arcing trot through the woods, she couldn't see a thing of the battle, only tree limbs she had to dodge to keep from being swept off the saddle. She rode down one slope and up another, working her way with the soldiers, skirting the battle noise. Finally the gunfire sounded behind her.

After she broke out of the woods and regained the road, Captain Spencer halted the troop and turned them back toward the north. "Form a battle line, pass it down." His whisper grated, harsh and hoarse.

Willa imitated the men around her and pointed Annie in the same direction. She didn't see any Yankees, just woods all around. Surely the Yankees had spotted the little Confederate force slipping around to their rear, and were getting good and ready to shoot her dead.

Every time she closed her eyes, she saw Stokes lying still, his face destroyed. Her heart hammered against her ribs and her breaths came quick and light. Sweat trickled down her spine into her waistband. She clenched her hands on the reins to control the shaking. Annie fidgeted underneath her, catching her case of nerves.

She concentrated on watching Captain Spencer. The sight of him, easy in the saddle, calmly waiting for the signal, steadied her. Unbidden prayers popped into her mind, pleas for strength and courage. *Don't let me be a coward.*

She drew the revolver he had given her, pointing it toward the ground in case it went off accidentally. Then came the opening notes of the bugle, Captain Spencer shouting "Charge," fierce high-pitched yips and yells, and the line surged forward. Too late to change her mind now. She and Annie Laurie rushed along, carried with the sheer power of the charging horses around them.

Puffs of guns smoke wafted through the brush in front, the Yankees fighting back. Willa was aware of Reynolds riding abreast to her left. Afraid she might fall behind, she pressed Annie to keep in sight of Captain Spencer.

She rushed through the place where she'd seen the gunfire. Then she spotted dark blue flitting behind a bush, raised her revolver, but lost sight of the target. The Yankees faded back, giving ground.

She followed Captain Spencer into a clearing, where a blur of bluecoats and horses tangled in a frantic mix. A Yankee officer beat one of his own fleeing men across the back with the flat of his saber. "Rally, men!" he hollered. "Goddamn you, stop them! Kill the sonsabitches!"

Then she heard Captain Spencer yelling, "Save the horses, kill the men!"

Pistols boomed. The Yankee officer faltered, staggered, dropped his saber and sank to his knees, clutching his belly, a stunned look on his face. Willa watched the blood pour out from between his fingers, watched him lie down on his side, drawing up his legs, and heard his screams.

She tore her gaze away from the stricken Yankee. At the edge of the clearing, other bluecoats were trying to mount and escape. Horses caught their panic, milling this way and that, wild-eyed and screaming, colliding with each other, stepping on men's feet and causing havoc. She heard grunts and groans and curses.

Reynolds barged right in front of her, and shot into a man who had just mounted. The bluecoat yelped, jerked, then fell forward onto the horse's neck and slid off, leaving a smear of blood on the saddle.

The metallic scent of human blood surrounded her, so strong she could even taste it at the back of her mouth.

She held onto her reins with one hand, revolver in the other, remembering she was supposed to shoot somebody with it too. She looked around for a somebody to aim at, but in the confusion she was afraid she'd hit a man from her own side instead.

A riderless horse slammed its chest into Annie, smashing Willa's leg and making Annie sidestep. Another bumped them from the off side. It was too much for the terrified mare. Willa clung as Annie whirled and bolted.

She hung on, sawing the reins with no effect, screaming "Whoa! Whoa! Whoa!" She lost a stirrup, regained it, and lost the other one. She clamped her legs around the mare's body and grabbed a handful of mane. Annie carried her off into the woods, whipping between trees and through brush. The mare scraped Willa too close to a trunk, banging her knee. Branches switched her face and she ducked to avoid them. She had no idea where she was going, just deeper into the woods behind Yankee lines.

She let go of the mane and pulled back on the reins with both hands, using all her strength. The mare slowed a little, running off her first panic. Willa was finally able to collect both stirrups and secure her seating. Much better. Now she had the leverage to regain control.

Just ahead, through a thinner place in the brush, she spotted a man lifting his rifle and pointing it toward her. A Yankee! She jerked the reins even harder and tried to turn Annie. The mare lurched. A flash and a bang and she heard the bullet whiz by. Seeing that he missed, the Yankee threw down the emptied rifle and ran.

Willa wanted no part of that Yankee, but couldn't seem to get Annie to stop. She yelled "Whoa!" and pulled back. The mare finally shifted into a trot. The Yankee looked over his shoulder, panic on his face. He was as much afraid of her as she was of him! Somehow, she still had the revolver, holding it in a white-knuckled grip along with the reins.

Then the Yankee stumbled, tripped over something and fell on his hands and knees. He dropped his rifle. Willa was upon him then, managing to stop Annie just before she ran by him. She raised the revolver, pointing it toward the man.

He twisted around, staring at the weapon. He yelled, "Don't shoot! I give!"

Willa sat on her blowing horse, watching the panting Yankee. His mouth hung open, gulping air, his face glowed red hot, greasy with sweat, as though he were about to have a sunstroke. No coat, shirt open at the neck showing curly dark hair. He was a big, robust man, with a full beard, a good ten years older than herself.

She wiped sweat out of her eyes and tried to figure out what to do next. It wasn't fair to shoot him after he surrendered. But what now? He was as dangerous as a rattlesnake.

"I'm taking you prisoner." Her voice sounded unsure, so she cleared her throat and repeated it with more authority. "You're my prisoner."

"Damn. Just my luck I missed. Damn, damn, damn. Just my luck. And a stripling, by God." He settled back on his elbows, glancing at his rifle, which had landed next to his foot. He still wore a revolver in his holster. Had he forgotten about it, or was it empty too? She wasn't as worried about his saber. It was sheathed, and he couldn't reach her with it before she had time to shoot him.

He looked back up at her. "You're making me nervous, kid. That pistol's shaking so hard it might go off by itself."

"Take off your gunbelt," she said. "Throw it over by your rifle. The saber belt, too."

He unbuckled the hardware, dragged it off his waist and tossed, clanking it down by his feet.

Willa pointed with the revolver to a spot a good ways from his weapons. "Now move over there."

After he complied, she dismounted and gathered up his weapons. Watching him as she worked, she hung the gun belt on the pommel of the saddle and stuck the rifle into the saddle holster.

"You better leave me be and save yourself," he said. "My friends are going to come along and kill you."

Did he know that for sure? There were bound to be other Yankees nearby, so she'd better split it back to her own kind. If she let him ride behind her, he could overpower her. But if she let him go, she would be releasing a menace.

She shook her head. "You're coming with me, but you have to walk. You lead the way."

He shambled to his feet, towering over her. "But *your* friends will shoot me as soon as they see me coming."

She kept the revolver pointed at his chest. "Just keep your hands up and pray they don't."

She pointed back the way she'd come. At least, she hoped it was the way she'd come. Gunfire cracked from all around, as though the fighting was going on everywhere at once. She had no ambition to be lost out in the woods in the midst of her enemies with this individual who looked mean enough to eat her for supper.

***

Jeff pounded over the rough country, giving chase to fugitives who had managed to mount and sneak away. He and his comrades had collected Yankees, mostly unhorsed or wounded. He'd sent men to escort them to the rear a few at a time, so his squad had steadily diminished in size.

His forearm stung from the bite of a bullet. He had wrapped a handkerchief around the bloody slice, only an inconvenience, not severe enough to keep him from his duties. He came suddenly upon a deep gully and Jeff reined in just before his mount stumbled over the side. "Halt!" he yelled to the men behind him.

The ravine was full of men and horses, full nearly to the top. He could have ridden across using the beasts and blue-clad bodies as a bridge.

Quinn reined in next to him. "Great God. A lovely sight. But this isn't our doing."

"We'd better find a way around them," Jeff said. "The horses won't want to step into that mess."

"That's what happened." Quinn scratched his chin. "Their own people ran over them."

Jeff nodded, noticing a man's flattened head that was stamped from cheek to ear by a purple horseshoe print. He turned and said to Will, "There lies 'every man for himself.' See what it'll get you? Always think of your comrades and act for the common good."

The boy had handled himself well, far better than Jeff had expected. He had gotten through the fight in one piece, even captured a stalwart Yankee all by himself. But at this moment, Will was swallowing hard and turning an unhealthy pale.

Jeff said to him, "You sick?"

Will wiped his mouth and shook his head no.

"You'll get used to it. You get hard."

Quinn reconsidered his earlier statement, musing, "Maybe we can take credit, after all. Sure must have thrown the scare into them."

Jeff spotted a hand upraised, as though a man pled for help. He heard a low moan from somewhere within the pile of broken and crushed flesh.

The poor devils would have to wait. Later he could detail a couple of men to drag the live ones out. They weren't going to go anywhere in the meantime. He guided his mount to the left alongside the ravine, down into a clear passage, and led his men across.

An hour later, encumbered by too many prisoners and too few men to guard them, he turned back. Some had managed to escape dispite his men's best efforts. Fresh men and horses could hunt them down later. This deep into Confederate lines, scattered Yankees wouldn't have an easy time keeping their liberty.

He returned to the ravine that had the bodies in it. A few Confederates were picking through the carnage, salvaging weapons, equipment, valuables, and haversacks with food in them. He watched one ravenous soldier cut the blood off a piece of bread and stuff the clean part into his mouth.

Somebody, maybe kindhearted scavengers, had pulled a couple of battered but living men out of the pile and laid them out in the shade. He had to pass close to the injured Yankees. One of them said in a weak voice, "Hey, Johnny. Do something for me, will you?"

He paused, drawing Baron to a stop a few feet from the man. "What is that?"

"Kill me."

Jeff blinked, caught by surprise. Then he said, "You want a quick way out?"

"Do it."

He recalled the stinking trail of vicious destruction the Yankees had left. Stokes, drilled through the face. Countless other dead friends, killed by men like this one. "My pleasure." He drew his revolver and leveled it between the Yankee's eyes. Those eyes looked right into his, then closed, prepared for oblivion.

He hesitated.

He'd killed plenty of men in hot blood or self-defense, but never by request.

In a like situation, he would welcome a bullet through the brain like he'd given that poor dying horse. Hell, it wasn't a year ago he almost did it to himself. Would have, too, had he not remembered taking one's own life was a mortal sin. Besides, he wouldn't mind killing another Yankee. He might even enjoy it.

That was what worried him.

He shook his head and lowered the barrel. "You're feeling hopeless right now. Give yourself a chance. Our doctors will take care of you." Easy words for him to say, but with those words he was probably condemning the wretch to slow death.

The eyes flew open. "Do it. I can't move my legs. My back's broke."

"Ah." Jeff cleared his throat. "Maybe you're mistaken. The doctor can tell about things like that better than you or I."

"I'll die anyway, in prison."

He shook his head no. "I won't make that judgment."

The Yankee turned his dejected face aside and Jeff nudged the horse forward. He glanced at Will, who had halted with him. The boy's face was set, staring at the crippled Yankee.

"I leave these things up to God." Jeff recalled his real feelings and condemned himself for a sanctimonious hypocrite. He led Will away from the ravine full of the dead and the better off dead.

Then he heard a pistol shot behind him. He started at the sharp, familiar sound, whipped his head around and looked over his shoulder. The woods blocked his view.

He heard Will's soft voice, right next to him. "That wasn't God, was it?"

Chapter Six

Willa staked, fed and watered the horses, then started a cook fire. Captain Spencer had promised to bring rations, and she hoped it would be soon.

By late afternoon, all the surviving Yankees had either surrendered or skedaddled, and the shooting was over. Tired but triumphant soldiers lounged about, smoking or cleaning their powder-fouled weapons.

The fright still came over her whenever she thought about what she had seen and felt today, the fear of dying, and the sickening sight of all those broken men and horses in the gully. She'd waded into the fighting, not knowing what it was going to be like, and it was worse than anything she'd ever imagined. She was over her head, far worse than when she had crossed that stream.

If it weren't for Edgar and Pa waiting for her at home, she'd just tell Captain Spencer she'd made a bad mistake and get out of this cavalry business. But she wasn't going to do that. She had to stick with the cavalry, the only hiding place she knew.

Someone rode up. It was Captain Spencer, sitting on a big sleek Yankee horse he'd captured. She worried that the bullet-slice on his arm was bleeding again, a red stain against the dirt-caked handkerchief binding it. The way he ignored it assured her it was not a serious wound. She stood up to meet him. He nodded to her in his formal way, taking in the cook fire and the contented horses. He dropped a couple of croaker sacks at her feet and said, "Supper for the troop, courtesy of Stoneman's has-been raiders."

Willa opened a sack, looking over the ham and green corn, no doubt stolen out of somebody's smokehouse and field. But her stomach wasn't asking any awkward questions.

"You acquitted yourself pretty well today," he said. "Bringing in a Yankee prisoner like that."

Better not point out that only dumb luck had turned her disaster into a triumph. "Thank you, sir."

He nodded toward a sapling. "Don't forget you're still green as that young pine over there."

"I'm learning, sir."

"Got a long way to go, but you do catch on quick. I'd better swear you in, soldier." He took off his hat and brushed back his hair with his fingers. She noted the hollowness of his cheeks, the darkness around his eyes, deeper than the gunpowder stains. He smacked his hat against his thigh. "No, let's do it later. I'm so hungry I could eat this fat Yankee horse raw."

The horse snorted and rolled his eyes as though he understood he might be supper.

"You scared him!" Willa said.

Captain Spencer cracked a smile and patted the horse's neck. "Never mind, old fellow. We've got better provisions tonight than stringy horsemeat."

Sergeant Quinn returned from posting guards and cast a hungry gaze over the provisions. "I'll divvy it up."

"A good haul." Captain Spencer dismounted and handed the reins to Willa. "Five hundred Yanks hors-de-combat. Lots of fine replacement horses, a wagon train full of provisions, two cannons, hundreds of sabers, rifles and revolvers. Not much ammunition. They said that was the only reason they had to surrender."

"Ha. Vandalism is such hard work. The poor things were too tar'd to fight." The sergeant's laugh sounded like a snort. "Most of them are sleeping like babies over in the bull pen."

"I hear General Stoneman was so humiliated over having to surrender he sat down on a log and cried like a girl." Captain Spencer eased himself to the ground then propped his back against a pine trunk, letting out a sigh. "I found Stokes and made arrangements to have him shipped home."

"Our little circle is getting smaller." Quinn shook his head, sorrowful.

"I'll write to his wife, maybe tomorrow." Captain Spencer took off his hat and rubbed his temple, a weary gesture. "You remember stopping at that old fellow's house? The drunk. Randall. Wasn't that his name?" He glanced at Willa. "You said you called by his place too, Will."

She stood frozen, holding onto his horse's bridle. "That's right, sir. Mr. Randall."

The sergeant spat tobacco juice. "Cranky old buzzard. Not a happy drunk."

"Up at headquarters I heard he got murdered by Yankee stragglers," Captain Spencer said.

"Murdered!" Willa yelped. The captain gave her a quizzical stare. She swallowed past her constricted throat, regretting her outburst, realizing she couldn't afford to show her feelings.

"Maybe he showed them his shotgun." Captain Spencer smiled without humor. "That would have been enough."

He must be mistaken. Somebody else, not Pa. She recalled wishing he'd died instead of Mama or Bobby. A wave of guilt washed over her.

"Strange." Quinn shook his head, thoughtful. "The Yanks didn't even take that route. They went down the east side of the river. Every last one, I could have sworn. I know it's peculiar. But some home guard major told a courier that Yankees killed the old fellow and burned his house." He glanced at Willa again. "Must have happened after you stopped by his place."

She rested her hand on the pommel of the saddle for support. Pa murdered and the house burned down. A home guard major said so. Edgar Dodds. It had to be him that told of it.

Captain Spencer's voice cracked through her shock. "You know anything about it, Will? See any Yankees when you were coming through there?"

She couldn't speak but managed to shake her head no.

He locked eyes on her. "You all right, Will?"

She shivered involuntarily and broke eye contact, dropping her gaze to the ground. Then she forced her voice to start working again. "I'll see to your horse now, if you'll excuse me, sir. Then I'll come back and cook supper."

"Never mind the critter, just cook." He stood up and stretched. "I'll get Reynolds to take care of him."

She tried to keep her mind on the cooking, but spilled the water for the coffee, dampening part of the fire. She willed herself not to fall apart at her personal catastrophe on top of the day's huge tragedies. Forcing herself to stay in control, she pitched a fresh log onto the fire and built it up again.

Tears welled into her eyes, but she blinked them back. She couldn't cry like a girl. And she didn't dare let on that the Mr. Randall the Yankees killed was her father. The other soldiers would ask questions, then ask around, and they'd be onto her. She couldn't stand to be found out that way.

She'd left Pa, then Yankees had killed him. If she had stayed home it wouldn't have happened.

Or maybe they would have killed her too.

She wished she'd just gone ahead and shot that Yankee instead of bringing him in alive. Maybe she'd get a chance to shoot more of them for Bobby and for Pa.

She recalled the one that asked Captain Spencer to kill him. Now she wished she was the one that had done it.

She ate a few bites of her supper, but the food tasted like bitter ashes. She choked on it, along with the grief and guilt.

Captain Spencer studied her, that way he had of looking right through her. "What's the matter, Will?"

"Nothing, sir." But his noticing brought the tears back to her eyes. She averted her gaze so he wouldn't see.

He leaned closer and touched her shoulder. "Look at me," he commanded.

Reluctantly she raised her head and met his gaze. What did he know?

"You've seen awful things today. Sometimes it doesn't sink in till afterwards. Go ahead and let it out. You'll feel better, and only a jackass would dare to make fun of you."

Grateful, she jumped up, ran into the woods, and threw herself down on a bed of pine needles. She sobbed, shoulders heaving, until she felt rattly and hollow inside. She sat up, hugging herself for a while, hiccupping, until her breathing evened out. "Damn you, Pa. Damn you for being a drunk and running me off."

Blame him hard as she could, she still couldn't make it his fault the Yankees killed him. She was the one who'd wished him dead, even if she did take it back.

She recalled better times. Pa had staked everything he was made of into the chunk of middle Georgia land, and it had given in return. He'd worked side-by-side with his people, taking advantage of the willing soil. The Randall family had worked into a rough sort of gentility, the beginnings of prosperity.

Then mama died.

So did Pa's spirit, or maybe it drowned. His drinking got worse, no matter how she begged him or how many jugs of Edgar Dodds' special recipe she poured into the ground.

She recalled standing in the red earth of her vegetable garden while Edgar showed her the agreement Pa had signed regarding her future. Then Pa asked him to supper to celebrate, making her cook for him and act the hostess. Naturally Edgar brought some of his liquid goods to share with Pa, and the two of them sat drinking and laughing while she hid in her room. But Edgar knew where she was.

She got up and wandered to the horse picket, shirt cuffs damp with tears. Annie Laurie stood switching her tail, and Willa walked over and rubbed the mare's velvety muzzle. She moved her hand to the warm neck while Annie flicked her ears, bent her head down then nuzzled Willa's pocket. "I don't have anybody left but you," she whispered. "Even if I went home, Edgar wouldn't leave me be." Her throat tightened in horror at the memory. She swallowed and kept talking to Annie. "Not after what happened. I've got nowhere to live. I have to stay with the cavalry. And all those bluebellies out there want to shoot me. Why, I could end up dead, just like Stokes!"

Here, at least, she had made a couple of friends. Reynolds, who seemed to like her and took time to give her revolver-loading lessons. Captain Spencer, who treated her as though she was worth something. His presence made her feel safe in the midst of the horror.

She stayed with the horses a little while longer before she felt a craving for human companionship. She longed to surround herself with her brothers, the soldiers.

After picking her dazed way back to the campsite, she paused in front of Captain Spencer, suddenly afraid his wound would fester up and he would get blood poisoning and die too. She made bold to mention it. "Are you going to see the doctor about your hurt arm, Sir?"

"No need." He glanced down at the dirty binding wrapped around the sleeve. "It isn't much of anything."

"I have some clean cloth. I'd like to see to it."

He shrugged. "It's nothing, really."

She stood her ground and clenched her fists. "I want to."

"It's that important to you?" He lifted a brow. "I guess it could stand a little attention, if you insist."

He stripped down to his bare chest, carefully peeling the sticky sleeve away from the wound. His body was muscular for a man so lean. The woman whose picture he carried probably liked the way he looked. If she didn't, she was a fool.

Willa tore her gaze away from him and found the white cloth in her sewing kit and a canteen full of water. Then she gently washed and bound the deep furrow in his forearm, willing her hands to work steadily. Stoic, he held his arm out and didn't say a word.

Her face was within inches of his, close enough for her to inhale his very breath. It smelled lightly of the ham she'd cooked for him, and of fatigue and endurance. She figured she smelled like that too. She breathed it in, an honest scent, good enough for both of them.

He thanked her for taking care of his arm, giving her one of his long, penetrating looks.

She caught her breath. Had she given something away? Did he suspect she was an imposter? Was he going to send her away in disgrace?

She shouldn't have pulled out her sewing kit. But soldiers carried such accoutrements. Bobby did, she'd even put it together for him. Maybe the captain thought she wasn't tough enough to be a soldier. After all, she'd gone off and cried, something soldiers weren't supposed to do, even though a Yankee general was weak enough to.

Should she beg him? *Please don't send me away. This is the only home I have now, the soldiers my only living kinfolk.*

"Raise your right hand," he said, lifting his own, palm forward.

"Do you swear to uphold the Constitution of the Confederate States of America?"

Weak with relief, she repeated "Yes, sir," for every question in the oath. In this way he swore her into the army.

Later, she curled up near enough to reach over and touch him. She flinched when big cold raindrops spattered on her cheek.

He got up and spread a rubber waterproof over her. Surprised at his thoughtfulness, she mumbled her thanks. He didn't say anything, but settled back in his place next to her.

Visions of Edgar and her father, Stokes and the dead Yankees in the gully galloped through her mind. She cocked her ears to the lengthening of Captain Spencer's sleep-breathing and watched his dark form. Knowing he was only an arm's length away sustained her through the terrifying and lonely night.

Chapter Seven

Jeff admired the scenery as he rode into Macon. Shade trees and gracious two story homes lined the wide streets. A Negro band fiddled in the town square, the members dressed up in red tuxedos. Ladies, young and old, stood along the sidewalks, waving their handkerchiefs to the soldiers, giving them the hero treatment.

He tipped his hat to them and held a smile so long he felt that his face would split. But it was a good change to win a real victory and save this town from the ravages of the enemy. Lately the Confederate army had done nothing but lose men and ground.

The harvest straggled along behind, captured artillery caissons and wagons heaped with weaponry. Other wagons carried groaning wounded from both sides, mercifully out of his earshot. The bullet that had grazed his arm hadn't disabled him, another mercy. The wound was a little fevered, but not enough to keep him from fighting. His new aide had done a good job cleaning and dressing it, a touch gentle as his wife's.

His wife. If only the pain of her remembrance were merely the physical kind. It would be easier to bear. She'd been taken from him, along with friends and acquaintances he dared not count, shaking his faith down to his boot-soles.

Just ahead, prisoners trudged on foot, surrounded by mounted guards. The Yankees had tried their level best to get into Macon. Only a few home guards, infantry, and a deep river had repulsed them until now. They had finally made it into town, but not on the victorious terms they'd envisioned. Forced to walk all the way from the battle site, a good 15 miles, the able-bodied prisoners were limping, almost to a man. Cavalrymen weren't used to walking. Besides that, most of them were barefoot, having *donated* their boots to needy Confederates. But they wouldn't have to walk much farther because there was a stockade close by the town.

He noted a crater in the street where an artillery round had exploded. Everywhere the invaders went, they bombarded inhabited cities, jeopardizing noncombatants. After a summer of siege, the buildings of

Atlanta were torn and crumbled. Macon had gotten off light by comparison.

Some of the Macon ladies didn't appreciate the Yankee presence and showed it. They shrieked insults at the prisoners as they walked by. He saw one woman stride up to a bluecoat and spit in his face.

"Tell the guards to look sharp and keep the civilians away from the prisoners," he said to Sergeant Quinn. "Some of the ladies are behaving badly."

After Quinn rode ahead to convey his order, Jeff watched a pretty blonde woman lean over a balcony that overhung the street. She picked up a chamber pot and slung the contents down onto the prisoners walking beneath. The wretch who got the brunt of the dousing halted, drooping, miserably wet from offal.

"No!" Jeff shouted. "There's no call for that kind of treatment. Those men can't hurt you now!"

The woman set down the chamber pot and looked right at him. Then she glided, head held regally high, from the balcony back into the house.

Just behind him, he heard Will's soft voice. "Maybe a Yankee killed that lady's brother. Or her father."

He twisted around to look at the boy. Will looked more like a proper soldier now that he was equipped with weapons and better-fitting boots. But he'd been silent, even tragic, all day.

"Still doesn't make it right. I doubt that individual is responsible."

"He might be."

Will's eyes were hot and his battered young face was set. The battle sure had a bad effect on him. Oddly, the boy hadn't started brooding and grieving until long after the shooting was over. Just when Jeff had figured Will was taking the awfulness just fine, the boy had suddenly spilled into tears, as though hearing about Randall's death affected him. Maybe he knew the old man better than he let on.

Never mind. He couldn't worry over every raw recruit and mother's son. Jeff wasn't Will's daddy. He wasn't anybody's daddy. He turned his back on Will and looked straight ahead.

A colored boy ran up to him and passed him a folded note. He scanned the neat small writing on the stationery, an invitation to dinner at a Mrs. Myron Mabry's home, celebrating the salvation of the city. In the note the grateful Mrs. Mabry urged him to bring all his men. Good for her. She wasn't snubbing the privates, who'd risked their necks for her property too.

The colored boy pointed her out. "Miz Mabry's over there."

Jeff looked up and spotted the dignified matron standing on the sidewalk smiling back at him. Two younger women flanked her, fresh in light pastel summer dresses.

The scenery is looking better and better.

He smiled at the trio and lifted his hat. The young ladies waved.

He scratched his chin. Good thing he'd taken time to shave this morning. He'd hate to look dirty-faced and stubbled for such lovely admirers. He needed to wash his clothes and take a bath so he wouldn't drive them out of their own house. Or worse, infest their home with his bugs. Better see that the whole troop looked to such affairs as well.

Jeff said to the colored boy, "Very good. We'll be honored to attend, all of us." He dug out a fifty-cent shinplaster and gave it to him. Then he took the direct approach, nudging Baron over to the sidewalk. Accepting the invitation from the lovely ladies in person promised to be a pleasant task

***

In camp, Captain Spencer announced that the whole troop was invited to supper at a Mrs. Mabry's home. The news brought whoops and cheers from the men, but Willa didn't join in. She had these men fooled about her sex, but what if a woman saw right through her?

Besides, she was in mourning, even if she couldn't let on. A party was the last place she wanted to go.

She managed to get Captain Spencer aside. "Sir, I can't go to supper at somebody's house. I don't feel so good."

"No excuses. A party will be good for whatever is ailing you."

"But I'm not presentable." She touched her face. "The bruises."

"Everybody's beat up one way or another, and it's warm enough to bathe in the river." He scratched his moustache. "I'm looking forward to a good time, myself. They are going to a great deal of trouble for us, and Mrs. Mabry's daughters are attractive."

"You'd pay court to them?"

"They'll be insulted if we don't." He drew up one side of his mouth in an amused half-smile. "You don't have to look so scandalized."

"Don't you already have a sweetheart? Or is she your wife?"

The smile fell off his face. "Jeannie. You saw her picture," he said flatly.

"You had it in plain view. Wouldn't she be hurt if you betrayed her so?"

He scowled. "Mind your own damn business, soldier."

"I'm sorry." She stepped back, startled. "I didn't mean any—"

"You *are* going to Mrs. Mabry's." His voice leveled but lost none of its intensity. "Get yourself cleaned up and decent, or else you are on latrine duty for the duration of the war."

"Yes, sir," she whispered, feeling shamed even if she was in the right.

He turned on his heel and stalked away, leaving her confused and desolate.

She'd never heard him curse before. No doubt she'd been presumptuous, but why did he get angry? Apparently he didn't like being reminded of his duty to his wife. Was he that faithless? Just when he had her believing he was a cut above the general run of men. Or were they all like that, tom cats who took every opportunity to stray?

Nonetheless, he'd given her an order, and she'd already figured out that didn't mean he was just asking. Better find a way to clean up for the party, because the captain sure wasn't going to take any excuses and let her get out of it.

She slipped down to the riverbank, knelt, and thrust her hand into the water. Another wicked hot summer day, sweat making her shirt cling to her back, and the water felt ice cold in contrast. Maybe a bath would rid her of the nasty little biting bugs she'd recently discovered. Now she understood why the soldiers were such persistent scratchers.

The river was brown, stained from red clay, but it was still cleaner than she was. She splashed her face, enjoying the cold shock. A dip in the river would be delicious, but she didn't dare take off any clothes in case a soldier happened by. Her clothes would dry on her body soon enough.

If only she had soap. But she'd have to make do without it. She was in the army now.

***

Willa stepped straight out of her element and into the Mabry home. A colored butler, wearing top hat and tails, met her at the door and ushered her and the other soldiers into the parlor, where lush carpet softened the tread of their boots. The room smelled harsh of tallow candles and furniture wax. The chairs looked unused, as though no one ever dared sit in them. Portraits of haughty strangers stared down from the walls. A buffet table was richly set with a gleaming silver tea service, a punch bowl filled with pink liquid, and platters piled with dainty light bread sandwiches. Along one wall a reception line of bright, smiling ladies stood in their colorful gowns.

What must it be like to live in such an elegant house? Her comfortable cabin seemed like a shack by comparison. She stiffened her back. Yes, she'd always been poor, but she wasn't ashamed. And she was as good as anybody living in a mansion.

She'd heard people all over town were putting on parties and picnics to treat the soldiers who had come to their rescue. The townspeople sought to accommodate everybody, from the big-shot officers all the way down to her. Maybe her hosts wouldn't look too far down their noses at her.

She glanced around at her companions. Reynolds grinned self-consciously and Sergeant Quinn was trying to pull his short jacket down to cover the patches in the seat of his pants. She realized they felt just as awkward as she did.

Captain Spencer, however, was equal to the occasion. He strode across the room and paused, drawing himself up elegantly in front of the oldest dowager in the reception line. "Mrs. Mabry, how lovely you look," he said. Then he took her hand in both of his and kissed it. The young ladies tittered and Mrs. Mabry blushed at his flattery.

Why shouldn't they be impressed? He was the best looking man in the room, tall and slim, as graceful on his feet as he was on horseback. Moustache combed and trimmed, uniform freshly brushed, rid of war-dirt.

It was hard to picture him as he'd looked yesterday, powder-stained, bloodied, exhausted, the haunted look in his eyes reflecting scenes of death. The coat sleeve hid the dressing on his gunshot wound. And his controlled expression hid whatever was going on inside his head. Those ladies knew nothing of him.

She moved, rather was shuffled, down the reception line. *Make the best of it.* She stopped in front of her hostesses. Imitating the men, she swept off her hat, and bowing from the waist and murmuring greetings. The ladies smiled their welcome. Up close, she noticed that the fine gowns showed signs of repair and make-do. Even old money couldn't buy new clothes these days.

She made it through the line and stood unsure, shifting her weight from foot to foot. What was she was supposed to do next? A servant brought a tray of party sandwiches and she took two. The ham was so thin it was transparent. Despite her unhappiness, she was hungry enough to bolt them whole, but forced herself to nibble politely.

She wandered to the buffet table, where a pretty young girl ladled punch into a crystal cup and handed it to her. Willa thanked her in a low voice and turned to face the center of the crowded room, sipping the punch. The lemonade tasted sour, as though the person who made it used long sweetening like sorghum syrup sparingly. She noticed other flavors she couldn't place.

Then it struck her that even the rich folks couldn't get enough of what they wanted. Mrs. Mabry and her daughters and probably everybody else in town had sacrificed precious stores of food, giving it freely to the soldiers. She turned back to the girl who gave her the punch, wanting to show appreciation. "This is nice, really nice. I haven't had lemonade in ages."

The girl lowered her lashes demurely. "It was the least we could do, after y'all whipped those Yanks that tried to invade us."

"Murderers," Willa said. "That's what they are."

"Is that how you got your face bruised? In the fight?"

Willa touched her cheek and nodded, although it wasn't the same fight the girl meant.

The girl bit her lip. "They killed my papa," she confided. "At Gettysburg. He was a colonel."

"They killed Pa and my brother, too," Willa said.

Neither of them spoke for a moment, a sympathetic silence. The girl at the punch bowl looked about sixteen, petite and ultra feminine, her hands smooth as though servants did all the hard work at her house.

Then Willa broke the silence. "I guess just about everybody's lost somebody."

"That's so." The girl cocked her head to one side, looking her over, then smiled and said, "I'm Martha Fielding."

"Will Barber."

Martha leaned across the table. "The fiddler's starting up, and I do so love to dance."

"Dance?" Willa swallowed, despairing at hearing the first notes of a reel and knowing a hint when she got one. "I, uh, haven't had much practice. We don't have time for such when we're out chasing Yankees."

"It should be easy for a gallant fellow like you. I'm a good teacher."

Willa swallowed past her tight throat. "Don't you have to stay here and attend to the punch bowl?"

Martha looked around and waved. "There's Emma. I'll get her."

Willa fought down panic, reminding herself if she was going to pass for a man she'd better always act like one, especially around women.

The girls returned and her new friend Martha gave her a radiant smile. Willa took a deep breath, leaned across the table and extended her hand. "Martha, may I have the pleasure of this dance?"

***

Jeff performed his duty and danced with every available woman, dowagers and young ladies alike. The warmth of the evening, the weight of his dress coat, the rustle of skirts and the press of female flesh combined to create prickly hot discomfort.

He escorted Mrs. Mabry's elder daughter to the punch bowl and took a liberal hit of the rum-laced lemonade. He smiled, made polite interested noises at Linda Mabry's flirtatious patter, and looked out over the ballroom. The ladies had provided well for his men. Even Will had a dance partner tonight. The boy seemed over his blues, was actually smiling and laughing and having a fine time with his sweet little partner. The rum-spiked the lemonade probably had loosened him up.

Perhaps Jeff shouldn't have lost his temper with Will when he'd mentioned his wife. But he hated explaining Jeannie. She wasn't anybody's business but his. At least Will wasn't likely to open his mouth about her again. He had made it clear the subject was off limits.

Into the house glided a new guest, an elegant, high-headed blonde woman who paused and casually scanned the crowd. Her gaze rested on Jeff and they locked eyes for a moment. Smiling at him, she shifted the fan she carried to her left hand, opened it in front of her face then turned demurely away to greet someone else.

He recognized the same woman who had anointed the Yankee prisoner with urine. This was a vindictive female, yet so bloody good-looking. And her deliberate flirting with the fan signaled her desire to meet him.

He nodded toward her and asked Linda Mabry, "Who's the latest arrival? I believe I saw her as we entered town."

"That's Clarissa McCrae." His hostess wrinkled her nose in obvious dislike. "I'm surprised to see her here. She has her own guests to entertain."

"Maybe her party was too dull."

"Clarissa McCrae is never dull," Miss Mabry sighed.

Jeff would have wagered that Clarissa was easily the most interesting female in this town. He gazed at her and met her eyes again. She carried the fan open in her left hand, further signaling a wish to become acquainted. Her smile dazzled him with its promise.

Contrasting her with Miss Mabry would have led to uncharitable comparisons he'd rather not contemplate for the sake of politeness. "Won't you introduce me?"

He sensed reluctance, but Miss Mabry played the good hostess and obliged him.

Clarissa McCrae delicately extended a gloved hand. "Captain Spencer? One of our esteemed saviors! Welcome to our city."

He unobtrusively noted her robust bosom, trim waist and the wedding band on her left hand. "The pleasure is all mine," he murmured.

Her pale blue eyes met his, sparkling ice. "I've heard all about you."

"Is that a fact?" He inclined his head, avoiding the bait. "I'm quite unremarkable."

"You're too modest. I'm told you are the bravest officer in Wheeler's Cavalry. Valiant to the point of recklessness, scorning the danger of enemy fire."

"Hmmm," he said. "That's some reputation to live up to." The flattery rang a warning bell in his mind, as flattery always did. What did she want from him? Might be interesting to find out. However, she would doubtless be disappointed to know the underlying cause of his rash behavior. How charming could a wretch on the brink of suicide be? There. He'd finally attached words to his despair.

He asked her to dance and promised Linda Mabry he would return soon. "Mr. McCrae is fortunate to have such a lovely wife," he said as he escorted her across the floor.

"He is unfortunate to be missing such a good time. He's been in Milledgeville on business all week. I don't expect him back until tomorrow."

"That long? Don't you think he's worried about his wife's safety while he's gone? I certainly would."

She laughed. "Whom should he fear more? The Yankee invaders, or one of our own men?"

He ignored the innuendo. "Doesn't he look after his wife?" His own words pained him. He hadn't done such a fine job either.

Her mouth formed a pretty pout. "Quite frankly, he's more worried about his precious holdings than his wife."

"He's not in the army?"

"And risk getting hurt? Ha."

"You're not painting a very flattering picture of your husband."

"Never mind him. I didn't come here to discuss *him*."

He smiled. "Men are such boring subjects anyway."

"That's a matter of perspective. I inquired about you because I wanted to meet you."

He raised an eyebrow. "Mrs. McCrae, you offer one surprise after another."

"Do I offend you?"

He lied smoothly. "I like women who can surprise me."

She lowered her long lashes, contrite. "I want to make sure you're not put out with me for my little performance today."

He shrugged, wanting to be drawn in, finding her easy to forgive. "I assumed you had a very good reason for baptizing that Yankee besides saving his soul."

She lifted her gaze back to him, eyes wide and innocent. "Nonetheless, you seemed offended."

"I don't believe in kicking a man when he's down."

"Fiddlesticks. The Yankees don't have the same scruples. And they have no business coming down here and destroying everything we've built up."

"I can't disagree with that."

She pressed closer to him, and he felt a spark like lightning jump between them. It was unbidden, unwelcome, and unmistakable. "I want to make it up to you, to prove I'm not such a bad person."

"On the contrary, I find you fascinating."

"Where are you staying tonight, Captain Spencer?"

"In camp, as usual."

"I have an extra room." She brushed nonexistent lint off her bosom. "You'll be much more comfortable at my house than in that dirty old camp. My home offers clean linens and a soft bed. All the comforts of home."

His throat went dry and the tickle of sexual desire centered in his groin. He'd lived celibate as a monk of late, and hadn't been tempted once until now. He studied her perfectly shaped face, her bold and direct gaze, and the mocking twist of her lips. "That's a tempting offer." He guiltily tried to push aside the image of Jeannie lurking in his mind. If he could only do the impossible and transform this woman into the one he wanted but couldn't have.

"I have other guests, so it will be quite respectable." Her fingers intertwined his warmly, transmitting her real intent. "I live a very lonely existence. It would be a pleasure to have an intelligent conversation with a man. I seldom get to do so."

He studied her, waiting for her to fill in the silence.

She tilted her head. "Do you think I'm too dangerous? Is the brave captain feeling a tremor of fear?"

He laughed low in his throat. "Is that a dare, Mrs. McCrae?" If she could read his mind and knew he wished she were Jeannie, she would not be flattered.

She lowered her long eyelashes demurely. "How much daring could it possibly take? I vow you'll have a pleasant visit."

He hesitated, torn, then pressed her hands in response, a confirmation no one but her might observe. "I'll be honored to pass the night at your home."

She purred, "How charming. You'll find me very hospitable, Captain Spencer."

She was beautiful and fascinating, if despicable. Maybe a night in her bed would help him forget his pain for a little while.

***

Willa and Martha Fielding hit it off very well. It was hard for Willa not to hit it off with a person who hung on her words, acted deeply impressed with every one, and offered a constant stream of compliments.

So that was how girls did it. That was how they got the men they aimed for to fall over them and do their asking. Her own experience with the opposite sex was limited mostly to existence with her father, friendship with her brother, and fending off Edgar. She'd had no idea how to attract a man, nor even wanted to, but Martha was giving her a fine example.

And convincing her she would be terrible at it. She felt unpolished and unschooled and plain spoken by comparison. Not that it mattered as long as she was playing the part of a man. Just as well. She would find it hard to fall into the role of helpless femininity.

Nor did she feel all that helpless, except when Edgar and Pa ganged up on her.

There. Just when she was able to forget for a moment, it struck her again that the Yankees had killed Pa. She blinked away the hotness that came to her eyes, and fought off a spell of dizziness and heat. Was she getting sick? "Would you like some more lemonade?" she asked Martha.

"I'd love some." The girl beamed at her, then fanned herself. "Even though the rum is making me giddy."

"Rum? There's rum in the lemonade?"

"Don't you like it?"

She glanced around, expecting to see men falling down with drunkenness like Pa did. Reynolds was laughing awfully loud with another soldier, but he didn't seem to be slobbering drunk yet. "You mean everybody is drinking rum?"

"The Mabrys had it stored away for a special occasion."

"Isn't there anything else to drink?"

"Don't tell me you're an old temperance prig!" Martha giggled. "And you've had as much of that lemonade as I did." She pointed to another bowl. "If you must, that one is *untainted*. But I'll have some with rum, if you please."

"I don't want to get you any more of that stuff."

Martha pouted. "Then I'll just have to find another dance partner."

"Never mind," Willa said. "I'll get it for you."

"I thought you would," Martha purred.

Sergeant Quinn was standing alone at the punch table. Willa slipped past him and filled a cup with the rum-laced lemonade for Martha. When she turned, she found herself face to face with Captain Spencer. A spectacular blonde was attached to his arm.

He acknowledged her with a preoccupied nod, then said to Sergeant Quinn, "Later this evening, I'm escorting Mrs. McCrae home. She has invited me to stay there, so I won't be back in camp tonight. You'll be in charge until I return."

Quinn looked over the striking woman and smiled. "Yes, sir. Enjoy yourself. Don't worry about a thing."

The captain nodded, then turned back to Mrs. McCrae, his expression softening. "Ready?" he said.

"Certainly." She was just about quivering, a cat ready to spring.

He moved off, the beautiful woman in tow.

"He's going home with her?" Willa said out loud.

"I hope to shout," Quinn whispered, grinning.

Willa stalked away and handed Martha her lemonade, her hand shaky. The more she heard these men talk, the less she liked them. Apparently Sergeant Quinn thought it a good thing for Captain Spencer to betray his wife.

Martha nodded toward Mrs. McCrae, who was gracefully swaying away with Captain Spencer. "That Mrs. McCrae better watch her p's and q's, or Mrs. Mabry and my mama and all the other ladies will refuse to receive her."

Willa stared after the woman, hating her.

Then Martha lowered her voice and giggled. "'Course, I can't blame her for wanting that captain of yours to pay attention to her. He is a fine figure of a man."

Martha was admiring her captain a little too openly for Willa's druthers. But she couldn't blame the girl, so she agreed. "He must be the handsomest man in the whole brigade." She meant it, too, even if he was behaving badly. Almost as bad, he wouldn't ever look at her the way he looked at that woman. After all, he thought she was a boy.

Willa lifted her chin. So be it. That was how it must be.

Chapter Eight

Next morning, Willa worked cottonseed oil into Annie Laurie's mane, untangling knots formed during the march. She yanked a twig out and tossed it aside, glad that horses didn't mind having their hair pulled.

No one else was around, and she had to talk to somebody. She leaned close to Annie's ear and said, "Have you heard all the talk around camp about Captain Spencer and Clarissa McCrae? Do you believe it? I tell you, Martha told me enough gossip about that woman to set a body's ears on fire."

The mare stood quietly, her eyes half shut. "Don't go to sleep on me now! Listen up." Willa blew in her ear, setting Annie to shaking her head.

"That's better. Huh. Captain Spencer spending the night with a woman he wasn't married to! Can you imagine? If he loves his wife so much how could he carry on with such a woman as Clarissa McCrae?"

She bit her lip. "That's not all. Have you heard the talk around camp? Even Joel Reynolds was talking about going to see women at a cathouse. I don't know much about that but he made it sound dirty. Men are all alike. Not a shred of morals where it comes to women." She combed through a section of freshly de-matted mane, rethinking that statement. "Except Bobby. He must have been one of a kind. Good thing Captain Spencer hasn't figured out I'm a girl. That way, he can't take advantage of me, too."

She wrinkled her brow, disturbed by the unasked for thought that she would have loved to switch places with Clarissa McCrae last night.

"Now he's even got me thinking bad things." Out of the corner of her eye she saw somebody coming and looked that way. "Look out," she whispered. "Mr. Tom Cat himself. Don't you wonder how much sleep he got last night? Doesn't look too perky. Serves him right."

She turned her back on the incoming horse and rider, and kept on working the remaining mats out of Annie's mane. She was so disappointed in Captain Spencer that she didn't even want to look at him. Yet she couldn't get away from him because she worked so closely with him. She had nowhere else to go.

He swung down from Baron and tossed the reins at her. "He's been fed and watered. Just unsaddle him and he's set. Mrs. McCrae provided us with everything we needed. She was most hospitable."

Hospitable indeed. Willa wrinkled her nose.

Wordlessly she took the reins and led Baron to the tie rope. She felt his gaze, studying her. "Something the matter?"

She shook her head. "No, sir."

"Do I sense an air of disapproval?"

She risked a glance at him. He was frowning, his head inclined, cocky-like, eyes half-shut but locked onto hers. "Sir, if I say what I really think, you'll put me on latrine duty for the rest of the war."

His frown deepened into a scowl. Then he took off his hat and ran his hand through his dark, thick hair. "Then keep it to yourself."

***

Jeff turned on his heel and stalked off. Why did he care a whit about Will's opinion? That kid didn't know a thing.

It wasn't any of Will's business that he'd spent the night sleeping on Clarissa's veranda, alone. He could have had a delightful night of lovemaking in a beautiful woman's soft arms, satisfying his desire, cooling his fires. A young man with unmet needs, he should have enjoyed her company to the utmost.

Making love to her should have been an easy pleasure, but it wasn't. Sure she'd been willing. He was the one who'd balked, tormented by bitter memory. How he had longed with all his heart that it was Jeannie he could lie with, not this shameless stranger.

Trying to soothe his misery with a woman he cared nothing for had been a mistake. And he'd be damned if he was going to allow himself to care for anybody ever again. He'd just be inviting more pain, too much pain for all concerned.

***

Willa managed to avoid her used-to-be idol most of the day, keeping her sulking to herself. But that night, after cleaning up the supper pan and tin plates, she took her usual place by the fire, far enough away so the heat didn't bother her, close enough so the bugs left her alone. She belonged there, and wasn't going to get run off just because she didn't want to be around Captain Spencer.

She watched him perform his usual ritual of reading the Bible and examining the picture of his wife as though he'd never looked at another woman.

He lingered over the picture longer than usual, sorrow lining the corners of his mouth. Repenting? Despite her disgust, Willa felt a stab of pain for him, and for her own losses. Even if he wasn't above taking up with another woman for a night, he still had feelings for his wife.

She leaned forward to lay another couple of sticks on the fire. Settling back on her haunches she said softly, "May I see her?"

He lifted his gaze from the picture and looked at her, frowning. She realized she had intruded again. She sat back and crossed her arms.

He shrugged and handed her the picture.

The face in the image was pretty in a delicate way, the expression pensive as in most Daguerreotypes, the subject having to sit still for a long exposure. The eyes showed a fire of bright spirit even through the flat brown and white tones. A halo of wavy dark hair framed the fine features. Willa envied her sweetness and femininity, qualities Willa had never learned to cultivate. "Your wife is lovely."

"More than lovely," he said. "I've never met anyone like her, before or since."

Willa handed it back, feeling bolder. "You really care for her, don't you?"

"Still do. That's the problem." He carefully filed the image in his Bible and closed it. "You love somebody, they just die and leave you worse off."

Die? All Willa could do was stare at him.

The lines around his mouth deepened. "I don't like to speak of it."

Willa swallowed past a lump, and stammered, "I... I'm so sorry. I had no idea..."

"She was too good for this world," he said softly.

It was the first time Willa had ever envied a dead person. Nobody had ever cared that much about her, even Bobby, and she guessed they never would. Certainly not Captain Spencer, and he'd said so. In more ways than one, he was beyond her reach.

He gave her a slight smile. "I don't know why I'm telling you anything about my wife. You're too young to understand."

She shifted her shoulders. "I told you I was eighteen."

"Oh, yes, I forgot." He lifted an eyebrow. "A full-grown man."

"I know about my brother dying. And my mother and my father. I understand plenty."

"Your father too?" He drew his brows together. "I stand corrected."

Willa fell silent, afraid he would ask what happened to Pa. She was so sick of making up stories. What if she got all tangled up and tripped over some contradiction?

"That young woman I kept company with, Mrs. McCrae. I'm afraid we wasted each other's time." He stared into the fire. "I hoped she would help me forget how much I miss Jeannie, but it didn't work. I won't be seeing her again."

She had thought unkindly of him, and it was a misjudgment on her part. She shifted again, but the guilt hung just as heavy.

He drew his gaze back to her. "Again, I keep telling you things. It's nobody's business but mine."

"I won't tell your secrets, Captain," she promised.

He was looking right at her, but judging from the distance in his eyes, he wasn't seeing her. "I remember how she laughed," he said. "Like tinkling bells. I didn't have much time to hear it. I married her when I was on leave. We were patrolling the coast in those days, and it wasn't too hard to get home once in a while, but it was never enough time."

"Did she know how much you loved her?"

He nodded. "I believe so. Still, I wasn't there at the end. She must have wondered."

"But you had a war to fight."

"Ha. Sounds noble, doesn't it?" His mouth twisted. "If I hadn't been so eager to get her with child she'd still be alive. I wanted to keep the family line going."

Willa wanted to reach over and touch his hand, show her kinship in grief, her deeply felt sympathy. But that wasn't something a cavalry private would do for his commanding officer. Instead, she shook her head. "Lord, Captain. You sure do take on a lot. You can't help it she died. Any more than I can help it the Yankees killed my brother Bobby."

"Where did they get him?" His voice lifted with interest.

"Virginia. He was in Cobb's Legion. Hit by an artillery round. They shipped him home, but we couldn't even tell it was him."

"I doubt he suffered, then."

"For the next year, I kept hoping somebody made a mistake and sent us somebody else, and he'd come walking through the door laughing like nothing happened." She grabbed a stick and flung it into the fire. Red sparks flew up. "Then I finally got it through my head I'd never see him again."

His nod said he understood.

She continued, though it hurt. "He was fine and brave. Generous, too. He gave me Annie Laurie for a going-away present when he joined the army. Took care of me, kept Pa from hitting me when he got drunk. I'd give anything to bring him back."

"That why you ran away from home? Your father beat you? Did he give you those bruises?"

She looked away and shook her head. "Bobby cured him of his hitting fits, and after I got bigger I learned not to let him corner me. Anyway, he's dead, too."

"It's worse for the survivors," he said. "I'm sure of that."

She turned and matched his gaze, studying him back. A sensitive face, gray eyes dark with pain. She sensed the depth of his wounds, and longed to cross the distance between them and comfort him. He was growing in her eyes, not shrinking like Pa did.

***

The road back toward Covington took Willa and her troop past the site of the battle. The ground was scarred with breastworks, blasted trees, fresh graves and cannonball craters. She breathed shallow through her mouth, but the stench of dead horses swelling in the broiling Georgia sun brought her stomach into her throat. The soldiers' mounts balked at the death-scent. Only curses and insistent kicks in the flanks got them moving forward again.

Millions of flies made a background noise of incessant buzzing. Swarms of them threatened to block out the sky.

Annie Laurie twitched her skin, flicked her tail wildly and shook her head to get rid of them. Willa followed the example of other troopers and tied a swatch of leaves to the mare's throatlatch. It fanned back and forth as Annie walked, discouraging the flies from landing and biting.

Still flies lit on Willa's face and licked her sweat. One flew into her mouth and she spat it out, disgusted. She had read of plagues in Egypt. Living through them couldn't be much worse than this.

Captain Spencer had said she'd get hardened to it. She was still waiting.

Because the troop did not ferry to the west bank of the Ocmulgee, she realized they would ride along the east side. Thus she would not pass by her destroyed home nor Edgar's spread.

Did he see to Pa's proper burial? She wanted to find out for herself, confirm it and close the matter, even if it gave her more pain. But she was part of a tightly disciplined troop of cavalry, so there wouldn't be any dashing off on lone side trips. Besides too much interest in the death of a man who was supposed to be a stranger might give her away. Also, the farther away from Edgar she was, the safer she felt.

So she hid her grief within, attended to the incidental drilling and instruction Sergeant Quinn threw her way, and even managed to laugh at the strutting, self-important little gamecock, General Johnston.

Next day Willa's brigade rode into Covington and camped on the outskirts of town. Good thing she could avoid staying smack dab in the middle of Covington. Townspeople knew Jason and Willa Randall, and somebody was liable to spot her. Local women came to camp from time to time to sell pies or take in laundry, but she avoided them. She didn't have enough money to pay for their goods or services anyway, and she figured a woman would likely be quick to see through her disguise. She'd been lucky at the dance and didn't want to take more chances.

She divided her last four roasting ears with Annie Laurie and gave the mare all the shucks. She'd been told they were to remain here for a few days to rest themselves and their weary mounts. Nobody had mentioned issuing rations.

She stroked Annie on the neck, letting her hand slide over the sharp withers. The mare had thrown off considerable weight during the past week of hard marching, and wasn't going to gain it back on grass and a little green corn. Annie hungrily nuzzled her other hand.

"I'll get you more corn, somehow," Willa promised. She glanced at the captain's horse, Baron. He looked like a rack of bones. Was Annie going to be reduced to that state too?

She carried the remaining two ears of corn to her campsite. Each of her messmates had contributed about the same amount for supper. Nobody had any meat left.

Captain Spencer had taken his revolver apart to clean it. Willa sneaked looks at him while she was cooking. She liked the way he looked, sitting in his undershirt Indian-style, bending over the components of the weapon that he had strewn over an oilcloth. His head bent in concentration, tendons and muscles working in his forearms and hands, the left one lightly dressed with a scrap of her own cotton cloth. She had changed the dressing for him earlier that day, and was glad to see little inflammation, only signs of rapid healing.

The sergeant sat idly smoking his pipe while Reynolds mended a hole in his shirt.

Funny thing, she didn't miss Bobby so much any more. And, she was ashamed to realize, she missed Pa not at all. The soldiers had adopted her, treating her like a kid brother. She had taken to them in turn. None of them had tents, but she didn't mind sleeping under the stars, as long as it wasn't raining.

She set a pot of water on the fire to boil. The corn wouldn't be as tasty without salt or butter, but her stomach wouldn't know the difference. She said to Captain Spencer, "After we eat this little bit of corn, we're out of food."

"Um-huh." He didn't even look up. "I took that up with the commissary boys. The answer was, in essence, 'Consider the lilies of the field.' I told them my men don't think much of lilies as rations."

She watched the bubbles forming at the bottom of the pan, then tossed the miserable small ears into the water. Plenty of corn grew on her land, which was just a few miles away. That would be enough for a few days' rations, unless the Yankees or other vermin had gotten it all.

"Both armies have eaten out Covington." Captain Spencer rammed a piece of cloth through the barrel. "I'll have to take out a party and do some foraging first thing tomorrow."

"Maybe I can find us something to eat," she said.

He glanced up from his gun cleaning and looked at her.

She took a breath. "You bought fodder from Mr. Randall, that man the Yankees killed."

He wiped off the outside of the barrel. "Right. That's where I figured to go. He doesn't need it now."

"Guess not," she breathed.

He watched her, giving her that feeling he wanted to screw open the top of her skull and peer inside. "Why do I get the feeling you know Mr. Randall better than you let on?"

She said the first thing that popped into her head. "I refugeed down there. He let me work some, for food."

She wished he'd quit staring at her. Maybe she'd just said too much. He said, "Is that why you got so undone after I mentioned he was murdered?"

She nodded, dropping her gaze.

"Why didn't you say so before now?"

"Didn't seem important."

"What else wasn't important enough to tell me?"

She picked up a twig and bent it between her fingers to keep from squirming. "Nothing."

"You know anything about the Yankees killing him?"

She shook her head no. "He was fine the last time I saw him, only drunk, but that never seemed to hurt him much."

"You sure acted like you just lost somebody that mattered."

She looked him right in the eye, not letting him know he'd guessed the truth.

"Were you there when we stopped by?"

She took a deep breath and nodded. "I was in the house."

"I thought there was somebody inside watching," he said. "Why didn't you come out and join up with us then?"

"Mr. Randall didn't want me to. He wanted me to keep on working for him and he was afraid you'd conscript me."

"Didn't need to. You volunteered." He looked right through her, then clicked the cylinder in place. "We'll start at first light, bring along a couple of wagons."

Chapter Nine

Willa rode up the drive to what used to be her home, and caught her breath when she saw the charred ruins. The cabin had collapsed into a black heap, the stout brick chimney rising from the ashes like a sentinel. Only a few half-burned timbers marked the site of her room.

If she ever found out which Yankees had done this, she'd kill them herself.

She swept her dry-eyed gaze over the property. "He had a vegetable garden planted over there," she pointed past the wreck of her home. "I used to tend it myself. Tomatoes, potatoes and pole beans, if nothing's eaten them up. See? The smokehouse is still there. Pole barn, too. Nobody bothered to burn them."

Captain Spencer turned around and called out, "Reynolds and Slade, get this wagon and take whatever truck is left. Check the smokehouse, too." He laughed without humor. "That's bound to be a futile quest. I don't see how Yankee stragglers would have failed to clean out a smokehouse."

"The cornfield is trampled down," she said. "But maybe there are a few good bushels left. Mr. Randall had an old plow horse hidden up the hill a ways. And cows."

"When we came here before, I suspected he had stock tucked away. Go see if the animals are still there. I'd pay a penny or two for a beef steak."

Alone, she skirted the ruin, looked over the garden, but found it dug up and stripped. The Yankee raiders had been thorough.

She rode beyond the garden to the family plot, a patch of ground bounded by a picket fence. In it stood Ma's gravestone and the memorial she had made for Bobby. Next to it, disturbed grass and a new mound of earth with a board stuck in the ground at one end. Someone had carved "Jason Randall - d July 30, 1864" on it, a crude and hasty job.

Edgar had done that much for her Pa, at least. She had no ambition to thank him, though.

She wiped her welling eyes and bit her lip. "Damn it, Pa," she whispered. "I would've never left you if you'd given me anything to stay for."

She rode up into the woods to the hidden paddock. It was empty, a section of rails thrown aside, leaving a gap in the fence.

At least old Standard didn't starve and thirst to death up here. That was worth something. Probably Edgar found him and the cows, if the Yankees didn't beat him to it.

She lingered at the paddock, dismounted and let Annie graze the new growth. She picked a sprig to chew and leaned against a fencepost. High-summer heat shimmered from the sunlit grass and a bumblebee lazed by, suspended in the steamy air.

She was fed up with grieving, sick of holding it in. She kicked at the fence rails on the ground. Then she picked up a stick, hefted it, and swung it hard at a fence post. She beat the post again and again, as hard as she could, until the stick broke in her hands. Then she threw down what was left of the stick and stood panting, spent. The abused post hadn't budged.

She sank to the ground and hugged her knees, feeling beaten inside. Before witnessing for herself the new grave and headboard, she had held onto a notion there could have been a mistake, that the Yankees had killed somebody else, not her Pa. But now she couldn't even hold onto that tiny hope. Her whole family was wiped out. So was her home. And her comrades were busy confiscating the little bit that was left. One hungry soldier had already started a cook fire.

She lifted her head. Let them have it. Her friends were making the best possible use of her last harvest. And they wouldn't even know it was hers to give. She was anonymous as well as disguised. Willa Randall had simply disappeared off the face of the earth.

Not entirely. Willa Randall had been replaced by an insignificant soldier boy.

Strangely content with that notion, she mounted Annie and rode back to the cornfield. The soldiers were picking through whatever the Yankees had overlooked, stripping stalks and throwing ears into the wagon.

Willa tied Annie, joined the men and gathered an armful of corn. She dropped it under the hungry mare's nose and left her munching her belly full. Then she set to helping the other soldiers demolish the last of her worldly goods.

***

Her stomach full of the corn she had roasted amongst the ruins of her home, Willa turned her back on the land. It didn't belong to her any more.

Captain Spencer said to her, "Good start, Will. Where to next?"

Uh-oh. Now he expected a tour of the neighborhood, and somebody was bound to recognize her. Worse, they were coming up on Edgar's place. "Uh, I only lived at Mr. Randall's a short time, and I didn't do any socializing."

He pointed down the road, to the Dodds' turnoff. "Where does that drive lead?"

She swallowed hard. What if Edgar were home, and spotted her? Or one of the field hands that used to belong to Pa?

"I don't know, sir."

"Let's find out." Captain Spencer wheeled his horse and started down the lane. Willa had no choice but to follow.

The lane to the house was pleasantly shaded with huge live oaks, but Willa broke into a sweat despite the lack of sun. She pulled her hat down low over her eyes and scanned the big house and gracious veranda, looking for Edgar. She didn't spot him, but Pa's buggy was parked next to an outbuilding. Standard and a spotted cow grazed in the corral. She knew that cow, having milked her often enough.

She nerved herself to point them out to Captain Spencer. "That's Mr. Randall's horse and one of his cows. The Yankees didn't get them after all."

"That's a comfort," Captain Spencer said, a touch of sarcasm in his voice.

What brought her comfort was the absence of Edgar's saddle horse. Of course, he would have gone back to duty in Atlanta. She exhaled, weak with relief.

A colored woman walked out onto the veranda, wiping her hands on a dust rag, eyeing the troop of cavalry. Willa recognized Daisy, the servant that ran Edgar's household. She ducked behind Captain Spencer, who lifted his hat and waved. "How d'you do, Auntie," he called out.

"Fine, sah. Jus' fine. What you gentlemens want?"

"We came to buy provisions."

Daisy clutched the rag and held it in front of herself, almost prayerfully. "You'll have to see Mr. Clavett, the overseer, about that. Major Dodds ain't here."

Captain Spencer arched a brow. "I know a Dodds back in Richmond County. Any relation?"

"Major Dodds' brother lived back east. Near Augusta, sah. But he dead."

He nodded. "That's the one. Is Major Dodds' title military or honorary?"

"Military, sah." The servant drew herself up proudly. "He a very important officer in the Georgia home guard."

"Then he should be happy to help the cause."

The overseer, Clavett, stepped onto the veranda, thumbs hooked in his suspenders. "What's going on here?"

"We need to buy provisions, that's all. We'll pay with vouchers."

"Worthless paper." Clavett ran his gaze over the troop, frowning. "Major Dodds won't like it. No, sir. Not a bit."

Captain Spencer turned to Willa. "Go check the smokehouse and see what's there."

She hustled Annie to the smokehouse, glad to get away from Clavett and Daisy. The hasp on the door was padlocked shut. Not wanting to ask for a key and risk being recognized, she yanked at it, but the lock and the door held fast.

She turned toward the house, then spotted two Negroes watching her. The light-colored one hung back, the other sauntered up. Josh, who used to be one of Pa's field hands. His face split into a sly grin. Drat. He'd recognized her.

"Hey, Miss Willa." He kept his voice low and conspiratorial. "You makes a fine lookin' soldier."

"Hush, Josh. It's not me. You never saw me."

"Major Dodds sure wants to."

She crossed her arms behind her back and clasped her wrist. "He's looking for me?"

"Huntin' high and low. He been round to the neighbors. Ridin' here, ridin' there." Josh laughed. "Even talked to us folks about you. That's how much he wants to find you. I gets a whole week loafing if'n I tell him where you is."

Panic seized her insides. "Say you won't tell."

"A week off be mighty nice." Josh looked her up and down. "You sure 'nuff got them soldiers fooled?"

"I *am* a soldier." She gathered her courage. "My name is Will Barber. Why's he looking for me?"

"What he told us? You bein' an orphan an' all." Josh frowned. "I was truly grieved to hear about Massa Randall, Miss Willa. What them Yankees done."

"Thanks for that. I guess Major Dodds wants to make me come live here with him."

"I believes he done said that."

"Never. Don't tell him. Please."

"You sure is a sight in them duds." He looked off, pulling his ear lobe. Playing games, the scamp.

Willa took a deep breath and held it. "I never told Pa I saw you slip off to see Lucinda over at the Copeland's that time. He would've whipped you good, too. If I told him."

He looked back at her. "You always treated me decent, Miss Willa."

"Then you won't tell."

Josh pointed with his chin. "Here comes one of them soldiers now."

She turned and spotted Reynolds riding up, then turned back to Josh. "Now hush up about me."

Reynolds reined in, looking from Josh to her. "Thought you was gonna check out the smokehouse, kid."

"It's locked." She turned to Josh, "Who's got a key?"

He cut his eyes from Willa to Reynolds, grinning like a fool. He lifted empty palms. "Not me, boss."

Reynolds drew his revolver. "That's what stopping you? Nothin' but a little old lock? Step aside, I got the key."

She slid away from the door and he shot at the lock.

He missed, shot again. General Johnston flapped to the ground, squawking in fright, and Josh hustled away. The lock exploded, shrapnel flying everywhere. A shard of metal hit the front of her jacket and bounced off.

She lifted the bar and stepped into the dark building. The savory aroma of cured pork brought saliva into her mouth. Her eyes adjusted enough for her to see a wealth of hams and sides of bacon hanging from hooks on the ceiling.

Reynolds poked his head in. "Jackpot," he crowed.

Willa looked over the meat, most of it cased in heavy cotton bags. Then she noticed some of it was in the burlap she favored using for meat storage. She touched one of the wrapped sides of bacon, then she was sure.

"Some of this meat came from Mr. Randall's place," she said. "How did Major Dodds beat the Yankees to it?"

"That's not a bit like Yankees to miss stealing perfectly good bacon," he agreed.

"And Yankees didn't take Mr. Randall's livestock. Major Dodds did. I'm telling you, it wasn't Yankees."

"Now it's us." Reynolds drew his saber and cut down a side of the Randall bacon with the ease of a man used to helping himself to what he wanted. "Catch."

Willa laid the hunks of smoked pig on the ground, feeling shaky. Edgar was hunting her, and Josh couldn't be trusted.

***

The next day, Willa sat cross-legged under a sycamore tree making a copy of Captain Spencer's report. A fresh breeze added to the shady comfort. She had come to feel easy with the horse and smoke odors of camp, the soft hum of conversations, the occasional hoot of laughter or voice raised in singing.

Still, it wasn't easy to keep her mind on her work, for worrying about Josh telling somebody he'd seen her. Where was she to go if she ran away again? She had made fine new friends in the cavalry, and didn't have any idea where else to hide.

That wasn't the only thing eating at her. Finding her own stored meat and Pa's horse and cow at Edgar's had raised unsettling suspicions that Edgar had something to do with Pa's death. Like he'd still been at her house before the Yankees got there.

That is, if there were any Yankees. Nobody but Edgar had reported them in the neighborhood, and that didn't make sense. She'd seen first hand that Yankees weren't in the habit of being stealthy. No, they seemed to enjoy leaving their mark everywhere they marched, destroying anything that didn't cut and run or fight back.

"Hey, Willy Boy!" She looked up, seeing Joel Reynolds amble up, waving a handful of paper money. "We got us a match tonight! General Johnston's fixin' to win his fifth straight fight."

"Guess I'll have to miss it." She wasn't as disappointed as she tried to make it sound. Watching chickens tear into each other didn't seem entertaining to her, but she dared not tell Reynolds so. He might think she was a sissy. "I've got picket duty tonight."

"Don't matter. You don't have to be there to place a bet."

She tried putting him off. "All I've got is about a dollar in change."

"You'll double your money."

"Isn't General Johnston getting a little too old for that? You shouldn't be fighting that rooster any more. He might get hurt."

"That trooper? He'd rather fight than eat. Give me that dollar, and tomorrow you'll have two."

Reluctantly she dug the coins out of her pocket. "If he loses, I won't have any left."

"Then bet half what you got."

She counted out fifty cents and gave the money to Joel. "That other rooster's liable to kill him."

"Naw. The general's invincible." Joel leaned closer to look at her work. "That official business?"

She nodded. "Captain Spencer wants to keep a copy of every report he makes."

"Anything in there about me?"

"I don't think so." She dropped her gaze to scan Captain Spencer's small, exact handwriting. "Even if there was, I wouldn't be allowed to tell you about it. Not without his permission." She looked at him and grinned. "You done anything lately to make the officers take notice? Sneaking off, getting into trouble?"

"Sometimes getting in trouble is worth the cost." He gave her a conspiratorial look. "I plan to slip off after the fight and spend my winnings."

"On what?"

"Millie. You know Millie? Woman that does washing for the officers. She let on she wouldn't mind picking up a few extra dollars."

"You're going to have her wash your uniform? That's what's got you all excited?"

"Don't be so dumb, Will." He shook his head and laughed wickedly. "I reckon I'm gonna get me some recreation. Have some fun. Millie's not the youngest gal I know, but she's got most of her teeth yet and she's a good kisser. I figure she's good at other things besides, and tonight I'll find out."

Willa swallowed hard. If her friend knew she was a woman, would he want to use her for recreation too?

"You don't have enough fun. The captain gets too much work out of you." Joel squinted at the upside-down writing as though by looking harder he could make it out. "You ought to come along with me. Millie might have a friend."

"I told you I've got picket duty." Wanting to change the subject, she remembered his defensiveness when she offered to teach him how to read. But she still believed she could do him some good and tried again. "After I finish this copy work, I'll give you a reading lesson. I owe you for taking me out target shooting and helping me learn this soldiering job."

This time Joel looked thoughtful. "It is awful boring in camp, ain't it?"

"It'll help you pass the time."

"Maybe I'll just give it a try. Not now, though. I'm busy. Tomorrow. Just don't tell nobody, hear?"

Willa watched Reynolds saunter off to drum up more bets then turned her attention back to the report. After she finished making the copy she stuffed the whole pad back into the saddlebag. Thirsty, she reached for her canteen and found it light, almost empty. She stood, stretched, slung the canteen over her shoulder and strolled through the woods to the stream that provided the camp's source of water.

Captain Spencer had insisted on designating an area far downstream for latrines, ensuring that the refuse did not seep into the clean water upstream. His company had a smaller sick call than most others. Willa suspected that his persnickety attention to such matters was one of the reasons for the general good health of his men, even if they did complain of hiking a ways to do their business.

Alone, she knelt by a calm pool and glanced at her reflection. She had to admit the haircut Captain Spencer and Sergeant Quinn had insisted upon smoothed out the hasty job she'd done on her own hair.

Remembering the party in Macon, and how Martha Fielding had flirted with her brought a grin to her face. Really, she made a nice looking boy, even if army life had made her too thin. Taken as a boy, her fine features made her look younger than her true age.

Willa scooped water to her mouth and slurped it, then filled the canteen. She sat back on a flat rock, enjoying the solitude. She squirmed underneath the bindings she kept across her breasts. They cut into her and needed adjustment. If she could be sure nobody would come along, she could fix it. Usually she managed such operations at night away from the campfires, where even if someone looked right at her they couldn't make out what she was doing.

Chafing from the restrictive cloth suddenly became unbearable. She must air herself out or she would die from sheer misery. Willa slipped behind a stand of bushes, alongside the stream, reached under her shirt, and untied the wrap from around her breasts. The instant relief felt delicious in contrast to her body's usual confinement.

How long could she hide here enjoying this small pleasure? She massaged under her breasts, soothing the impressions the bands of cloth had cut into her flesh. She looked down at the filled-out shirtfront and smiled at the thought of Captain Spencer seeing her like this. Of course he mustn't, but was it possible he would appreciate her true form? Or if he realized she was a woman would he want to use her? What would it be like? She had taken unexpected pleasure in the few times he had touched her shoulder or arm in a comradely manner. Could she actually like whatever it was men did to women?

Everything in her experience told her men set the rules and women must obey. Men did as they pleased and women did what they were told. Men had the power and women had to accept it. Was Bobby like that too, just treating her well because she was his sister? She thought less often of him these days but constantly of Captain Spencer. She recalled the reverent way he always looked at that picture of his poor dead wife and was sure that neither Pa nor Edgar had ever shown such affection for their late wives. She didn't know whether Captain Spencer was a rarity, but she liked his way and found nothing to fear in him.

She glanced down at the strip of cloth in her lap, the bit of her costume that kept her breasts in check, kept them from giving her away. She sighed, resigned to the continuing discomfort and awkwardness of passing herself off as a boy. She could stand it. That minor annoyance was nothing compared to what would happen if the men discovered her truth and returned her to Edgar.

She was about to reach under her shirt and restore the bindings when a soft boot-tread made her realize she was not alone. A soldier came into view on the other side of the stream. He stopped and stared at her, a bemused look on his face.

Willa froze, her hands clutching the cotton strip. His approach had been silent, from the far side of the stream, behind the cover of brush.

She recognized him, another of Captain Spencer's men. Canfield, was it? She'd never had much to do with him. He wasn't in her mess and seemed to prefer scouting duties, ranging ahead and away from the troop. A loner, a virtual stranger to her. His blue-eyed gaze was planted right at her breast level, and the slow smirk moving up his face told her he was onto her.

"Afternoon, Private Canfield," she managed to say.

"So the captain's new aide has hidden talents." Canfield licked his lips, grinning. He planted his feet in an arrogant posture and hooked his thumbs in his belt. "Seems instead of a pretty boy he's got hisself a pretty girl. That does relieve my mind."

Willa felt a chill start in her belly and spread outward. "You shouldn't sneak up on people. It could get you shot."

His face was sharp and sly, foxy. Her instincts told her this was not a man she could trust if in fact such a man existed. He rubbed his chin thoughtfully. "Do you reckon the captain would mind sharing the wealth?"

She settled her hand on her revolver grip. "I don't know what you're talking about."

His eyes glittered with amusement but he kept his distance. "I'll even pay you. I've got good Yankee money, too."

"Leave me be," she snapped.

"You won't sell nothing with that prickly attitude." He shrugged and unslung his canteen from his shoulder, setting it down next to the stream. "I reckon you won't mind me doing what I came to do."

"The stream belongs to everybody," she said levelly.

"That's a fact." He knelt down and held his canteen under the surface, letting it fill then glanced up at her again. "If you set up shop, you could make a right good living. Better than any poor old soldier boy makes risking his neck."

"I'm not out to make a living." She clutched her bindings, wanting to hurry up and replace them under her shirt. "Not like that."

"What is your game, then? Why are you going to all this trouble?"

"That's none of your business." She lifted her chin. "I have my reasons, and I'll thank you not to noise this about."

He shrugged. "I won't. Provided you do me a favor."

"What favor?"

The smirk came back. "You're pretty. Even with short hair and trousers. A damn sight easier on the eyes than the rest of the camp followers. I haven't been blessed with the company of a good-looking woman in longer than I care to mention. It's been lonely, and men are such poor company. I figure it wouldn't do either one of us any harm if we slipped off into the bushes and took a roll. Our little secret."

She recoiled, shaking her head.

"Holding out for the captain?" He snorted. "Won't spread your legs for lowlies like me?"

"Don't touch me. If I don't shoot you for it, he would."

Canfield continued to regard her, the smirk still set firmly on his face. "Change your mind, I'll be around."

She watched him leave then she fumbled the bindings back into place and hurried back to her campsite.

What would Canfield do? Would he tell anyone? Would he ambush her and force himself on her? As long as nobody else knew her secret, Canfield had an advantage, and might try to extort something from her. She tried to think clearly.

If she continued to stick close to Captain Spencer, Canfield wouldn't have a chance to jump her. Did he have anything to gain from tattling on her? He didn't realize Captain Spencer didn't know she was a woman. The scout apparently assumed she was the captain's property.

She took heart in knowing he had none of the legal rights over her that Edgar claimed. Still, she felt endangered and exposed. Should she run again? Where could she go? Or should she wait and hope nothing came of her encounter with Canfield?

The frightened thoughts beating about her head calmed instantly when she saw her captain sitting on a campstool signing the reports. He glanced up at her and smiled, not a sly grin or a smirk, but a genuine look of welcome, as though he were glad for her company. Maybe it was her imagination, but she believed he smiled more often lately, wasn't quite as grim. What would he do if she threw her arms around him? Imagining his astonishment almost made her laugh, but her longing was real.

As she saluted he said, "At ease. Go about your business, Will. How about fixing us some of that ham for supper? And those corncakes. Nobody in the regiment makes them better. "

She grinned with pleasure at the compliment. "Whatever you'd like sir." She squatted by the modest fire and started building it up for cooking. "Maybe tomorrow I can find some peaches and make a cobbler. Do you like cobbler?"

"Never turned it down yet." He actually sounded cheerful.

If her simple corncakes made him happy, what would cobbler do for him?

Maybe everything would still be all right. Even if Canfield told Captain Spencer, none of them knew about Edgar's claims, so whatever he might do about it, he wouldn't send her back to her legal guardian. She'd stay and take her chances, clinging to the small hope that she could maintain her role and make the people who mattered keep on thinking she was a boy.

Chapter Ten

Edgar Dodds rolled out of bed sweating after another night of fitful sleep. He had been dreaming of trying to get inside Willa Randall. All the while she kept fighting, fighting, fighting.

He'd never wanted a woman so much. Not being able to have her was driving him crazy. He had to do something about it. Now. Being forced to kill that drunken fool didn't help either. Willa was a danger to him as long as he couldn't control what she might tell people. Besides, once he had her under his authority, Randall's land was his.

Edgar sat on the edge of the mattress staring at his officer's frock coat hanging on the back of the chair. The power just wasn't enough. There was always somebody over him bossing him around, telling him what he could or couldn't do. He felt trapped at his post just east of Atlanta.

His damned army responsibilities were keeping him from what had become most important. Finding Willa. Edgar stood up and fished in his jacket pocket for the scrap of Willa's underwear. He rubbed it between fingers and thumb and sniffed it, his desire growing unbearable. He must find her to satisfy his many needs.

He had convinced himself that she hadn't fled to Atlanta. He couldn't do anything further here, and he couldn't continue leaving the search to underlings. Even if she turned up close to home, word wouldn't get to him for at least a whole day. Plenty of time for her to disappear again.

Edgar stuffed her drawers back in the coat pocket and pulled on his trousers. He was through letting his duties stop him. Time to pay Governor Brown a visit. If the governor wouldn't give him leave time, he'd just hand in his resignation and walk away.

***

Huddled in a poncho, Willa listened to the soggy night sounds. The windless air smelled of musty rotten wood and moldy pine straw. Big raindrops plopped from the trees and dripped off her hat brim. Water leached through holes in the rubber fabric and seeped into her clothes, spreading chill. She walked a short beat, her footsteps padding softly on the sodden leaves covering the ground.

The wet darkness absorbed whatever light the brush and trees admitted. She couldn't see her fellow pickets, though they were posted within hailing range. Likely she couldn't see intruders coming down the bridle path either, not until they were right on top of her.

So she listened, anxiously classifying each sound. The sodden woods were charged with noises. Water dripping from saturated leaves, a hoot owl, the panicked rustle of a small animal her feet disturbed.

The trail she looked down led to her own property as well as the Dodds' place. Beyond her back her own troop lay sleeping. They occupied the southernmost campsite of any unit in Wheeler's division, the one farthest from the Yankees, so Captain Spencer had told her. Still cautious, he had seen fit to post pickets, and she could swear she saw enemies skulking in every deep shadow. Whether they would take the form of Yankees or that sneaky Canfield, she couldn't predict.

What was that noise? Was she hearing things now?

Footsteps, muffled on the spongy earth. She spotted a vague movement, a figure walking toward her along the bridle path.

She slipped behind a tree, groped underneath the poncho for her revolver, yanked it out and thumbed back the hammer. She raised it with shaking hands and aimed at the center of the moving shadow.

She strained to see an outline. Her heart pounded fast. Whoever it was couldn't possibly make her out behind the tree trunk. She waited, throat constricting. Did she really have the upper hand? Could she keep it?

She let him come on, closing in, walking like somebody who had a long way to go and not much time to get there, carrying a bundle. She made out a wide-brimmed hat and work clothes. He didn't look like Canfield or a Yankee.

Now the man was only a few paces away. "Halt or I'll shoot!" Her voice split the quiet. "Who are you?"

The man froze. She heard his harsh breathing.

"Who are you?" she repeated.

"Josh." The voice was familiar. "Who you?"

"Josh! What are you doing here? It's me, Willa." She realized they were both whispering.

"Oh, my, my, my. Miss Willa." He didn't sound sly this time, just relieved. "Thank the Lord."

She lowered her revolver and carefully released the hammer. "I almost shot you. Better turn right around and get home."

"I didn't tell, Miss Willa. I swear I didn't tell on you."

"What are you doing out here?"

"It was Gabe that told. He told on both of us. How I talked to you and all."

She felt cold spread from the pit of her belly, spilling into her whole body. "Edgar Dodds knows where I am?"

"He'll know soon enough, Miss Willa. Mr. Clavett sent Gabe after him."

She shuddered.

"I didn't tell 'em a thing. Mr. Clavett whupped me, but I still didn't tell on you. Didn't tell him nothin'. It was Gabe done all the talkin'."

She stared at the slave who used to belong to her father, now to Edgar. Just like her land, and her. "You're running away, aren't you, Josh?"

"Mr. Clavett whupped me bad, Miss Willa. He had no call to hide me like that." His voice trembled with anger. "I stay, I'll kill him."

She started to tell him she knew how he felt, then hesitated. Things were different for them. He was a black man, a slave, and she was a free white woman.

Unless Edgar enslaved her, too. And Pa had given him that right.

"You gonna turn me in?" He drew back his shoulders. "Might as well shoot me if you gonna do that."

She sucked in a long breath then shook her head. "The cavalry camp is behind me. Pickets on either side of me. You understand?"

He nodded.

"Slip around toward Copeland's place then straight north toward the Yankee lines. Stay as far from Covington as you can. Soldiers are camped all over the place."

"Bless you, Miss Willa."

"Now we're even. Don't let them catch you, hear?"

She watched him glide away, blending into the darkness.

"You there, Will?"

She whirled toward the voice. Corporal Harris. What did he see and hear? And what was the punishment for helping a slave escape?

She didn't care. Knowing what Josh faced, she had to let him go, law or no law.

"Here." She squinted to make him out in the shadows.

"Who's out there?"

"Nobody."

"I could've sworn I heard you challenge somebody."

She forced a laugh. "An owl. It was only an owl, that's all, catching a mouse. I didn't realize what it was and called out to it."

He laughed too. "All right. Holler if you see anybody." Then he was gone.

She took a deep breath, removed her hat and knocked the rainwater off it. Canfield's knowing about her was a mere nuisance compared to this. Next thing, Edgar would show up and tell the officers who she really was.

Then Captain Spencer wouldn't have any choice. After he got over the shock of finding out she was a girl, he'd have to turn her over to her legal guardian.

She'd run for it before that happened.

***

The next morning, Jeff returned from headquarters with his new orders in his pocket. His troop was among those picked to carry out a raid behind enemy lines, cut the Yankee supply line and break the siege of Atlanta. He was spoiling to get started. Well rested, the men were getting stale. They'd been sitting around camp bored, gambling over cockfights and spending their mounts' strength in horse races.

He guided Baron toward the horse picket area. Will was with the horses, as usual, his back to Jeff, packing provisions in his saddlebags. The mare stood saddled and ready. The aide must have already heard about the orders to pull out. So much for military secrets.

The new uniform Jeff had requisitioned from the quartermaster fit Will much better than the sloppy old clothes the boy was wearing when he joined. He was as literate as he'd claimed and had turned out to be a satisfactory aide, still as earnest and eager to please as the first day he'd turned up. The bruises had faded from his face, leaving the effeminate features unmarred. As always, seeing Will gave Jeff an undefined sense of pleasure. He enjoyed having the boy around and found himself seeking his company. From the beginning he had noted Will's misplaced hero worship. That was as diverting as it was silly, but it wasn't what made Will so companionable. Some magnetism between them had forged a deeper bond despite Jeff's belief that it was better to stay aloof. He didn't want to foster the attachment, but didn't know how to deter it.

Will started and whirled, a look of sheer panic. Then his eyes met Jeff's, his features relaxing a bit, but still wary. The aide drew himself straight, threw out a salute, then walked over smartly to hold Baron's halter while Jeff dismounted.

"Why so jumpy?" Jeff said. "You're off picket duty, no Yanks coming to get you today."

The boy's face reddened. "I'm not afraid of the Yanks, sir. Want me to unsaddle him and rub him down?"

"Fine. Get him fit out for the raid."

"Raid?" Will tied Baron to the picket line, his voice lifted with interest. "When are we leaving?"

Jeff leaned against a tree trunk, crossed his arms and raised an eyebrow. "Don't you know? Isn't that what were you packing for?"

A nervous laugh. "Oh, yes. The raid."

Jeff rubbed his jaw, suddenly suspicious. "You weren't getting ready to take French leave, were you?"

Will shook his head no, his gaze dropping away, studying the ground. "Oh, no, sir."

"Good. I didn't take you for the deserting kind."

Was that a guilty look? Will would have plenty of chances to light out during a raid behind enemy lines, if he chose. Maybe that would be for the best. Jeff hated to see an underage kid getting under his skin then taking man-sized risks that would get him killed. He wouldn't make much of an effort to track him down if he did desert. He decided to drop it. "Have you been practicing your saber drill?"

A quick nod. "I sure have. Sergeant Quinn is a real taskmaster. Joel Reynolds took me out target shooting. I did pretty well. He says I have a steady hand. And I've been practicing the mounted drills."

"Good." He wished he didn't have such strong misgivings about the boy jeopardizing his life. But he was a volunteer, for God's sake. Nobody had forced him to join. Jeff studied him. "You're a bit slight yet. You need to build up your strength. Your shoulders and arms are kind of puny. If you get into hand-to-hand combat with a stalwart Yankee he'll break your head off."

Will flushed under his tan. "Yes sir. But I'm stronger than I look."

"When you get into a scrap, always use your gun first, saber as a last resort."

"That's what I figured, sir."

"You'll do. You're from up Ringgold Gap way, aren't you? That's behind the lines, maybe we'll head in that direction. Maybe you'll get to see your old home." Jeff watched for a reaction.

Will set his strong little jaw and narrowed his eyes, the old having-something-to-hide look. "My home is gone and so are my people."

"You don't have anybody?"

"I have friends here in the cavalry. Don't they count?"

"Sure," Jeff agreed. "We watch each other's backs. Just like brothers."

Will rubbed Baron's arched neck. "My home is in the saddle, and this troop is my family of brothers. I don't want to go back to where I used to live. There's nobody and nothing left."

Jeff shifted on his feet. How could he have suspected this loyal soldier was about to desert? On a sympathetic impulse he clasped Will's shoulder. He wasn't prepared for the trapped look on his aide's face and the flinch under his grip. He let his hand drop. "What's the matter? I wasn't going to beat you."

Will flushed again under his tan and averted his eyes. "I know. I'm sorry, sir."

"Carry on." Jeff walked away, flexing his hand. Something about the way that shoulder felt under the shirt… The boy's flesh and bone had a womanly texture to it. He glanced back at Will and their eyes met again, but Jeff shook his head and kept on walking. No. It couldn't be. The boy just needed to muscle up. That was the only odd thing he had noticed.

He shook his head again, angry at the sexual stirring he felt. He'd been away from female company for too long, and the deprivation was making him peculiar. Unwanted memories of Jeannie's sweet body pressed next to his plagued his mind. What would bring an end to his sadness? Would it take a Yankee bullet to put him out of his misery?

***

When he got home, Edgar Dodds found Clavett lounging on the porch swing like he was the rightful lord of the manor. A jug of home brew perched on the swing next to him. What the hell went on when the proprietor wasn't home, anyhow?

"Hey, boss!" Clavett stood up, beaming like his horse had just won a race. "You got the message, I see."

Edgar jerked the sweating gray to a stop. "What message?"

Clavett wrinkled his brow as though thinking was hard labor for him. "Ain't Gabe come back with you?"

"What the hell for? Man, tell me straight out what you're talking about."

"Hell, I gave him a pass." Clavett wiped his mouth, still grinning." I told him to find you and tell you."

"Never saw him. Tell me what, damn you!"

Clavett laughed out loud, ignoring Edgar's temper. "Who we witnessed in the flesh, right here on your own property."

"Not Willa Randall?"

"The same." Clavett rocked on his heels in enjoyment and laughed out loud. "All done up in soldier duds. Wearing a hog leg. Riding with a cavalry troop. That same bunch came by here and like to cleaned us out while you was gone."

"Dressed as a boy?" Edgar stroked his beard, his rage turning into excitement. "Damnation. Why didn't I think of that before?"

"Soldiers took all the meat we brung from Jason Randall's place and then some."

"She's with the cavalry? Which cavalry? Speak up, Man!"

"Some a' Wheeler's. They're camped up near Covington." Clavett nodded in the direction of the town. "She must a' brung them here on purpose, Major, knowing we had plenty of provisions."

Edgar tightened his fists on the reins. "When?"

"Two days ago. Gabe wants his week off work."

"To hell with that." Edgar curled his lip. "If that lazy black bastard don't show up soon, we'll be hunting for him, too."

"Gabe saw Josh talking to her, but he wouldn't own up. I did my best to skin it out of him, I really did." Clavett's eyes shined and he licked his lips. "Want to know what I did to him?"

"Later. Get on with it," Edgar snapped.

"Now Josh is missing, too."

Edgar glared at the worthless overseer. "Why you ain't out looking for him?"

"Got no help I can trust. I got to stay here and take care of your business." Clavett shrugged. "Don't matter. Sooner or later, army'll pick him up."

"Was Gabe telling the truth about Willa? Did you see her yourself?"

"If I'd a' spotted her, she'd a' never left the place," Clavett stated.

"Then I'll be off to Covington."

Clavett again wrinkled his forehead in the effort of thinking. "Ain't you supposed to be in Atlanta, Major?"

"Not any more," Edger told him. "I turned in my resignation."

"I'll be damned. They took it? Just like that?"

"Tell me everything you can about what unit she's in, who's commanding."

Clavett scratched his belly, another aid to thought. "I got the vouchers that officer in charge signed."

"Quit wasting time. Hurry up and find them. Don't those damn fools know she's a girl? Or are they stooping far enough to recruit females these days?"

He watched the overseer saunter into the house to find the papers. Damn Willa Randall. Consorting with common soldiers. He'd fix that.

***

News that the cavalry was vacating Covington had persuaded her to stick with Captain Spencer just as she'd made up her mind to bolt. Riding behind the lines and leaving Edgar behind was the best idea General Wheeler had ever thought of, in her estimation. She'd never met General Wheeler, but her good opinion of him was bolstered by his decision to send her away from Edgar's clutches. He was a genius and a saint, rivaling only Captain Spencer in his perceptiveness.

As long as she could keep up with the cavalry, deception intact, she could remain close to Captain Spencer and far away from Edgar. She was satisfied with that.

However, she had a new problem in the person of the scout, Canfield. It seemed he had more business with Captain Spencer than usual. Today he was less inclined to range off apart from the column, his mere presence making her jumpy and out of sorts. It didn't help that he gave her knowing looks from time to time, making sure she didn't forget he knew all about her and would use it against her when it suited him.

"Will!"

Captain Spencer's voice broke into her worried speculations. She jerked to attention. "Sir?"

"Peach cobbler. Here's your chance!" He pointed toward a stand of small trees to the right of the trail. "You have my permission to break ranks and gather us some peaches."

"Get me some while you're at it." Reynolds tossed her his haversack and she caught it by the strap. Laughing, she snatched Sergeant Quinn's out of the air as well.

Captain Spencer handed his over. "Look sharp and don't get into trouble. You can catch up with us easy enough."

Willa veered Annie down the little slope leading to the orchard, eyeing the branches for ripening fruit or hidden gunmen. Stopping at a promising tree, she picked a golden peach, rubbed it on her jacket and took a bite. Her whole being delighted in the burst of flavor and sang for joy at the nourishment. The sweet juice ran down her chin and she wiped it with her sleeve. She threw the pit on the ground with the littering of peaches that had fallen off the tree unused. Then she began her project of making sure at least a portion of the fruit would not be wasted. She snatched fruit from the low branches and stuffed it into the four haversacks she carried.

Lately Captain Spencer had been assigning more of the foraging and food procuring duties to her because she was good at it. She took pleasure from both the praise he dealt her and from the satisfying act of gathering food for their little group. Anything she did well made her more useful and justified her position.

She heard a horseman approach. Quickly she let go of the peach in her right hand and snatched her revolver from its holster, then looked to see who was coming. Canfield.

"What do you want?" she snapped.

He reined in, grinning. "No need to point that thing at me. I ain't ever forced myself on a woman yet. They're generally pleased to see me."

Willa waited, unwilling to put away her weapon on his say-so. "Anyways, you seem right irritable. I thought a little scratching in the right places would do us both good." Canfield's manner was affable, as though he believed she could be persuaded.

"I told you to leave me be. Nothing has changed."

"I've been watching. Captain treats you like his aide, not like a woman he's bedding. He doesn't know about you yet, does he?" Canfield's gaze wandered to her chest.

"Just you, Canfield." She sighed deeply. "You're the only one."

"That's purely amazing." He snorted with laughter. "Then it'll be between us. I can keep a secret."

"Good." Willa drew herself straighter. "I expect you will. What good would it do you to tell anybody?"

"What good would it do me to keep my mouth shut?"

"I'm one more trooper," she told him. "Captain Spencer says we're always short handed and outnumbered. Someday I might be a help to you."

"Oh, I doubt that." He shook his head, emphasizing his disbelief.

"It's possible. The other thing you want me to do is impossible."

"The other thing…" He glanced at the revolver in her hand, still grinning. "You want me to believe you'd blow my head off before you'd let me touch you."

She sat quietly, feeling Annie stir underneath her. "Another man tried to force himself on me and got his head cracked open for his trouble." She wished she felt as brave as her words. She had no idea what effect threatening this man would have on him. And on her, as a consequence. "Truly, Mr. Canfield, I'd rather be on friendly terms with you. We're both good soldiers and we're on the same side. Can't we just leave it like that?"

Canfield studied her for a long moment, his expression sobering. He nodded toward the haversack in her left hand. "You better finish picking them peaches. Captain will wonder where you've been. I'd hate to be accused of taking pleasures I never got to enjoy."

She nodded and watched him ride over to another part of the orchard and fill his own haversack. She'd fended him off this time, but if he were determined to cause her problems, she couldn't think of any way she could stop him.

***

Edgar looked for the encampments, figuring he couldn't miss them. Army camps all smelled of cook smoke and latrines from a long ways off, and cavalry camps stank even worse from the refuse of many horses. But all he found when he got to the first one was charred remains of campfires and grazed-out fields.

He ranged over the countryside and found other such sites deserted as well. Maybe they had moved to a better grazing area. He hustled his faltering mount toward Covington to make inquiries.

The streets were unusually quiet. With cavalry camps nearby, he'd expected to find the streets and stores and other establishments jammed with soldiers loitering about looking for food, drink and amusement. Today he spotted only Mrs. Bales and her daughter strolling arm in arm along the sidewalk, and one-legged Old Man Sykes sitting on a rocking chair in front of his dry-goods store.

He greeted Sykes, a long-standing acquaintance. "What happened to all the cavalry camped just outside town? They pick up and move?"

"You're a military man, Dodds." Sykes spat onto the street. "Don't you know? They went a-raidin'."

"Raiding? Where?"

"Behind the Yankee lines. Where else?" The old man scratched under his armpit.

Damn. She'd brought the soldiers to steal his property then she'd given him the slip again. It should have been a simple matter to explain to the cavalry officers that they had recruited a woman by mistake, and he would be glad to take her off their hands. He had planned to go easy on her when he found her, try to make up to her and get on her good side. But she had just about outrun his patience. "Which way did they go?"

"Up towards Social Circle, most likely, to get around the Yankee pickets," Sykes said.

"You know anybody that's got a fresh horse I can borrow? This one's about give out. Besides that, I need provisions."

Sykes laughed. "Not hardly. Yanks been through here twice, stealing. Then come our boys. Every one with a worn out nag and an empty belly. Couldn't hardly get 'em to pay for nothing. Seem to think we owe them for the protection. But I ask you, who's gonna protect us from them?"

"It's a scandal," Edgar agreed. "They even got to my place. I'm filing a formal complaint. Get that captain who raided my place busted clear down to private."

The old man grumbled some more, but Edgar turned away, losing interest.

No choice but to follow. All that cavalry should be easy enough to track, even if he was hours behind them.

With any luck, he'd evade the Yankees and track down Willa Randall once and for all.

He kicked his stumbling mount into a canter. No time to spare horseflesh.

Chapter Eleven

Willa was hungry, tired and sore. She'd been riding for the past two days, skirting the Yankee picket camps, north past Marietta, ever deeper into enemy-held territory

Captain Spencer had explained they were going to live off the enemy for a change. But the locomotive her brigade had captured earlier today sure wasn't edible. The fruit and the small store of provisions they'd brought with them had gone quickly, leaving their haversacks and their stomachs vacant. Still, knowing Edgar would never find her on this march made the hunger and weariness worth enduring.

She glanced over at Reynolds, who was busy stuffing General Johnston into a saddlebag. Fortunately, the rooster had survived his latest fight and had made Willa fifty cents richer. She'd spent the profit on lye soap. Last night she slipped off in the dark and enjoyed a good scrubbing in the river.

A scout returned. It was Canfield, guiding his horse through the scrub between pines. He reined in where Colonel Crews waited with other officers. Captain Spencer was with them, listening, alert but outwardly relaxed. She could have sworn Canfield shot a knowing look her way as she strained to hear what the men were saying.

"What do you think is going on?" she asked Reynolds, who waited next to her. "I can't make out a thing."

"We come up here to raid, so I guess we're raiding. You better get ready to fight. I smell one coming."

She checked the caps on her revolver to make sure they were seated properly, then sighted down the barrel at a pine sapling. She was sure she would have been able to hit it if she'd been allowed to discharge her weapon. After practicing her marksmanship, she could hit most any man-sized target she chose, provided her hands weren't too unsteady. Funny, they didn't shake like this during target practice.

Captain Spencer rode to where she waited, near the head of the troop, then stood up in his stirrups to make an announcement. "Wagon train ahead, and a herd of beeves." His eyes gleamed with excitement. "We're going to capture the train and get us some beefsteak for supper. File right by fours."

"Now you're talkin'." Reynolds urged his horse forward and Willa fell into place beside him.

Now that she was in motion, some of her tension lifted. Annie moved ahead willingly, giving Willa a sense of control. She bent low over the mare's neck and whispered, "We know how to do this now, don't we?"

Soon, ahead of her, a bugle sounded charge. Shouts and gunfire began. She burst into the open and slowed Annie to steer her around a wagon that moved into her path. Another burst of gunfire exploded, and the Yankee driver screamed, fell forward and came to rest slumped over the wagon tongue. The near mule went down, thrashing and braying horribly, jolting the wagon to a stop. A blue-uniformed soldier dived behind a wheel and aimed his rifle toward one of her comrades. Willa reined to a stop for a better chance to shoot at him, fired but missed. His rifle flashed and barked. She raised her revolver with both hands and shot at him again. He scuttled out the far side of the wagon, leaving his rifle on the ground.

She looked around, saw Captain Spencer and turned to follow him up the line of wagons. He appeared to be chasing a group of Yankees who had abandoned the fight and were running away on foot. One of them turned and pointed a revolver at him, but Captain Spencer fired first. The Yankee staggered backward, clutching his middle, and sagged to the ground.

She rushed past the shot Yankee, alongside Captain Spencer, to catch the rest of the fugitives. The swift horses quickly gained on the three runners.

One stumbled to a halt and turned, eyes wide, mouth open, foam flecking his beard. He raised his hands.

Captain Spencer didn't stop. "Watch him!" he shouted to Willa.

She brought Annie around, pointing her revolver at the Yankee.

"I'm unarmed." He was wheezing, staring up at her, eyes wild and hands trembling. "Threw down my rifle back there. It was empty anyhow."

He wasn't wearing a gun belt, but she wanted a sure way to control him and keep him from rushing her in case he changed his mind about surrendering. "Get down. Face down and stretch out your arms." He obeyed.

The gunfire had dwindled into intermittent shots. Was the fight already over? She looked past her prisoner at the dingy white canvas tops of the wagon train. Confederates rode back and forth gathering prisoners together. Now she saw cattle, a milling herd. Joel Reynolds climbed into one of the wagons, revolver ready, investigating. Then he jumped down and went through the pockets of the dead driver.

She let out her breath. They had gained victory, that quick. "You people sure didn't put up much of a fight," she told her prisoner.

"We didn't expect a lot of gray devils to come screaming down on us like that. We were outnumbered."

Between her and the wagons lay the man Captain Spencer had shot. He sat up, blood oozing between the fingers splayed over his belly. He looked down at the damage to himself, his expression bleak.

Steps and hoof beats came up behind her. She whirled, revolver in hand, but relaxed when she saw Captain Spencer riding back hustling the two caught Yankees in front of him. Canfield had joined him and herded the unhappy pair from behind.

"We did it!" She lifted her hat and shouted. "We whipped 'em and got the whole kit and caboodle!"

"Tonight we feast. Fresh beef." He looked at the man she'd ordered to the ground and said, "All right, Yank. You can get up now and join your buddies."

"What about—?" She cut her eyes at the wounded Yankee, then caught her breath. A revolver had appeared in his hand and he was lifting it, the barrel wavering, toward Captain Spencer.

She stabbed her revolver toward the Yankee, jammed back the hammer and fired. Stricken, he twisted and grunted as the bullet punched him, but his gun discharged anyway.

"Damn you!" she screamed.

She shot him again and again and again.

He fell back, jerking with the impact of each bullet. His body stiffened, writhed, and went limp.

Willa's revolver hammer clicked on empty cylinders three times.

Captain Spencer grabbed her arm. "You can stop shooting now."

She shuddered, looking him over, but didn't see any sign of injury, thank God. "He was trying to kill you!" she cried.

He studied her from underneath his hat-brim. "Anyway, he didn't." He shrugged, cracking his half-smile. "I guess you saved my miserable life. Thanks."

The prisoners stared at her. They seemed menacing, like devils in the flesh. She started reloading, her hands trembling, and fumbled with the cylinder, suddenly inept.

"Calm yourself, Will." Captain Spencer said softly, still holding onto her arm with firm, steadying contact. "He's dead. You can't make him any deader."

"He was going to kill you." The unbearable awfulness of what almost happened twisted her insides.

"Soldiers kill other soldiers. It's our job."

One of the prisoners shook his head sadly. "Guess Taggert knew he was dying. Wanted to get the Johnny that got him."

She whirled to him. "Not my captain."

Captain Spencer released her and watched her finish loading her revolver. "I'll take these fellows back and turn them in. Go through the corpse and fetch his weapon." He hesitated. "I'll mention your quick thinking in my report." He glanced at the riddled Yankee and lifted an eyebrow. "And your thoroughness."

"Thank you, sir," she breathed.

She noticed Canfield watching her. He wasn't smirking now. She met his gaze and saw something different in his eyes. Was it respect? "Quick reflexes, Will." Canfield rubbed his jaw thoughtfully then touched his hat brim in a kind of salute. "I guess you're onto your game after all. Only a damned fool would mess with you." He flashed a quick grin at the captain then the two of them rode off, the prisoners walking ahead of them.

Willa watched her commander's upright, intact back for a moment, thankful that the one bullet the Yankee had managed to shoot hadn't hit him. Then she remembered the awful feeling, the need to strike out, anything to stop that Yankee from shooting him.

She rode up to the man she had destroyed. Annie balked, unnerved by the smell of blood. Willa dismounted and tied the mare to a tree, then stalked over to the corpse, fascinated and repelled at the same time.

He was lying on his back, still clutching his revolver in his bloody hand. His face was blank, his features relaxed. His heavy lidded blue eyes staring at nothing. She ran her gaze down his body. Besides the gory hole Captain Spencer had blown in his belly, she noted three other red tears in his clothes, into his arm, chest and shoulder.

She swallowed the beginnings of nausea. "I'm not sorry," she told the corpse. "Better you than Captain Spencer."

She bent over, grasped the barrel of the revolver and carefully pointed it away from herself, then pulled it. The hand clung to the handle, dead fingers refusing to let go. She shuddered and gave it another yank. Finally the fingers slid out of the trigger guard and the arm flopped onto the belly. The grip had blood smeared all over it, so she wiped off all she could on the grass.

She mumbled, "This time I was able to stop you, Yankee. I won't let the damned Yankees kill everybody I love—"

She shook her head, adding, "And my commanding officer."

***

Edgar swore and kicked the dead horse.

Worthless animal, giving out under him like that. How was he going to catch Willa now?

He'd ridden for hours without seeing a living soul. The Yankees had turned this part of Georgia into a wasteland. Everywhere he looked, he saw ruins of houses burned down or deserted, the livestock driven off. Fields lay in weeds, whatever crops anyone had tried to grow trampled. Nothing left for him to ride or eat, either.

He uncinched the saddle and yanked the saddlebags free. Then he hoisted the gear over his shoulder and trudged north, following the hoof-mangled road. Somewhere, somehow, he'd find another horse to ride.

Willa Randall wasn't going to get away from him, even if he had to walk all the way to Tennessee.

***

Reynold's rooster crowed, loud enough to jar Jeff out of his dream of making love to a woman. Perplexed, he realized the woman was not Jeannie. Great God, she resembled Will.

The fantasy shrank away, but not his erection. He stared at the gray predawn sky, mentally grasping at the gossamer threads of his lover's features, the soft lips, the firm body moving in rhythm beneath him, not wanting to believe what his mind had presented.

The vision faded away, leaving only Will sharing his waterproof against the night drizzle, snuggled right into his side, warm and vital, always sticking close like a faithful puppy. At some point during the night the boy had thrown his arm over Jeff's waist, further entangling them.

He picked up Will's arm and gently moved it away. Not for the first time he realized the bare skin felt softer than he expected. Will mumbled in his sleep.

Jeff pillowed his head on his hands and stared at the lightening sky. What was happening to him? The boy was getting to him, no doubt about it, and he was sure he didn't like what Will did to him. This was lust, pure and simple. Directed at a *boy?* Jeff wasn't built that way, never had been, and didn't understand such inclinations. But here it was. He'd better send Will away as soon as he could work it out.

Jeff turned his head and looked at his aide's serene face. He noted the full lips, smooth immature cheeks, fine nose and cheekbones, adding up to soft good looks, just like the girl in his dream. One of these days his voice would change, his skin would coarsen, and he'd start sprouting a beard. The sooner the better.

Unless a Yankee bullet cut off his future.

Certainly he was protective of Will. Nobody better give Will a hard time or they would have him to answer to.

And Will sure was protective of him in return. He'd stopped the Yankee that had tried to kill him, and in a fit of rage seemed to take it personally that the poor wretch drew a bead on his captain. Despite his previous indifference to death, Jeff was mildly surprised he was grateful to live another day. Enough of his despair had lifted lately that he started to see benefits in staying alive. He'd even caught himself laughing out loud once or twice. Was it a betrayal of Jeannie to enjoy his existence without her?

Whatever Jeff's state, the boy had gotten attached to him, like it or not. Jeff knew better than to allow himself to reciprocate, get that fond of anyone, a bad mistake that could only lead to heartbreak. But here he was, having fantasies about Will.

Whatever was ailing him, he'd better get rid of the cause as soon as the opportunity arose.

***

The blisters on Edgar's feet were giving him fits. Yesterday he'd walked into the night until he'd found a deserted shack to sleep in. This morning he'd started trudging all over again.

He heard hoof beats pounding up behind him, but didn't wait to find out whose they were. Slowed by the heavy saddle he carried, he stumbled across the ditch and threw himself into the woods. He dropped the saddle and lay face down behind a screen of bushes.

He felt the trotting hoof beats pound through the ground and heard the clank, clank, clank of sabers and the huff of hard-ridden horses. Cavalry. He squinted up through the leaves. They weren't slowing, must not have seen him. Dark blue uniforms coursed by. Yankees, no doubt trailing the same Confederates he was after.

They were chasing Willa.

When they caught her, they wouldn't realize she was a woman, all done up in a Confederate trooper's uniform. They were as likely to shoot her as any other Confederate soldier.

He watched them pass, envying them the fleet horses. He hoped that when he found Willa she was still lively enough to give him everything he wanted.

His empty stomach rumbled. Damn that worthless plug for giving out on him. Damn Old Man Sykes for not furnishing a fresh horse and provisions.

He watched the receding backs of the last of the Yankee soldiers, then waited a few minutes longer before poking his head up to look in every direction. After he was sure nobody else was coming, he slung the saddle over his shoulder and kept on walking.

Chapter Twelve

Jeff ripped open the wooden case marked "MILK" and a dozen small tins clattered to the ground, more spoils of war. The Confederates had occupied Dalton after chasing the small Yankee garrison into earthworks at the edge of town. Other units had laid siege to the dug-in Yankees, who hadn't given up yet, judging by the persistent crack of guns. He'd been sent to secure the railroad depot and claim supplies. His men weren't complaining. Sane fellows, they would rather forage than dodge bullets.

He picked up a can, shook it and listened to the swish of liquid inside. Then he knelt, set the can back on the ground, pulled out his penknife and chiseled a hole into the top of the tin.

A few white drops leaked from the slit. He sniffed them, suspicious of the unfamiliar product. The odor was milky and sweet, not at all sour. Then he touched the tip of his tongue to the liquid to sample it.

"No lie," he said. "Real milk, preserved in a can. It's a little thick and scorched tasting, but not bad. I've heard they had such, but it's the first time I've sampled any." He tossed a can to Will. "Everybody get some. They'll fit in the saddlebags real handy." He glanced around. "See if you can find any grain for the horses."

Reynolds kicked aside an empty crate and swore, saying, "They didn't leave enough forage to feed a goat." The other men went about their salvaging, carrying crates outside to load onto wagons.

Jeff watched Will grab a croaker sack and bend over to gather a supply of the milk tins. He noticed, not for the first time, that the boy's hips seemed unusually wide for his build. Shaking his head at the ridiculous thoughts that persistently leapt into his head, he reached for a couple of cans and added them to Will's cache.

Gunfire snapped from a new direction, close by. He ran to the door and looked out. The pickets posted at the edge of town were galloping in. One turned in the saddle and fired over his shoulder.

He cupped his hands around his mouth and yelled, "What's the matter?"

"Yanks!" a soldier shouted back. "Yankee cavalry!"

Jeff turned and shouted into the building. "To horse! To horse! We're under attack!"

Quinn grabbed a last handful of plunder and started for the door, followed by the rest of the boys. Will ran toward Jeff, slinging the loaded croaker sack over his shoulder. In his haste Will must have come down wrong on his boot-heel. He lost his balance and tripped.

Jeff threw his hands out to right Will and caught him. Will piled into him sideways, skinny shoulder catching Jeff on the ribs, the sack full of cans thumping him in the side. Jeff braced himself and didn't go down, but yanked Will upright, his hands clutching the boy's chest.

Grasping at . . . what?

Through the front of Will's jacket each of his hands caught a firm mound of flesh he felt through a tight layer of cloth. Will tensed in his arms, then pulled away. Jeff let go.

Will turned to him, terror on his face. "Sorry, sir. I didn't mean to do that. I—"

"Tripped." Jeff finished for him. "Get moving."

Will whirled away, gripping his precious sack. Jeff drew his revolver and sprinted after him out the door. Already he saw bluecoats at the end of the street.

***

Leaving Dalton was swifter and less glorious for Willa than entering. Yankee infantry had arrived in force to save their little garrison and it was the first time since she joined the cavalry that she experienced being driven away from somewhere.

Being chased off left the same nasty taste in her mouth she remembered from when Edgar had driven her away from home. At least this time she was in good company. Her comrades rode close behind and around her, looking just as frustrated as she felt. Even Reynold's jaunty rooster appeared a little crestfallen.

She also remembered Captain Spencer catching her as she stumbled, and the rough feel of his hands across her tightly contained breasts. Had they given her away again? At least Canfield was keeping his distance, as though he had decided she wasn't worth the trouble.

The shooting kept up sporadically behind them. Then, a little ways out of Dalton, she heard gunfire somewhere ahead of their part of the column. She swiveled her head to look both ways, alarmed. Were they surrounded?

Captain Spencer shouted, "Forward, trot." He didn't look in the least unnerved. But then, nothing seemed to frighten him. She feared he didn't love life enough, and that he might throw it away like a used handkerchief. She longed to tell him he was far more important to her than he could possibly know.

The horses picked up speed and surged forward toward the action. Then they halted, piling up in a jam along the road. The heavy rump of a horse squashed Willa's leg and she shoved it away.

"Dismount to fight!" yelled an officer to their front.

"Count off! Dismount to fight!" Captain Spencer shouted.

Willa sounded three. Drat. That meant she would have to fight instead of holding horses. The glory of battle had lost its shine for her, soiled by blood and dirt. But this came with the role she'd taken, and she wouldn't shirk her duty. She dismounted and handed Annie off to the lucky Owens, who had sounded number four.

She cradled the carbine the army had issued her at Covington and rushed forward with the others. She took her place in a field where ragweed and dog fennel grew waist high. Reynolds crouched a few feet away. Captain Spencer strode down the line, calmly inspecting his men.

She loaded her carbine and made herself ready, her hands slick and damp on the barrel of the weapon.

Captain Spencer paused in front of her, studying her face, one eyebrow cocked as though in inquiry. He ran his gaze down to her chest and back to her face, and she felt her face flush.

Just then a courier rode his horse through the weeds and stubble, calling for him.

He spun, waving his hat. "Here," he shouted.

The courier reined in and saluted, "sir, Yankee skirmishers ahead. Colonel Crews directs you to move your troop to the right to receive them, double quick." The courier pointed across the rocky field. "Near about that stand of oaks."

Captain Spencer turned to his men. "Attention! Re-form and march. Double quick. Follow me."

Willa trotted after him, watching for his signal, then dropped behind an outcrop of granite. The short run had made sweat pop out, tickling the back of her neck, rolling down into her undershirt, soaking her chest bindings.

She glanced at Captain Spencer, crouching only a few feet away. He was busy watching for the enemy, making sure his men were positioned right, all the tasks an officer must execute.

In the distance she made out the glint of sun on the many bayonets of Yankee infantry, in force, intending to punish Wheeler's Cavalry for their audacity. She cradled the stock of the carbine against her shoulder, rested her cheek on the hard wood, and waited.

Captain Spencer yelled, "Here they come! Hold your fire 'til you can't miss!"

The gleaming bayonets surged closer in the shimmering heat. Willa heard the hurrahs of the enemy floating her way. Wanting to kill her. Flags fluttered above the line of blue. Still she waited, rigid with fear.

Artillery opened up. The whiffle, whiffle, whiffle of a round flying overhead, then the shock of an explosion behind her. She glanced backwards, noting the blossom of red earth that marked the blast. A bullet cracked into her rock, chipping off a shard. The impact stung her hand. She snatched it to her mouth and touched her tongue to the hurt place. No blood, but a dark swelling had already started under the skin.

The enemy was within range now, and from her left she heard the order to fire. Captain Spencer echoed it, slashing his saber downward. She squeezed the trigger, deafened by the crash of the volley. Some of the Yankees disappeared, leaving gaps in their line.

She reached her sore, shaky hand back for a paper cartridge load and tore it open with her teeth. She reloaded her carbine with the black powder, trying to slow her movements so she would get the order of the drill right. Load in nine times.

She rammed the ball home then lifted the weapon to her shoulder and steadied it against the rock while she aimed. Fire and smoke spat out of the barrel. She knelt again to repeat the loading procedure. Stinging sweat trickled into her eyes.

She glanced to her left, where Reynolds lifted his carbine and fired it. To her right, Captain Spencer deliberately raised his revolver and squeezed off round after round. Realizing she was right between her two best friends steadied her.

Faced by continuous fire, the Yankee line slowed down. Some went to earth and others dropped back, discouraged, leaving their dead and dying comrades behind. A writhing form caught her eye. She jerked her gaze away from it, down her own line, which appeared intact. Further down, where the trees and rocks were not as thick, she spotted gray bodies lying on the ground, a couple of fellows dragging off a wounded man. Out of his mind with pain, the soldier thrashed, kicked and fought his rescuers. She heard the screams and felt the man's agony in her own gut. She wished she didn't feel so much.

"Look sharp, boys," Captain Spencer called out. "That was just a little test. They'll be trying again."

She took advantage of the breathing space to drag off her hat and wipe her brow with her sleeve. Smoothing her sweat-damp hair back, she squinted into the heat-shimmering distance and saw more blue coats advancing behind the ones they'd repulsed. She heard drum rolls and made out the mounted men riding back and forth among the ranks.

They were bringing up reinforcements. Please, God. No.

A courier raced up to Captain Spencer and hollered something about an order to mount and pull out. The answer to her prayer. The horse holders rushed up with the skinny animals and Captain Spencer ordered everybody to mount. She found Annie Laurie, grabbed the reins and swung into the saddle.

She fled with the rest of her troop as fading gunfire rattled behind them. After it died out, Willa settled Annie into a less tiring trot, keeping her even with Captain Spencer's mount. Every time she glanced toward him, his gaze met hers, his expression thoughtful, perplexed, studying her.

He knew.

What was he waiting for? Why didn't he confront her? This was sheer torture, trying to guess what he was thinking. Did he consider her a freak, a hoyden, a woman so hard she could pass herself off as a man?

She crossed an arm over her bound chest, trying to imagine what he felt when he grabbed her. Remembering what she had felt, his arms enveloping her, his breath warm against her cheek. She had wanted to rest in his embrace forever. Instead, terrified of discovery, every time he'd touched her she had thrust him away.

She'd been longing to reveal herself to him, make him understand her admiration had grown into a deeper yearning. What was the use? He couldn't possibly care for her beyond friendship. She was aware of her utter lack of femininity, and she'd seen the picture of his ideal woman, his dead wife. A model of soft womanliness, so different from Willa she might as well not claim to be the same sex.

Surely he would drum her straight out of the cavalry. Then where could she go? She was at home in this troop, among these men. It was her only home.

Later, Captain Spencer called the troop to halt at a stream to water and rest the horses. He handed Baron off to Reynolds and strode up to Willa.

"Tie your mare and come with me, Will." His voice was stern. "We have a few things to discuss."

She followed him away from the other men, knowing she was doomed. He stopped and turned to her. His gaze raked her up and down as though he could see through her clothing, to see her femininity. He knew the truth without needing to touch that femininity, as she had so often wanted him to do.

"Please explain, Miss. Why did you join my troop?"

She lifted her shoulders, stiffened her spine, thrust her chin forward, and tried to bluff her way through. "*Miss*! You calling me a girl?"

He locked eyes with her and raised a brow. "I could have the regimental surgeon examine you, but that embarrassment isn't really necessary, is it?"

Knowing she was trapped, she let her shoulders droop. "Damn."

"I'm afraid living with soldiers has enriched your vocabulary." He cocked his head to one side. "Had I known a young lady was in our midst, I might have been more discreet with my own speech. Now I know one of the things you're hiding. Tell me the rest. What is your real name?"

"Willa Randall," she admitted, studying her boot-toes.

"Any relation to—?"

"I'm Jason Randall's daughter."

He nodded. "That explains a few things. But why did you join the cavalry?"

"I didn't want to be Willa Randall any more. She wasn't any better off than a slave."

His smile went sardonic. "Not good enough. You want me to believe you've been putting up with dust, dirt, bugs, short rations, long marches and risking your delicate female neck every day just because you were unhappy at home? Some of our men were shot today and only by the grace of God you weren't one of them. Life at home couldn't have been any worse than this."

"It was." How could she make him understand? She lifted her eyes to meet his gaze. "Pa was going to make me to marry a mean, disgusting man. I had to run away."

"Lord." He lifted a skeptical eyebrow. "Who could be that unbearable?"

"Major Dodds. We foraged at his house. Remember?"

"You prefer this misery to what he offers? A nice home with servants and plenty to eat? What the hell did he do to you?"

She glanced away from him, remembering the shame of that evil night, then looked back at him, imploring. "I'd rather not talk about it, sr."

He stood watching her, stern-faced, but giving her time.

"My father is dead," she continued. "The rest of my family, too. You've seen my home. There's nothing left of it. No place to live, nothing to live on, and him the nearest neighbor. He and Pa made an agreement. With Pa dead, Major Dodds is supposed to be my guardian until he makes me marry him."

"You just traded one disaster for another." Was that a shadow of sympathy in his eyes? If only he would take her part like Bobby would have. But what could he do even if she told him everything? Would he be able or willing to keep Edgar away from her?

"Please let me stay with the troop. I can ride and I can shoot. I'm a good soldier."

He shook his head. "We don't risk women's lives in combat."

"I've been doing just that these past two weeks! Risking my life fighting Yankees, doing everything you said. Have I complained? Have I complained even once?"

"I must give you credit." He cracked a smile. "You are an audacious female. Fooled me all this time."

"Then let me stay. I can keep on fooling the other soldiers."

"What am I to do with you? A female, for crying out loud."

"I can hold horses and cook. All the things I've been doing all along. Keep me on as your aide." She set her jaw, hating having to beg. "Please. Just don't tell anybody. Nothing has to change."

He shook his head again. "That's not possible. Anyway, everything has changed as far as I'm concerned."

"Then what? You're not going to leave me here, behind enemy lines, are you? I'd be a prisoner, at the mercy of those Yankee soldiers."

"You'd be a civilian," he said slowly. "A noncombatant."

"Most of the people in these parts have left home because there's nothing to live on. Besides, would the Yankees respect a woman out here all by herself?"

He ran his hand to the back of his neck, riffling the hair. "I must admit this is an inconvenient place to get rid of you."

"Get rid of me?" Tears sprang into her eyes. She blinked to banish them. "Haven't I been a good soldier? I've followed every order and I've been fighting the Yankees as good as anybody. You know very well what I've done. Just because I'm a female—"

"I apologize." He clasped her arm, then withdrew his hand, suddenly awkward, as though she had changed into something unfamiliar, not to be touched. "I'm not faulting you. I wouldn't even be here to consider the problem if you hadn't saved my neck. You've been holding up your end, even if you are the wrong sex."

"Then let me stay in the cavalry. I told you the truth when I said I never meant to go home again. Then I'd belong to Major Dodds, and I'd rather die."

He looked away, then back at her, frowning. "All right. I guess I can't do anything about you until we return to our own lines. So far, I'm the only one who knows. Keep it that way. Otherwise, people will likely make wrong assumptions about you."

"What assumptions?"

He let out his breath. "They will likely call you a camp follower, making a living off the men."

Just like Canfield, until she set him straight. "You know that's not so!"

"Of course, but who would believe us? For God's sake, to think we've been sharing blankets all these nights, and I never even suspected! I'll be damned if I'll let us be dragged into a scandal. Neither one of us would ever live it down."

She recoiled from his heat, realizing she had compromised him and jeopardized his standing as an officer. He probably despised her for it. Her longing for him to care about her was nothing but a fool's daydream. He couldn't possibly want her. How could he want a girl who looked and acted like a man and got him into trouble?

"I'm sorry," she murmured. "I ought to tell you, somebody else knows. Canfield caught me out, but I don't think he's told anybody."

"Canfield?" Captain Spencer gave her a sharp look. "What has he done to you?"

"Nothing. He left me alone. He couldn't have told on me, or you'd have heard about it, wouldn't you?"

He nodded. "I'll speak to him anyway. Make sure he keeps his mouth shut. When we get back, I can say you deser—"

"Will Barber would never desert!"

"Then I'll say you're underage. How old are you, anyhow?"

"Eighteen, just like I said."

"No matter." He waved his hand. "I'll figure something out. I won't throw you out with nowhere to go. You deserve better."

"You won't turn me over to Major Dodds, will you?"

"Are you already married to him?" He studied her face.

Meeting his eyes, she said, "I got away from him before he could get it done."

"I hope you're telling the truth this time." He exhaled. "I won't do anything about you yet. That guardian business, I don't know. It bears investigating."

That was the best she could ask for. "Thank you, sir." She felt her shoulders relax. "That's fair. You are a kind man."

His features tightened and went stern. "No more fighting Yankees. From now on, stay in the rear."

"Can't I even defend myself?"

"Of course. Keep your weapons for now." His eyes betrayed an edge of anguish. "And for God's sake don't get yourself killed."

***

Edgar shifted directions, attracted by the faint curl of smoke, his tired footsteps slow and heavy. Although he'd dropped the burdensome saddle hours ago, his arm still ached from the labor of holding it in place. He should have abandoned it long before it wore the groove in his shoulder.

Smoke oftentimes meant cooking. This time, it had better. He was perishing from lack of food. He'd tightened his belt two whole notches since leaving home. The memory of the last hurried meal taken at his place—ham, cabbage and corn bread—filled his mouth with saliva.

Closer now, he inhaled the fragrance of bacon, wishing he could eat the air. His mouth watered fast as he could swallow.

Might be Yankees doing the cooking.

Still, given the choice between starvation and capture, it was worth risking.

Unless they shot him on sight. Or called him a spy, held a drumhead court marshal and hanged him from the nearest tree.

He'd better watch himself. Hungry was better than dead.

His stalking gait went stiff with fear. If a picket called out, he'd have to cut and run.

The trail opened up, a clearing, a field lying fallow. He paused and stood still at the edge of the woods, studying the view before him.

Beyond the field, spread a scattering of rough log cabins that looked like plantation slave quarters. Smoke rose from one of those chimneys and a wagon was parked next to the cabin. A mule grazed in a nearby corral. Besides something to eat, Edgar needed that mule.

He worked his way toward the cabin, sticking close to the underbrush in case he had to slip back into hiding. Only one window on the near wall, but he couldn't see into it. A cultivated garden spread behind the cabin and chickens strutted around the yard.

A couple of hundred yards away, a pair of brick chimneys stuck up, a pile of burnt rubble around them. He realized he was seeing what was left of the main house.

The cabin door opened. He froze, waiting to see who came out.

Two little brown children ran outside. The chickens scattered, squawking. One of the brats, a boy, grabbed a low-hanging limb on a chinaberry tree and swung, holding his knees up so his feet wouldn't drag the ground. The smaller one, a girl, stood watching, thumb in mouth.

Watching the peaceful domestic scene, Edgar relaxed. Apparently, the owners of the property had abandoned the place to the pleasure of their slaves, and to his pleasure as well. He knew how to handle coloreds. He'd been doing that all his life. He'd get his dinner, for sure. The mule, too.

He strode up to the colored children. The boy, maybe six or seven years old, spotted him, let go of the limb and stepped back, round-eyed, whites showing. The girl kept on sucking her thumb.

"Your mama inside?" Edgar said, motioning toward the cabin.

The boy nodded.

"Anybody else in the house? Any men?"

The boy nodded again.

"Come here, honey." Edgar scooped up the girl and held her in the crook of his arm. She took her thumb out of her mouth so she could cling to him for steadiness. She felt rigid against him, scared. He figured she made a good insurance policy, in case somebody had a shotgun stashed in the cabin

The door opened again. Edgar faced it and quickly drew his pistol. A white-haired black man stuck his head out, staring at the pistol, just as wide-eyed as the brats.

"Grampaw!" The girl started wiggling, trying to get away. Edgar squeezed her harder and she kicked at him. The small bare feet banged against his thigh with little effect.

Edgar grinned at the old man. "Howdy, Uncle. Fix me a plate. I'm just in time for supper."

***

Jeff escorted Willa Randall back to the stream where the men were resting, her face drawn with despair. He wished she'd proven him wrong about his suspicions. He would have been embarrassed, but he wouldn't have this problem. Will was a female, and that fact created a tangle of complications.

What a blind fool he'd been, not recognizing her deception sooner! He shook his head, his lips twitching into a rueful smile. Still, who would have expected a girl to masquerade as a boy so she could join the cavalry? And he wasn't the only one she'd gulled. As far as he knew, the whole troop, aside from Canfield, was taken in by her bold act.

Hindsight was dead center. He'd had plenty of clues. Her proficiency at cooking, an unusual skill in a boy. Her slight shoulders, liquid grace, delicate features and underlying gentleness. Her extreme modesty about keeping all her clothes on even when she got soaked fording a river. His unaccountable fascination with her, as though part of him had sensed the truth from the beginning. That same sneaking part of him rejoiced in verifying Will's true sex. He was relieved to know his lustful thoughts were only the healthy response of a man to a young woman.

Still, another worry replaced that one. Was he making a mistake, letting her continue the game a little longer? Even if he tried to shield her from the action he was still risking her life. The fact that young boys exposed themselves to fire was unfortunate; a young woman doing the same thing was unthinkable. After today's fight he'd counted two men in his troop seriously wounded and another missing, probably in the hands of the enemy, dead or alive he couldn't ascertain. No one had seen him fall, and he wasn't on speaking terms with the Yankees to ask if they had him. Such tragedies weighed endlessly upon his mind. He wished he could shut down the part of him that cared.

Why in heaven's name would a woman prefer this frightening, exhausting life to marrying Major Dodds? Was the man that insufferable a monster? Her life was in jeopardy as long as she rode with the cavalry, and he didn't want to be responsible for the death of another woman, even if he did like having her around. Yes, he had to admit he enjoyed her company.

But he couldn't leave her stranded behind enemy lines, not a friend in sight. She didn't deserve that sort of treatment, certainly not from him. The only way she had wronged him, a little deception aside, was by volunteering to join his troop. She had performed bravely, without a whimper. In fact, he hadn't spared his aide a whit, something that must change. He'd never expect a woman to take care of his horse as well as her own, cook the meals, run errands for him, carry a gun and expect to use it.

After they continued the march she rode alongside him, easy in the saddle as any trooper. He studied her, resting his gaze on the curve of her neck. Intriguing girl. He should have been repelled by a scrappy female who wore a soldier's uniform. Instead, it was as though the scales had fallen off his eyes and he could see her as she really was for the first time. Her sun browned, hollow cheeks, short amber hair and lean boyish figure appeared merely unconventional, certainly not unattractive. The expressive green eyes were positively lovely. Dressed right, her hair grown out properly, she'd be a beauty.

He felt responsible for her, even if he couldn't afford to let himself like her too much and set himself up for another heartache. That was going to be the hard part. He had to keep her close to him for her protection, yet keep his emotional distance. Could he really do that? He feared his emotions were already involved and had a will of their own.

And for the time being he had to keep on hoping nobody would find out he unwittingly recruited a female. Unwittingly? Witless, they would call it. Word would spread and so would the laughter. He'd suffer too much compromise and loss of respect to lead effectively. They would accuse the girl of immorality, and assume he'd been taking advantage of the opportunity.

A temptation he'd better withstand.

***

Willa caught Captain Spencer staring at her again and gave him a tentative smile. He didn't return it but his eyes softened before he adjusted his hat brim self-consciously and redirected his attention to the trail ahead.

Of course, he was displeased; her presence was bound to cause him trouble. Naturally, he had a lot to sort out as far as she was concerned. But the way he looked at her made her hope he had already forgiven her for getting in his way.

She had often wondered what he would think of her if he knew her as a woman. He didn't act as though he wanted to take advantage of her. Despite her fears, she'd known all along he was an honorable man like Bobby. But then, she wasn't a woman fit for his affections. His tastes obviously ran to ultra feminine beauties like his Jeannie. Willa still looked like a boy, and must continue to do so if she was going to save them even more trouble.

Captain Spencer's decision to let her take refuge in the cavalry for the time being brought her some comfort. So far his knowing about her wasn't as disastrous as she'd feared. Also, Canfield had lost the advantage he'd held over her because now he couldn't tell Captain Spencer anything he didn't already know. Probably Canfield wouldn't bother her again, and if he did, her commander would put a stop to it. She could relax her guard in Captain Spencer's presence, for the first time since she had met him. When they were alone, at least, she could be herself, and that would be a great relief.

Later that afternoon the cavalry called a halt for the night. While Captain Spencer issued instructions to Sergeant Quinn on setting up camp and posting guards, Willa led Baron and Annie to a likely spot for a horse picket. She tethered them to a couple of trees and let them chomp on bushes while she set about unsaddling them. She started with Annie, unbuckled the cinch and hauled off the saddle. As she began to work on Baron, she heard Captain Spencer behind her, saying softly, "I'll get that."

She turned to him and whispered. "It's my job."

He shook his head, smiling faintly. "I'll be taking care of my own horse from now on. I'm relieving you of your duties."

She unbuckled the cinch. "Captain, I expect to pull my weight."

"All I expect you to do is cook, and only because you're good at it. You're the only one in our mess that doesn't desecrate the mealtime ritual with burnt offerings." He moved closer and lifted her hand away from the saddle. "The rest is too much for you."

She stood firm. "It wasn't before, and it isn't now."

"It's different now." He shouldered her aside and loosened the cinch. "What has it cost you? Women are not cut out for this life. You're wearing yourself down to the ground. I've noticed you've gone off in weight and you're always dead tired."

"Everybody's dead tired. Not just me."

He pulled off the saddle and hefted it to a spot away from the horses. "You're the one I'm concerned about."

She planted a fist on one hip. "The men think I'm your pet as it is."

He turned to face her, his expression resolute. "That's none of their business."

"We have to keep doing things the same way." She was in the habit of obeying her commanding officer, but she wouldn't keep quiet when he wasn't talking sense. "Aren't you afraid you'll lose their respect? And what about their respect for me? They're used to seeing me do for you and take care of your horse. If all that changes, what are they to think?"

"I'll tell them you're ill."

"They'll say I'm malingering."

"Damn it, Will, I mean Willa." He took off his hat and ran his hand backwards through his hair. "What am I to do with you?"

"I'm sorry." She looked at the ground. "I never meant to cause you a problem."

"A complication." He reached around and touched her back as though he were going to draw her closer. This time she brought her gaze up to meet his and did not flinch or move away. He kept his hand there as though he'd gotten used to what she was. "If I can keep you safe and undiscovered until we return to Georgia, it'll be fine."

"I'd just as soon we never go back." She'd been this close to him before, but not since he'd found out about her. His hand, light and warm on her back, flustered her but she tried not to show it. She glanced around but didn't see anyone watching. "I don't have anywhere to go."

"I've been thinking about that. I'll send you to my home in Augusta."

She felt the sting of tears and blinked to dispel it. "Your home?"

"It's the best I can do."

"Thank you, sir." It was all she could do to keep from throwing her arms around him in gratitude. "I'd like that."

"See if you're still thanking me after you've been there a while." He offered a rare grin. "My mother does love a worthy project."

Willa glimpsed movement through the trees. "Somebody's coming," she hissed.

He stepped away, breaking contact, and she turned her attention to Annie.

From the corner of her eye she watched Captain Spencer take a rag to Baron and wipe him down. The impression of his hand on her back and the kindness in his eyes remained with her, teasing her with hopes she dare not cherish.

***

Duties fulfilled for the night, Jeff wolfed the beefsteak Willa had roasted over the fire, bounty from the supply-train raid, along with the inevitable corndodgers. Lately he took more pleasure in food, and in life in general. Thoughts of wanting to join Jeanne in death had fled.

Should he feel disloyal or liberated? He opened the Bible to his wife's picture and studied it in the fading light, true to his evening habit. What would Jeanne think of this extraordinary young woman who dared to pass herself off as a soldier and didn't shrink at doing everything that role required of her?

He decided Jeannie would have liked her. Who wouldn't?

Willa stretched out nearby on her blanket, looking as weary as he felt. He'd tried to lift some of the burden off her, but she was hard to persuade. Of course she was worried she'd be found out by the rest of the men and had to keep up appearances. He had to support that as much as he could and protect her at the same time. It wasn't going to be easy. One small favor, nobody seemed to notice any difference in the dynamics between him and Willa. Quinn was so worn out that he nodded off open-mouthed, snoring, his half-eaten plate of food sliding off his lap. Reynolds, as usual, wandered off to join a card game.

Jeff picked up his waterproof. He motioned for Willa to follow him, bringing her blanket. He unrolled the blanket a good distance from the other men while she watched. "Same as usual, we share the waterproof," he said in a low voice. "You're right about one thing. We can't let on anything has changed."

She just stood there looking at him, lovely eyes wide. The thought of this fine young female body lying next to his all night brought an unwelcome rise of desire. Lord, this was going to be hard.

"I don't like this any better than you do, but I'm trying to protect you the best way I know how. It's a little late to fake respectability, but I assume you are untouched and I will honor that." Didn't he sound pious? If she knew what he really wanted to do, would she run away from him just as she'd run from Edgar?

She gave him a resigned smile. "I trust you like my brother." She unrolled her blanket beside him and tucked herself inside it, pulling the edge up to her chin. Then she turned her back to him.

He resisted an impulse to touch her cheek and stroke her short amber hair. What was she doing to him? He'd already let his tightly leashed feelings stray too far, and he'd better bring them back to heel before he lost control. "I'll consider you my sister, and we'll do fine."

It sounded easy. But he was going to have a tough time ignoring the warm, vital woman lying right next to him.

He'd sure better ignore her, before she became important to him, like Jeannie, then dropped out of his life forever. He couldn't allow that to happen again. His wounds had never completely healed, and he couldn't afford to let Willa reopen them.

If he did, he'd bleed to death.

Chapter Thirteen

Willa startled awake, a hand jerking her upright. She stretched in the saddle and squinted at Reynolds, who was hanging onto her arm.

"You fall off, you're liable to wake up looking up the barrel of a Yankee carbine," he said.

"Thanks." She looked around to see whether anybody else had noticed her lapse. Captain Spencer had turned in the saddle to look at her, his handsome face lit with amusement. Drat. Caught her dropping off in broad daylight. She'd seen the men fall asleep in the saddle often enough too, but he'd still use it against her.

Let him. Even that just showed his concern for her, and she had no right to complain. He'd been nothing but kind ever since she'd been forced to admit her secret. He'd been kind before that too. And the offer of letting her live at his home was a generous gift. She didn't make anything more of it than his being a good man. After all, she was only Willa Randall, no doubt the most unfashionable girl he'd ever seen. Heck, it was worse than that. She didn't even know how to act feminine.

Doubtless his mother would be scandalized at the whole situation.

Reynolds said, "You see me sliding, do the same for me, hear?"

She nodded, grateful he was willing to admit he could fall asleep too. "I'll look out for you." He did look worn out like everybody else in the troop. Back and forth marching between Dalton and Chattanooga had exhausted them."

She pointed out a road sign to Reynolds, "Chattanooga again. I'm getting dizzy."

"So are the Yanks," he said. "They keep on following us, their feet will give out."

"Never mind them. Our horses are giving out." She patted Annie's neck and shifted in the saddle. "Not to mention my rump."

"They don't know which place to fortify next." Captain Spencer said. "They have to move their men around to accommodate us. Reinforce one place, then the other."

She wasn't sure which side was doing more accommodating, but didn't say so. Good soldiers didn't complain. They just kept on doing their jobs. And as far as she was concerned, she was still a soldier, even if Captain Spencer didn't agree.

She slid her hand into her pocket and pulled out a handful of parched corn. Eating that would keep her awake, at least as long as it lasted. She'd grown fond of the crunchy stuff. Just a few kernels kept her mouth busy, tricking her hollow stomach into believing it really had something in it.

Then Captain Spencer whipped his head around and drew his pistol. "Look sharp," he snapped. "On your right."

Willa fished her weapon out of the holster and peered into the woods. What had alerted him? A cocking gun, a flash of blue uniform, the sound of a misplaced hoof step? She was getting used to such alarms. They were often genuine, dangerous enough to keep her on edge. Yankee cavalry intermittently dogged their flanks, slashing in at every chance to shoot or capture whomever they could get to.

Two bangs in quick succession, flashes of gunfire, right where he'd said to look. She aimed and shot toward where she had seen the flashes, aware of Captain Spencer and the others firing at the same time. He yelled, "After 'em," and she wheeled Annie to follow his charge. Others tore into the brush with them.

The Yankees mounted and pounded away. Willa gave chase, yelling and shooting. Keeping Captain Spencer in sight, she pushed Annie faster, faster, feeling the animal power surging underneath her.

She broke into a meadow and saw the Yankees clearly now, a half dozen fleeing across the field. At the far edge of the field stood fence posts.

Then Captain Spencer reined Baron around in a wide arc. "Go back! Go back!"

The fence posts moved, and she realized they were men. Bluecoats, lots of them, raising rifles and firing. She swung Annie around, hearing bullets cut through the air near her head, thankful these Yankees weren't better marksmen.

Captain Spencer ranged beside her, his eyes spitting anger. "Why aren't you in the rear?" He held his voice low, controlled, but furious.

"They started shooting so I had to shoot back."

"I don't give a flying damn. You are a noncombatant."

"The Yankees don't know that, sir. Neither do our men. You said I could defend myself."

He shook his head, frowning. "That wasn't what I meant, and you know it. Taking off after them is not self-defense."

They intercepted the column ahead of where she'd left it, hailed the men and identified themselves so they wouldn't be fired on. She didn't see Reynolds and realized she didn't see him join the chase.

"Where's Reynolds?" she asked Captain Spencer.

He looked around. "Was he hit?"

Willa gripped the reins. "I don't know. Maybe he was." She wheeled Annie and retraced the route of the column.

Then she spotted him, halted on his mount alongside the road. Reynolds' horse was munching at bushes, pulling off whole swaths of green and crunching peacefully.

She rushed to Joel Reynolds, realizing he really was in trouble.

He was lying over his horse's neck, face gray as his uniform, his hand pressed to his side. Blood, oozing through his fingers and soaking his coat, had run all the way down his trousers and dripped off his boot-toe.

His eyes glazed and staring, he raised his wobbly head and looked at her with a grimace that passed for a grin. "Bastards couldn't even shoot me out of the saddle."

Captain Spencer reined in next to them. "How bad?"

Reynolds let out a hard, cackling laugh. "Look for yourself, Jefferson."

Captain Spencer took the reins to Reynolds' horse and said, "Will, prop him up and we'll bring him along. We can't stop here."

She nudged alongside Reynolds, grabbed his arm and supported him as they hustled forward. She felt him struggling to keep his seat, then his strength faded and he passed out. His head drooped forward, dead weight, his beard brushing his chest. It took all her effort to keep him from sliding out of the saddle. Still the blood poured out.

"He fainted." Her eyes blurred with tears. "And he's bleeding to death."

Captain Spencer looked over his shoulder at the wounded man. "We'll stop here and see what we can do. Hold the horses and look out for Yanks."

She drew rein. As the officer dismounted and took hold of Reynolds' belt, she jumped down and helped ease Reynolds to the ground and onto his back. Captain Spencer ripped the blood-saturated shirt open. Then he yanked a wadded-up handkerchief from his pocket and mashed it into the big hole in the man's side. Willa gathered the reins of all three horses and watched.

The bleeding slowed. But Reynolds lay limp and unmoving. Then he convulsed and relaxed, his jaw dropping slack, his eyes half open.

Captain Spencer grabbed Reynolds' wrist and except for his probing fingers, froze perfectly still. He dropped the wrist, ripped his hat off and threw it on the ground next to Reynolds. "Damn it to hell!"

Willa wiped her sleeve across her damp eyes.

Captain Spencer glared at Reynolds as though angry with him for dying under his hands. Then he picked up his hat, knocked the dirt off and stood up. "I guess the bullet tore him up inside." His voice was bitter. "I don't know what all happens or how to fix it when you get shot. All I know is law and planting, not doctoring."

"I want to find the murdering Yankee that got him," Willa said.

"Forget that. We'll never catch him."

Willa spotted General Johnston scratching the earth nearby. She swallowed to moisten her dry throat. "I've got to bring him along."

"Sure," Captain Spencer said, his tone telling her he was humoring her. "I'll lay Reynolds across the saddle, take him where we can bury him properly."

She looped the horses' reins around a bough, then started toward the bird. It squawked and ran away from her. The rooster flapped up to a branch, high out of her reach.

"Stupid chicken," Captain Spencer said. "Let him go."

She looked over her shoulder at him, but he turned away and she couldn't see his face.

"Let's get out of here before we end up like Reynolds." His voice sounded husky. He cleared his throat. "I won't be responsible for getting a woman killed."

"You wouldn't be," she said. "My life is my own concern."

"Like hell." He turned back to her, anguish twisting his features. "Not since the day you tricked me into letting you join up."

"What would it matter if I got killed?" She lifted her shoulders and let them drop. "There's nobody left to grieve for me anyway."

"Nobody but me." He looked down at Reynolds' lifeless body.

She recalled the homage he paid his dead wife every night. This was a man who couldn't help feeling deeply. And he did care about Willa, even if it was only worry that she might come to harm under his command. She touched his arm. "Don't talk that way. I don't aim to get killed."

"You will if you don't quit running out into the thick of things and chasing Yankees."

"It's hard to sit by and watch."

"Then I'm begging you." He took her hand. His was bloody from the effort to save Reynolds. His gaze held hers, burning with an intensity of feeling. "Damn it, Will, you get killed. . ." He slid his free arm around her back and drew her to him. She yielded, resting against him, taking comfort from him, wanting to comfort him in turn. Two comrades united in common distress, nothing more, though she could lose herself in his

116

embrace. He smelled of horse, burnt gunpowder and sweat. He felt strong and vital, as though nothing could harm him, but that was a lie. He was just as subject to sudden death as Reynolds.

Annie Laurie nickered. Captain Spencer tensed and broke off, looking past her shoulder. "Great God, Will. Yankees catch us like this, all they'll need is one bullet."

She let her arms fall away from his waist. Then she helped him haul Reynolds over the horse's back and lash him to the saddle. She mounted Annie Laurie, leading Reynolds' horse, rushing alongside Captain Spencer to catch up with the troop. Jackknifed over the saddle, the body jiggled, the arms and legs dangling limp.

**

"I am the resurrection and the life. Whosoever believeth in Me, though he were dead, yet shall he live." Jeff closed his Bible, hoping the words he read out loud weren't just a cruel hoax.

He stood, watching Willa, Owens and Smith shovel dirt back into the hole they had dug under the shelter of a huge oak.

The girl was taking it hard. She'd asked permission to help bury her friend and he'd given her the detail despite his reservations. Grave digging wasn't women's work, nor was fighting, but she obviously cared not a fig for such distinctions.

Tearless and set of face, ignoring the drizzling rain that had set in, she attacked the damp, heavy clay as though it were a mortal enemy. Each shovel-full made a sad plop as it landed on Reynolds' body.

The dead man's personal effects lay in a saddlebag at Jeff's feet. He'd see that they were delivered to his family, back home near Augusta. No wife and children, thank God. His death had also grieved Jeff despite his best efforts to remain detached. If anything happened to Willa, he feared he would fall apart.

He pocketed the Bible, continuing to study Willa, a bundle of contradictions. She should have seemed out of place among the troopers, unmistakably female ever since he'd learned to see beyond her disguise. But she fit in nonetheless, willing and brave.

She fit in his arms, too. Settled in like she was made for him. For a brief moment the boyish facade had vanished, revealing the warm, vulnerable woman underneath. A woman who needed protection and comforting no matter how fiercely she tried to hide it. Despite her wrong-headedness, he couldn't help but admire her fortitude.

She threw in the last shovelful, tamped it down with her foot then turned to him, eyes tragic. She swiped at her rain-misted cheek with her jacket sleeve, smudging it. "Wild hogs could dig him up. And how will we ever find him again, once the dirt settles?"

Owens leaned on his shovel. "He's not going anywhere, Willy boy. He's buried deep enough."

"At least find some stones and mark it." Jeff reached down and hefted a small chunk of granite near his boot-toe. "Plenty of them about."

Willa lifted another rock and piled it on top of the grave mound, then straightened and looked at him. "I find a board, I can carve his name on it."

"Ammunition crates." Jeff nodded. "Come on, Will. Let's go to the ordinance wagon and pry off a likely board."

**

Willa started through the dripping woods, a shortcut toward camp, Captain Spencer walking close enough to brush her sleeve. She was grateful he had come with her. He cared about his men, whether he wanted to or not, and she could see he was just as grieved as she was about losing Reynolds.

"We haven't had much chance to talk lately," he said. "Too many people around."

She sighed. "Things sure have changed, now that you know."

"That's so. You can be honest with me now. No pretending."

She kicked a clump of moss. "I'd rather keep on pretending. Keep on being a soldier."

"Deny what God meant you to be? You want a good womanly cry? Nobody can see you here. I'll even stand guard for you."

"I'm through crying." She clenched her teeth.

"I hate to see you get hardened. It isn't right for a girl to know this kind of hell."

"It's just as tough on the men. Some of them even get killed."

"I have to give you that," he said.

She dropped her gaze to the ground. "I sure will miss him."

"I'll even miss his stupid chicken," he admitted.

"I don't have enough friends to spare any."

When he laid his hand on her shoulder and squeezed it, she lifted her eyes to meet his sympathetic face. She softened against his hand momentarily.

His features stiffened, as though guilt-struck, and his hand fell away from her. "That could've been you we just buried. I have to keep you away from the fighting. For your own good."

She smiled bitterly. "Just like Pa always used to say when he got out his razor strap. 'For your own good.'"

She felt him grip her arm, harder this time. He spun her to face him. "The truth, Will. What really drove you to join the cavalry?"

She glared down at his hand, jerked her arm free, and shifted her gaze to meet his. How could she trust anybody enough to tell them? Even Captain Spencer?

"The truth, Willa. You owe it to me."

She gnawed her thumbnail and cut her eyes toward the deep woods, wanting to run away.

"Must be an ugly secret you don't want to talk about. But you are my responsibility. How can I know what I am to do with you if you won't tell me what you're afraid of?"

"I didn't do anything wrong."

She risked a look at him. His face was full of concern. "Nothing but a whole lot of lying," he said.

"I had to lie before, but I'm through with that now, at least with you." She stuck her fist on her hip, recovering her bravado. "Swear you won't tell anybody."

"Don't you trust me by now? I swear."

"All right." She took a breath then forged on. "I told you Pa insisted I marry Major Dodds. So I ran away."

"Why just then?"

"He tried to make me . . . you know what." She bit her lip, mortified, feeling her cheeks tingle. "Remember the bruises on my face the morning I caught up with you? He hit me when I wouldn't let him touch me."

Outrage darkened his face. Could he be angry for her? "That low-down scoundrel!"

Assured, sensing he was on her side, she got the rest out. "I knocked him out cold and left home. Afraid of what he'd do when he woke up. Pa was sleeping off a drunk when I walked out." She hugged herself. "Last time I ever saw him."

Again he gripped her arm again, more gently this time. "I'm sorry."

She looked into his eyes, searching them for scorn, feeling defiant. "Now you know why I'm here."

"You did what was right, defending your honor."

"Major Dodds didn't think I deserved any." She squared her shoulders. "I don't think the Yankees killed Pa. I think he did it."

"Can you prove that?"

She shook her head no. "I don't know how."

"You can't go around accusing Dodds of murder just because you have something else against him. I've studied law, Willa. It would be your word against his."

"You don't believe me?"

"It's not me you'd have to convince."

She'd known it all along. Not a thing she could do to get Edgar what he deserved. "All I want is to stay away from him."

"He frightens you so much you'd rather risk getting shot by a Yankee?"

She looked off, sorting out her thoughts, then back to him. "Major Dodds pretended he was doing everything for my own good, but it was a lie. Here, at least I know who my enemies are. And I like being with the soldiers. People I can count on. Honorable men like you. Before that, there was only my brother Bobby, and he got killed. Like Joel Reynolds was." Her chin trembled, fighting back tears.

He drew her to him, and she buried her face in his chest, feeling protected and safe. His earthy smell was so familiar, everything her life had become.

His voice rustled soft next to her ear. "What you must have gone through!" His fingertips lifted her chin, forcing her to look up at him. "Tell you what. You'll be safe from him at my house."

At the mention of his home her heart lifted, full of fresh hope, and she gave him a grateful smile.

He bent his face down to hers, his lips grazing hers then settling on them, forcefully. His mouth parted and he clasped her harder to him. She yielded, opening her own lips and catching his in soft bites. His tongue darted in between, startling her, but she accepted the sensation because she trusted him.

What was happening to her? A fire kindled low in her belly and her knees went watery. She wanted him closer yet, wanted to crawl inside his very skin. She clung to him, wanting more of him.

***

Voices. Laughter. Jeff jerked his head up, let go of Willa and took a staggering step backwards. Great God! What was he doing?

Resourceful and swift, Willa bent over and snatched up a stick, laughing. "Better act like we're just looking for firewood," she whispered. Of course she was used to playing games of deception. Damned good at it, too.

He peered through the dim woods, made out a couple of soldiers approaching casually, not acknowledging his presence. He felt a shudder of relief. The boys must not have seen him and Willa kissing. Good thing. Wouldn't that have caused a stir!

He must have taken leave of his senses, giving in to the girl's tantalizing presence. He'd felt sorry for her. That was all. He'd consoled her by taking her into his arms and that led to a dangerous progression.

Hating his own weakness, hating the play-acting, he grabbed a couple of dry sticks and tucked them under his arm. His body's reaction to her nearness gradually came back under control.

"Hey, Willy boy! Captain! Jeff recognized Owens' voice.

"Hey yourself." Jeff tried not to reveal the disgust in his voice.

"What you skulking in them woods for, Willy?" Smith called out.

"You got a sweet young thing hid in them bushes?" Owens added. "No hoarding yer women, now."

Willa laughed hysterically, her eyes wild. "Sure, fellows. That's just exactly what we got. Girl friends!"

She turned her back to the approaching soldiers, grinning, and blew Jeff a kiss.

Quirky woman. She did have a peculiar sense of fun. No telling what she'd say or do next. He wanted to know more of her, but he couldn't bring himself to fall into that black hole until the war was over and the dead were buried.

She watched him, smiling, green eyes alight. The soft fire in them, meant only for him, spooked him even worse than the unexpected intrusion had.

He studied her, analyzing the warmth and the passion that her nearness aroused in him. Would he have lost control like that with any female, or just this peculiar version? He pictured her hair long, styled in ladylike fashion. Smooth, fine-featured face shades paler, protected from the sun. Wearing a dress. The vision was growing stronger and stronger every time he looked at her.

The past two nights had been torture, her sleeping next to him. His awareness of her female body, firm, warm, packed with life and energy. How he'd wanted to hold her, embrace her, and experience her womanly truth. He had tried to attribute his fever to his own healthy lust plus the knowledge of forbidden fruit within reach. But it ran deeper than that. He'd been fond of Will the boy, but he was fascinated with Willa the woman.

Feelings it would cost too dearly to indulge.

He let out his breath. "We better find that marker board. Before it gets too dark."

She ducked her head and started walking away, fast. He strode after her, neither of them saying a word until they reached the ordinance wagons.

He explained his purpose to the officer in charge, then broke a likely board off a partially empty crate and handed it to Will. "Good enough?"

She ran her hand over the rough surface. "I'll carve his name on it. After I fix supper."

"Better try to find some dry firewood. No faking this time. I'll help you."

Another shy smile. "Nice to have company."

Why was he giving into his urges like a lovesick fool? The sooner he returned to Confederate lines and restored her to civilian life, the better. In the meantime, staying aloof wasn't going to be easy, because he must keep her physically close for her own safety.

He had assumed the role of Willa's protector, but who was going to protect her from him? Contemplating the irony, he reached down, grabbed a heavy stick, and stepped on it, breaking it in two.

He must police his feelings and never again lose control.

Chapter Fourteen

Willa walked through the leaf-dampened woods to the bank of the Tennessee River with Captain Spencer. Her raw nerves made his closeness painful. Cordial but remote, he had cooled to her ever since their kiss. Yet, he insisted she stick within his sight so he could make sure she didn't get into trouble.

She'd changed her thinking from hoping he wouldn't take advantage of her to wishing he would. That embrace had awakened feelings in her she'd never before experienced. Nothing in her life had prepared her for this strange hunger. She could have sworn Captain Spencer only let go of her because he didn't want to get caught tangled up that way with another man. Yet he acted tense and bothered toward her. She must not have measured up. Of course she didn't. How could he possibly think her boyish appearance attractive? So far he hadn't taken back his offer to let her stay at his home, but that didn't mean anything. He would do the same thing for any old stray.

She paused at the drop-off and looked across the river, wary despite the picket line at their backs. Enemies could be hiding on the far bank, so she slipped behind the screen of a lush willow and hunkered down. Captain Spencer glided into position next to her.

They'd been following the bank for miles, looking for a place to cross, but she knew this wasn't the spot even before she looked. No river that rushed and roared so loudly was safe to cross.

She looked down the short bank, where water lapped below her boots. In the middle, the savage flow boiled and churned, fed by the steady rain. Whitecaps sheared where currents ran in conflict. Through the leaves she watched a log rush downstream, hit a submerged obstacle with a thud so heavy she felt it jolt the earth through her soles. The log hung there for a few seconds before it scudded away.

Captain Spencer scratched under his moustache, then spoke as though thinking out loud. "At least it's quit raining for the time being. River's still rising, though. I'd lose half the men and all the horses if we tried to swim that flood."

She sure didn't want to try it. But sooner or later they'd have to find a way across the river. If they didn't find one soon, the pursuing Yankees were liable to trap them.

"Sometimes it pays to be a lowly captain. I can rest until the generals figure it out." He yawned. "Think I'll go for a swim anyhow, clean up and rinse out my clothes."

Both of them could stand such improvement. Her clothes had clung wet to her body for several days running. Now drying, they smelled like mildew, not that she took much notice. Amazing what she'd learned to tolerate in the past two weeks.

She fished into her pocket and found the slick lump she'd been saving. "You can have some of my soap."

He knitted his brows. "Soap? Where did you get that?"

"Peddler came into camp, down at Covington. All he wanted was fifty cents. I used my winnings from General Johnston's fight."

"As long as you're willing to share . . ."

She handed the little cake of yellow lye soap to him, managing a wry smile. "See how much you're going to miss me after you kick me out of the cavalry?"

His right eyebrow lifted. "Isn't Will getting pert?"

She cocked her head to one side. "I'll sure miss you."

Instead of answering her he drew back the corners of his mouth in an expression of exasperation. He transferred his papers, watch, and other personal effects into a saddlebag and threw it over his shoulder. She followed him downstream and they found a little protected cove where the current was still. Other soldiers had found it first and were splashing in the water like schoolboys.

She gazed out at the swimming hole, longing to join them. But they were all half or wholly naked, and she sure couldn't skin down like that. Nor could she jump into the water fully clothed without getting some hard teasing.

Captain Spencer must have read her thoughts. "Tell you what. After I clean up, we'll go a ways farther down and find you a private spot. Then I'll stand guard while you bathe."

"I'd like that." She gave him a grateful smile.

She watched him shed down to his union suit, then slip off the top part. She wanted to squeeze the flexing muscles of his arms, run her hand through the shadow of dark hair across his chest, and feel the tight ripple of his hard abdomen.

He was the only man she'd ever wanted to touch that way. What would it be like to bury her face in his chest, fold herself into his sinewy body, and revel in his strong arms; arms that gathered her close to his heart. Not just when something awful happened, but for herself, because it would be right.

She frowned at her own craziness. Why was she still holding onto such foolish notions, like there was any hope? No, Captain Spencer had finer taste in women than Willa Randall.

He laid his saddlebag, boots, hat and gun belt at her feet. Then he draped his jacket and trousers over his arm and strode toward the brown water, soap in hand.

She sat down cross-legged in the deep shade of a sycamore and chewed a twig. Smith shouted for her to come on in, but she pretended not to hear. She picked at her stiff and dirty trouser leg, wishing Captain Spencer would hurry and finish his bath so she could find her own swimming hole.

She batted at a deerfly, then took off her hat and fanned herself as she watched him scrub his clothes at the water's edge, working up a lather with the soap she'd given him. He slathered his hair, his face, his arms and upper body with suds, then he splashed himself to rinse, wrung out his clothes, and set them on a stump on shore. He turned and waded deeper into the river. Swimming with long strokes, he made himself look as masterful in the water as he was on horseback. Even from a distance, she envied his obvious pleasure in coolness and cleanliness.

Finally, he emerged from the water and strolled toward her, carrying his dripping outer clothes. His wet underwear clung to his lean hips and bulged slightly over his privates. She tore her gaze away from there and up to his face. He'd shaved this morning, so his cheeks were clean and smooth, free of stubble, gunpowder stains and campfire soot. He pushed a wet black forelock away from his eyebrows and slicked it back, then stopped in front of her, a little frown darkening his sun-browned face, like he was still trying to sort out what he should do about her.

Martha had called him a fine figure of a man. Even half-dressed and soaking wet he filled that impression. It sure wasn't for her sake he was so cursed good-looking.

***

Jeff ignored Willa's open stare and handed her the wet lump of soap, smaller by half. "Now we'll find a place for your bath."

He pulled on his damp clothes while she stood up and waited. He buckled the gun belt around his waist and hefted the saddlebags, then set out. Truly, he didn't relish the sweet torture of guarding Willa while she stripped off her outer clothes and rubbed herself with soap. But somebody had to take care of her. As the only responsible man who knew her secrets, he was stuck with the job.

They chose a rocky little pool well away from camp traffic—a private spot where no one could see them, screened by trees from both banks.

She handed him her few belongings, removed her hat and boots, then skipped into the water fully clothed.

He leaned against a pine tree and watched her immerse her head and surge back up, sputtering happily. She settled in water that covered up to her neck. Now she was squirming under the surface. Taking off her clothes? He locked his gaze on her, trying to see into the brown water. His throat closed at thoughts of smooth legs, tidy buttocks and a flat little belly. He imagined her breasts freed of their bindings, spilling out under the water.

She scooted up to a rock, laid her clothes out on it, worked up a lather with the soap and scrubbed her face and arms with a soapy rag, just as he'd pictured. He watched her movements, which were sensuous and lingering, her facial expression blissful and sweet.

He shifted where he sat, the usual unwelcome physical reaction plaguing him. Lord, how he wanted to join her in the water. Join with her in there. Fold her into a mating embrace, their slick wet bodies sliding in rhythm together. He pushed away from the tree trunk, stepped forward, then hesitated.

What was he going to do? Ravish her? Not hardly. He took a deep breath and looked away from her. Then he cut his eyes right back, unable to resist, feeling like a voyeur.

She rinsed the clothes, soaped her hair and massaged her scalp. She threw back her head, eyes shut, lips parted, glorious in virginal womanliness.

She threw him a beautiful smile. Didn't she understand the effect she was having on him? It hurt to watch her, yet he couldn't tear his gaze away.

She arched her head back into the water, elbows upraised, rinsing her hair. The roundness of the top of her young breasts barely broke the water's surface, but rode up and down with her movements. A gentle wake rippled from her toward the shore where he stood.

Lord, how he wanted her. Like he'd wanted no woman since Jeannie.

Willa would consent, he was sure. The way she looked at him, the way she had melted in his arms convinced him she had fallen in love with him. Bad judgment on her part. The physical act of making love to her wouldn't make him fall in love with her, would it? Couldn't he take his pleasure and let it go at that, as he'd just stopped short of doing with Clarissa?

But Willa was different. She was innocent and vulnerable. He was sure she had no idea what she was doing to him. He'd want to shoot the cad that took advantage of her.

She slipped her face underwater and came up shaking the wet from her head, her short-cropped hair standing up in a spiky halo. Then she ran her fingers through it, slicking out more water. She glanced at him again, crossing her arms over her breasts, suddenly shy.

"I'd better get dressed," she said.

He felt a tug of disappointment, but he ought to be relieved. In a moment she'd be back in her sexless soldier's uniform, and he could go back to trying not to think of what the trousers and jacket hid.

She didn't ask him to turn his back, but swam to where her scrubbed uniform waited on the rock. Then she worked her clothes back on, all under water, everything but her jacket, which she threw over her arm. Soaking wet, she arose barefoot from the pool and climbed onto the bank toward him. The wet shirt clung to her, showing a hint of her female shape. Suddenly he realized it didn't matter what she wore. It was the woman underneath he wanted.

Good sense told him to run like hell. But he didn't.

Knowing he'd regret it, he stepped right in front of her, blocking her. She hesitated, looking confused. "What is it?"

He reached out tentatively, caressed her damp cheek with his fingertips, and stroked back a wet lock of hair. She stared right into his eyes, her head cocked to one side, lips parted in an uncertain smile.

He traced her lips with his finger. "You are beautiful," he said.

Her eyes widened, startled. "I am?"

It amazed him that she didn't even realize it. He cupped her chin in his hand and she didn't resist. Her cheek softened into his palm. She shut her eyes and rested her face in his hand, her smile still shy, but he sensed her trust, that she would do whatever he asked.

In her innocence, did she have any idea what he really desired of her?

Sighing, she pressed her body against his, inviting him. At that point, he was a goner.

He drew her into himself, locked his arms around her and felt her yield against him. He brought his lips down on hers, brushed them open, then pressed, hungry, in deepening assertiveness. She shivered, kissed him back, her lips pliant. She didn't retreat from his hardness against her belly.

Her hair smelled clean, fresh, of the lye soap. Her chilly clothes warmed to his body heat. The damp wool let off a pleasant animal scent. He breathed it into himself, feeling intoxicated.

Her bosom pressed against his chest, he ran his hand up to explore, and found her breasts firmly bound. "You hide your womanliness, but it's there," he murmured. He reached for her buttons, eager to free her breasts, take them in his mouth, work the nipples with his tongue until they hardened like his own manhood.

She stood unprotesting, eyes softly closed, letting him unbutton her shirt. He loosened the bindings and the fabric fell around her waist. Her breasts sprang forward in joyous liberation. He filled his hands with their soft firmness, then bent down to kiss each damp nipple. His desire so intensified that he felt as though he would explode if he didn't take her, right now.

Breathing deep, he filled his mouth with her breast, his need overwhelming his caution.

Willa gave in to the warm, flowing sensations of his touch. His tongue caressed her nipple, reawakening that urgent yearning in her center.

Standing in front of him half naked should have sent her into spasms of mortification. Instead, she felt a shy pleasure in revealing her femaleness to him. She relished his enjoyment and wanted to give him whatever it was he wanted, knowing little but that she wanted something from him too. She wanted him closer, near enough to share the same skin.

He released her breast and circled his arms around her, drawing her to him. Again he kissed her, his lips parted and damp. His tongue played around her lips, exploring between them. She opened to him, liquid fire tingling throughout her body. She pressed herself tight to him, feeling his male part clapped hard between her legs, thrusting against the cloth that kept them apart.

He let go of her, tore off his jacket and spread it on the ground. "God help me, I want you." His voice was husky, his expression intense with longing.

Should she be afraid? She recalled Edgar's rough demands, her revulsion and resistance. But this wasn't Edgar, this was her beloved Captain Spencer, a man worthy of her trust. Besides, she knew about risks. This was one of the few she'd taken lately that wouldn't kill her.

She reached for him and grasped his hands. "Show me," she whispered. "I want to know everything about you." Again she lifted her face to meet his lips. His mouth came down on hers with deepening urgency and she clasped him hard to herself. They settled on his jacket in one motion, as though they'd decided to lie down together at the same instant. He stretched out next to her, shifted one leg between hers, straddling her thigh. She felt the bigness between his legs, like a stallion's contained within the trousers.

His lips captured hers again, and again his tongue ran between her lips, inside her mouth. She groaned, caught up in the strange sensations and longings that burned in her core. He shifted again, placing both his legs between hers. She felt the tantalizing pressure of his maleness bearing down on her secret places, and moved with an urge to push back. She heard him groan and whisper her name.

Jeff fumbled with her trouser buttons, then his, and soon their clothes no longer separated their bodies. But he paused, suckling her breast, running his hands down her unclothed thighs, kissing her neck and her chest and her belly in a frenzy of passion. His hand moved to her center point, caressing, his fingers probing into places no one else had ever touched, stoking new fires she'd never before felt.

Then he took his hand away, let himself down and thrust his hips downward, searching, pausing at her gates. She arched to meet him, knowing exactly what to do even though she'd never done it before. She brought his male part in, welcoming the warm hard press of him, ignoring the stretch of her untried interior. She felt no pain, just a tingle, warmth and an irresistible urge to push back and take in his whole length, in rhythmic stages. He was wonderful to hold, solid and strong and virile.

He moved slowly in her, bringing her to a peak of excitement. Then he suddenly caught his breath, exhaled with a sharp cry, withdrew and settled his hardness onto the soft flesh just outside her opening, still thrusting. The hot damp press of his male part against her body made her insides ripple and she wanted him back inside, where he belonged. She wrapped her arms around him, caught up in the churning violence of her own release.

Then he relaxed atop her, spent. He lifted onto his elbows and kissed her. "You are exquisite."

She shook her head, smiling, languid. "Now I know what the fuss is about. We don't need anything but us. Nothing else in the whole world." She fingered his hair, stroked his cheek, ran her hand down his back, loving him. "Why did you do that? Come out just then?"

He rolled off her, leaving his arm across her breasts. "I don't want to harm you by getting you with child."

She was aware of the fertile dampness he'd spilled between her legs, outside, where it couldn't create new life in her. The thought of his dying seed made her sad.

***

Jeff's sense of well-being dissolved into shame. Lord, what had he set loose? Giving into the passion of the moment bore consequences he wanted no part of. Now she was wrapped up with him sexually and emotionally, and how could he justify that? He wasn't able to take her, heart and soul. If only she would be as detached as Clarissa would have been, satisfied with a single night of passion, then back to life as usual.

But she wasn't, and he'd already done the damage. He'd taken her virginity and abused her trust. Some protector he was.

The honorable thing to do was to marry her. But that wouldn't be right, either. She deserved a man who could open up and love her as she ought to be loved.

"You'd better get dressed." His voice sounded rougher than he intended. He rolled away from her and dragged his trousers back on.

Willa sat up and slipped back into the water to rinse herself. She reemerged, smiled at him then gathered her clothes, and set about assembling her disguise. He stole a glimpse of her slim body, catching her before she hid the graceful slope of her shoulders under the bindings. He longed to reach out to her, caress her from one end to the other, lose himself inside her again. But he forced himself to turn away from further lovemaking.

Lovemaking? That wasn't it. He had just given in to the lust of the moment, taking advantage of a young girl's misplaced affection for him.

Better end it now and hope it wasn't too late. "I apologize," he said in a low voice. "I must have lost my reason for a moment. What I did was inexcusable. I won't ever touch you again."

He turned away from the humiliation on her face.

Chapter Fifteen

Edgar Dodds followed the courier to Colonel Crews' headquarters, a wooden country church. No colonel in sight, just two lean, sunburned soldiers lounged in the front yard. Seated on campstools, the pair faced each other over an ammunition crate, squinting at their cards in the fading light. They weren't wearing jackets so their rank insignia was missing. He reckoned their combined ages equaled his own, so they couldn't be very important. But they were positioned so he had to pass them to get to the tent.

The one facing him glanced up and mumbled a warning to his companion. He laid his cards face down, lazed to his feet and saluted Edgar's major's insignia. The other soldier followed suit, and Edgar noted that his shirt fell open, unbuttoned halfway to his waist. Still the young fool ran his impertinent gaze over Edgar's home guard uniform, the dress sword, and the plume in his hat.

Edgar felt a twinge of dissatisfaction. A week of hard travel and no chance to clean up—he must look damn near as disreputable as the rank and file.

The courier told them who Edgar was, and they introduced themselves, both so-called staff officers. The half-dressed, impudent fellow called himself Captain Langston, his consumptive-looking partner, Lieutenant Graham.

Langston dismissed the courier and turned to Edgar. "So, sir." His drawling voice was lazy, just short of insolent. "Here we are standing on Tennessee soil. What could possibly bring a Georgia home guardsman out from cover and clear across the state line?"

Edgar tapped his riding crop against his boot leg, seething. How dare Langston imply he was a bombproof officer? "It is imperative that I see Colonel Crews about your insubordination, plus another urgent matter. I presume he's inside?"

Langston shook his head no, didn't look nearly as cowed as he ought to be, though maybe a shade less cocky than before. "The colonel is not available right now. He is meeting with General Wheeler about other urgent matters. Perhaps if you made an appointment?" Langston inclined his head, still looking like he thought he was the superior.

"I order you to take me to him."

The two officers exchanged glances then Langston said, "I already have my orders, sir, from Colonel Crews."

"Must I remind you that I am the ranking officer present?"

Langston gave him a skeptical look. "I can't help that, sir. If I can assist you in some other way—"

"Are you Colonel Crews' orderly?"

"I'm on his staff. Inspector general for the brigade."

"Inspector general?" The stripling had a little authority after all, but he looked like the one who needed an inspection. "Let's start over." He took a breath, calming himself. "Perhaps you could assist me with this predicament. Even though it's a matter to be handled with the utmost discretion."

Captain Langston offered a campstool with exaggerated courtesy. "Have a seat, sir."

Edgar reluctantly accepted. Was he wasting his time with these underlings? He would rather go straight to the top, to Major General Wheeler himself. Though Colonel Crews commanded a brigade, Richmond hadn't yet bothered to give him the general's title.

Because Crews wasn't available, Edgar would have to chance talking to Langston. "No sense mincing words. I have reason to believe a young woman masquerading as a soldier has joined your brigade."

The two cavalry officers exchanged bemused glances and looked back at him. "A young girl, sir?" Langston repeated.

"I said, a young woman. She was spotted among a detachment that foraged at my plantation near Covington, under the command of a Captain Spencer."

Langston crossed his arms over his bare chest and chuckled. "That's unlikely. I'm pretty sure Jefferson Spencer can tell the difference between a man and a woman."

"She was in disguise, sir, wearing a soldier's clothing and hat. I understand she was seen carrying a pistol. One of my nigras who spoke with her used to belong to her father."

Langston smirked. "He wasn't pulling your leg?"

"My people wouldn't dare lie to me."

"Maybe old Jeff has something good on his hands he hasn't been willing to share." Graham grinned, then broke into a coughing fit.

Edgar slashed his crop, scattering the playing cards. "If he's touched her, by God, I'll kill him. She is my fiancée."

Graham grabbed for his hand of cards and the chips. "If you please, sir!"

"So." Langston crossed his arms and cocked his head to one side. "Why would your intended want to join the army, if you don't mind my asking, sir?"

"She hasn't been quite right in the head since her mother died." Edgar shook his head sadly. "Her father was a drunk. A weakling. Bad enough he wasn't much of a father to her, then the Yankees killed him. The poor girl must have completely lost her mental balance over it."

"Oh, I heard something about that old fellow." Graham hawked his throat clear. "Yankee raiders. They burned his house south of Covington."

"Exactly," Edgar said. "They were neighbors of mine, and I am legally responsible for Miss Randall now that she's an orphan. We are betrothed, and her father appointed me her guardian before he was killed. I'm still willing to take her in despite her touch of lunacy." He shook his head again. "Can't imagine that young lady facing the danger of being in the army."

"Nor can I." Langston's voice was level, but the skin around his eyes crinkled and the corners of his mouth twitched. The fool thought it was a joke. "We'll certainly check into this, sir."

"I expect more than that, Captain Langston." Edgar drew himself up straight, controlling his fury. "I expect you to escort me straight to this Captain Spencer's camp without further delay. That is an order."

Langston covered his mouth and glanced sidewise at Graham. "Yes, sir. We'll clear this up straightaway."

"You'd better. Your cavalry's reputation certainly doesn't need to be stained by the presence of a female trooper." Edgar tsk-tsked. "This brigade could easily turn into a laughing stock."

Langston's eyes flashed, less amused now. "We are far from that sorry plight, sir. Our military accompli—"

"I'm sure, I'm sure." Edgar waved his hand impatiently. "Now you will take me to this Captain Spencer so I can find Miss Randall and take her home, if it's not too late. I fear for her, sir. I fear for her very life."

"Yes, sir," Langston drawled. "We'll give the matter all the prompt attention it so richly deserves."

Graham covered his mouth with the handkerchief and studied the ground. The corners of Langston's mouth started twitching again.

Edgar stood up, eager to force these insolent pups to their duty. He needed them to find Willa, despite their sloppy attire and thinly veiled ridicule. "Now. Or I'll have you both arrested for failure to follow orders."

"There's no call for threats," Langston said softly. "I said I'd take you there." He stood up and started buttoning his shirt. "I'll handle this, Graham. Can't have everybody gone. You stay here and cover HQ."

Graham slumped back down in his campstool without so much as a "yes, sir." No doubt disappointed to be missing out on the excitement.

Clearly, neither of them believed a word he said and thought he was making a fool of himself. He'd show them who the fools were, by God!

***

Willa poured Captain Spencer a fresh cup of coffee and handed it to him. He took the cup from her, thanking her with a cool smile, taking care not to let his hand contact hers, giving the formal officer-and-aide routine, even after what they'd done together. None of the men were present to make such a show necessary.

She returned to the campfire, confused. He was acting as though nothing had ever happened between them. Yet, she felt changed, through and through, awakened to feelings she'd never known before.

Incredibly, he had said she was beautiful. Womanly. And he'd kissed her. Caressed her lovingly, longingly. Came down on her, mated with her, joined with her in a union that was sacred to her, made her believe he wanted her, cared about her. He'd accepted her love and in one beautiful lesson taught her how it could be between a man and a woman.

Then he'd denied her, turned away and coldly cut himself off from her.

She glanced over at him. He was leaning against a tree, watching her, the shadow of his hat brim hiding his eyes. Then he looked away, quite deliberately.

It was like a slap on the face.

Suddenly furious, she lunged to her feet. "I'm not good enough for you. Is that it?"

He whirled back to her so suddenly his coffee sloshed over the rim. "What? Is that what you think?"

"You're no better than Edgar. I hate you!"

He blinked, his controlled expression wavering, then going hard. "Fine. It's all for the best."

She pivoted and stalked off toward the woods.

"Where are you going?" he said.

"To see to my horse," she flung over her shoulder. "Do I have your permission to be excused, sir?"

"Go, then." He turned his back.

Damn him. Mean as a snake, deep down inside. Couldn't count on him for anything that really mattered. Just like every man she knew but Bobby. He was perfectly willing to have his way with her, then discard her as though she had no feelings.

She ought to saddle Annie and ride away, anywhere, as far away from him as she could travel.

From the corner of her eye, she glimpsed the movement of men walking toward the campfire. She paused in the shadows and watched the staff officer and another officer, a darkly bearded man, approach. Even in the dark she recognized his form and walk. Oh, no! Her insides convulsed with fear. How could it be him, this far from home?

Edgar. He'd finally run her down.

Captain Spencer stepped forward to greet the two men.

Willa veered the other way, hoping Edgar hadn't spotted her yet. Forcing herself to walk calmly, not to call attention to herself, she glided deeper into the cover of the dark woods.

Fighting back tears, she battled her way through the underbrush toward the horse picket.

How on earth could he track her all the way up here, deep into Yankee held land, clear to Tennessee? Why would he go to all that trouble?

He must be obsessed, wanting to find her so badly he'd risked his life, everything. How could she keep on escaping a man so determined?

Edgar had all the legal rights. He practically owned her. That was how the authorities would see it. Captain Spencer would finally be rid of her. She hoped he would be satisfied.

She would keep on running, lose herself in hostile territory. Even the Yankees didn't scare her as much as Edgar did.

***

Jeff resisted the impulse to run after her, take her in his arms and allow his true feelings free rein. He'd seen her pain and desperately wanted to sooth her, to make amends, to make things right between them. He wanted to keep her by his side forever.

No. Nothing was forever. He clenched the coffee cup in both hands. How in the hell did he ever let himself get cornered like this? Something was bound happen to her, and this time it would kill him too.

His own guilt stabbed him in the gut. She hated him, all because of his loss of control. It wouldn't happen again, that was the right thing to do. He couldn't use her this way. He had to think rationally. The sooner he sent her away the better it would be for both of them. At least he'd had the presence of mind to make sure he didn't get her with child.

He noted the two men approaching but didn't recognize the officer with Captain Langston. He was a major, but not cavalry. What was he doing here?

He saluted, noting the thinly suppressed smile on Langston's face, as though he were about to pull a joke. The major's gaze darted about, searching. He was a burly man, his beard matted, his expensively tailored uniform torn and dirty.

Something was up, and he sensed he wasn't going to like it.

"What can I do for you, gentlemen?" He started to tell Will to boil more coffee then remembered anew her stalking off, hurt and angry.

"Captain Spencer, this is Major Dodds, with the Georgia Home guard. Chased us all the way up here." Langston shifted his weight from foot to foot, obviously trying to keep a straight face like he was really enjoying himself. "He has made statements we are compelled to investigate."

Dodds, in the flesh. The very man who'd brutalized Willa. Jeff felt his back stiffen, instant loathing as he studied Dodds. Puffy cheeks, mean little eyes, not a good face. If he'd ever doubted Willa, something about the man would have convinced him she'd told the truth. "What statements?"

Dodds fixed him with a haughty stare. "First off, you've been to my place, but unfortunately I was attending to duty in Atlanta at the time. Had I been there, I wouldn't have allowed you to plunder my smokehouse."

Jeff met Dodds' withering look squarely with one of his own. "Surely, sir, you didn't chase the cavalry all the way into Tennessee to grouse about the meat we *purchased* from your overseer to keep my men from starving."

"Sir, do you wish to file a formal complaint?" Langston asked Dodds. "Although I'm sure Captain Spencer followed legal procedures. He's very precise."

"In time, Captain Langston. I have more urgent concerns." Dodds jabbed a finger toward Jeff. "See here, Spencer. My fiancée, Miss Willa Randall, was seen with your troop. I've come to take her home where she belongs."

Jeff lifted an incredulous eyebrow, faking disbelief. "Your fiancée?" He took a deliberate sip of coffee, stalling, waiting for Dodds and Langston to rush in and fill the silence.

Langston said, "Yankee stragglers killed her father, and she must have run for her life. Major Dodds theorizes Miss Randall posed as a man and you mistakenly let her join up about the time Stoneman raided middle Georgia. Didn't you recruit a young soldier then, the one you've been using as an aide? What's his name, Will Barber?"

They had him, only a quick inspection from the truth. Lying now would only make things worse.

He shrugged as though nothing much out of the ordinary had occurred. "She had me fooled, all right. I did recruit Willa Randall, believing her to be a boy. After we were well behind enemy lines, I found out different."

Langston blinked. "Then it's true. I'll be damned."

Dodds took a threatening step toward Jeff. "Where is she?"

Jeff ignored him and turned to Langston. "Surely you appreciate my concerns with Miss Randall's welfare. I wasn't about to abandon her behind enemy lines or to reveal her sex to the other troopers. I took the only course available, keeping her safe until she can be delivered back to friendly territory."

"Why didn't you report this, ah, irregularity—to headquarters?" Langston asked.

"I'd never heard of a precedent." Jeff smiled easily, shrugged again. "Who ever heard of a woman joining the cavalry? I saw it as a minor matter, best handled at the company level, well within my authority."

Langston let out his breath. "Whatever the case, Major Dodds is willing to take her off our hands. It seems to me that is the ideal solution."

"Not for Miss Randall, I'm afraid," Jeff said.

"We could discharge her before anybody else in your troop knows a thing," Langston said. "Better for morale."

Jeff let out a contemptuous snort. "Of course you'd be happy to let Major Dodds solve the problem of a errant female breaking regulations and clean up the mess for you."

Dodds stood with his hands clasped behind his back, looking smug. "Of course I'll be discreet. If you wish, I won't say a word to anyone about this scandal."

"Scandal?" Jeff's jaw clenched in anger as he thought of this man pawing that innocent young woman. His woman. He'd be damned if he'd let Dodds get his hands on her again. "By what authority does Major Dodds claim her guardianship?" Jeff looked him up and down, frowning, letting his contempt show. "His own say-so?"

Still smug, Dodds slipped a piece of paper out of his wallet and handed it to Langston.

Langston struck a match to read the document. "It's a will signed by Mr. Jason Randall, making Major Dodds executor. It states here that the major is to be in charge of Miss Willa Randall's affairs in the event her father passes away before she marries Major Dodds. It names him her guardian." The staff officer glanced up from the paper at Dodds. "Looks clear to me, sir."

Dodds grunted his satisfaction.

"Let me see that." Jeff snatched the document, and scanned it. He needed more time to think. Whether the will was legal couldn't be decided on the spot, but Dodds's demand would put her under hir control in the meantime.

He could come up with one sure way to override Dodds' authority, and he was the only man available to provide that means, if she was willing. She hated him, but didn't she hate Dodds even worse?

He stared at the damnable words on the agreement. Edgar Dodds would destroy her, and Jeff would never forgive himself for letting that happen.

So much for not getting attached. Oddly enough, his decision felt liberating.

Dodds tapped his riding crop against his boot-top. "See here, Langston. We've stalled long enough. Captain Spencer, I must insist you produce Miss Randall immediately."

"The sooner she's off our hands the better," Langston said. "Where is she?"

"Not so fast." Jeff shook his head no and smiled, hoping he looked more relaxed than he felt. Then he handed the document back to Dodds. "You can't have her, nor can any other man. You see, Miss Randall is about to become my wife."

He let out his breath. There. Once the vows were taken, she would be out of Edgar Dodds' reach forever. A safe interval afterwards, he'd offer her a quiet annulment to let her out of a union she had never bargained for. If she chose to stay with him instead, he would cherish and honor her as she deserved. The possibility that she might make that choice warmed him against his will.

The corners of Langston's mouth twitched up in a smirk. Dodds went pale and opened his mouth like a hooked fish. Then his face turned red and a vein on his neck popped out. "You have no right! She's my fiancée, not yours!" He shoved forward, right into Jeff's face. "Damn you, Spencer. She's mine!"

Jeff stood his ground, inhaling the rotten smell of Dodd's breath. "She is a free woman, sir. You don't own her. I insist we let her make the determination."

"What determination? I have the papers," Dodds blustered. "Since her father is dead, I'm her legal guardian. He appointed me before he died."

"After she becomes my wife, that's all over with. She'll be under my protection and authority. Then we'll contest the balance of her estate." Jeff turned to Langston. "We'll need the chaplain straightaway to get this settled."

"How the devil are you going to maintain a wife while we're on this campaign?" Langston said.

"I'll send her home as soon as it's practicable. In the meantime, she's not an official problem. Not your concern, only mine."

Langston looked doubtful. "You'll have to consult with Colonel Crews."

"Fine. I'll consult. After Miss Randall and I see the chaplain."

Dodds said to Langston, "Are you going to let a lunatic decide her own fate? The girl doesn't know what's best for her."

"Sir, I refuse to stand here any longer and listen to you insult my bride." Jeff took a step toward Dodds, hands fisted. "I must insist on a private word with you."

Edgar went pale, the anger draining from his face. He actually looked frightened. He lifted a shaking hand to his pistol grip. "Are you calling me out, sir? I refuse to fight with you."

"Then get your hand away from your weapon." Jeff led off, letting Dodds fall in alongside, careful not to tempt the bastard with a view of his back. Once he was sure they were out of Langston's earshot, he stopped, faced Dodds and said in a low voice, "I know what you tried to do to Willa. You're bleeding lucky I didn't kill you on sight."

Dodds crossed his arms, his mean little eyes narrowing. "What the hell are you talking about?" he said between clenched teeth.

"After I caught on who she was, she told me why she ran away from you. Marks on her face proved it. She was beaten up pretty bad when she found us."

"I didn't do nothing to her. She's been making up stories." Edgar sneered. "Seems to me you're pretty damned easy to fool anyhow, seeing as how you let her join your troop."

"She thinks you killed her father too. Not a bad theory. We didn't come across any Yankees in that area. If it was Yankees, they would have cleaned out Randall's livestock and meat. But we found all that on your property. How did it get there?"

"I found it and saved it for her. Her property was in my care."

"Why didn't the Yankees take it, considering they were supposedly there first?"

"Ask them."

"That paper you showed Langston gives you a lot to gain with Randall dead. Seems to me she has quite a case against you."

Dodds wiped sweat off his forehead. "She has nothing. You can't prove a thing."

The sorry bastard was right. Jeff may be rusty on lawyering, but any fool could see the only case he really had was pure conjecture and bluff. "Make any further trouble, and I'll make our suspicions public. I am only forbearing for Willa's sake. She has been through enough grief."

Dodds' eyes narrowed. "You haven't been bedding my fiancée, have you, Spencer?"

Jeff clenched his fists, feeling his face heat up. "I'm warning you. She's not your business any more."

"If you bedded her, I'll kill you."

"Come near her again once we're married, and you're the dead man. That's a promise."

Dodds gave him a deadly look, then turned and walked back to where Langston stood. Jeff followed, keeping his thumb hooked in his gun belt, his hand distrustfully covering the revolver butt. To Langston he said, "Would you please send for the chaplain? I'll go explain things to Miss Randall."

"I'll go get him myself," Langston said. "I'm sticking around for the wedding. I wouldn't miss this . . ." he walked away shaking his head and grinning.

"I'm going with you, Spencer," Dodds said. "I want to make sure she understands exactly what she is doing."

"No question she will. The same things she understood when she ran away from you."

Chapter Sixteen

Willa made up a story about carrying a message for Colonel Crews and had no trouble with either the horse guard or the picket. Everybody knew she was Captain Spencer's pet aide, and neither trooper so much as raised an eyebrow.

She didn't know quite where she was headed, but she sure knew what she was running away from: Edgar's cruelty and Captain Spencer's indifference.

Upstream along the Tennessee River was Knoxville, she'd heard. She didn't know a soul there, not such a bad thing—nobody to turn her over to Edgar. She didn't have any money, but she knew how to work. If she got desperate, she could sell Annie Laurie for good money, although that would be the last resort. Annie was her last link to Bobby, who'd turned out to be her only friend in the whole world.

Even after she'd been stupid enough to believe she'd made another one.

She wiped tears from her eyes and pushed on through the darkness, listening for the rush of the river at her left. Moonlight dappling through the trees helped her find her way.

***

Edgar walked with Spencer to the horse picket, hatred burning like acid through his veins. He had come this far to retrieve Willa, only to find this tough-looking younger man in his way. Probably got his way with her, and that notion made him shake with fury. To make the situation even worse, Spencer had him worried he'd challenge him to a duel, a frightening proposition. Out here he wouldn't be able to control the stakes and it would be a fair fight with a fit opponent, turning the odds deadly.

Spencer had to go, but it was too risky to take him on directly. Better be ready, have things more in his own favor when he dealt with that one. And it would require careful calculation. If Spencer dropped his guard, shooting him here would be dangerous, but it could be done. He'd have to do it right then whisk Willa away before anyone caught on. Behind enemy lines, nobody was likely to come looking for him. He'd just shed his gray uniform, become a peaceable Union sympathizer, lie low in Knoxville and wait until it was safe to go home.

He didn't care how long he waited, as long as Willa was warming his bed.

But it was clear Spencer wouldn't give him an opening. He kept Edgar within his line of vision, not presenting his back for even a moment.

Edgar made out a line of cavalry horses standing in the dark, heads drooping, drowsing in the dark. "Will," Spencer called out.

A man's voice answered. "He's already gone."

"Gone!" Spencer barked. "Where?"

The horse guard stepped out of the shadows and saluted, looking puzzled. "Sir, you're the one that sent him."

"Sent him where?"

"Said you told him to take a message to Colonel Crews. Seemed to be in a big hurry." The soldier nodded toward the horses. "Saddled his mare and lit out like ghosts was after him."

"Which way?" Spencer said.

"That was the funny part." The soldier lifted his arm and pointed west. "Colonel Crews' headquarters is that a way, but Will took off east instead, along the river. I figured he knew something I didn't."

"Damnation," Spencer said.

"Something wrong, sir?" the soldier said.

Spencer turned to Edgar, his face working. "She must have seen you. She thought . . . oh, hell."

"She?" the guard said, looking confused.

"Never mind," Spencer snapped. "Get Baron's saddle."

Edgar reached for the lead-rope of one of the horses. "I'm going too."

"You'll stay here," Spencer said.

"I outrank you, damn it. You've got nothing to say about it."

"This isn't Atlanta." Spencer took a menacing step forward. "I take no orders from an out-of-place home guard major who bought his commission from his statehouse cronies."

"That's it." Edgar felt hot blood rush to his face. "Stop right there." He whipped out his pistol and cocked it, regretting this wasn't the right time to send Spencer to hell. He'd save that luxury for when they were alone. "Guard, you're a witness to a captain disobeying a direct order from a major. Blatant insubordination. This man is under arrest."

"Horseshit," Spencer said. "Put that hog leg away."

"Unbuckle your gun belt and hand it over," Edgar said.

Spencer obeyed, tight-lipped with anger. Fine. Let him be good and mad, give an excuse to plug him, as if one was needed.

Edgar pointed to the horse he had started to untie, "Guard, saddle this one for me. Looks fresh enough."

The confused guard looked past Edgar to Spencer. "Captain?"

"Do it," Edgar snapped. "Or you're under arrest too. Then saddle his nag. He's going with me."

"Guess I am." A change had come over Spencer, his voice soft and calm. "It's all right, Smith. Do what he says. We'll sort it out later." He stood by quietly while the guard threw the gear on the horses. Edgar wasn't fooled by his silence. The bastard had collected himself, was outwardly unworried, biding his time, arms folded over his chest, eyes watchful, the most dangerous kind of enemy he could have.

"Mount up and lead off," Edgar told him. "Take me through the picket posts."

Spencer obeyed without saying a word.

***

Jeff saw no choice but to respect the weapon pointed between his shoulder blades and escort Edgar Dodds out of camp. The most important thing was finding Willa before she got too long a lead. He'd play along for the time being and deal with Dodds when he got a chance. So far, Dodds hadn't given him an opening, not without making sure Jeff got shot for his efforts. But the paper major would probably make an awkward move sooner or later. He'd just have to wait until then.

He found the picket on duty right where he'd left him. The soldier said he'd let Willa pass through his post only a few minutes before, supposedly carrying a message. He pointed out the eastward direction she had gone, again along the river.

How was she likely to play it, given that she was terrified of Dodds and expected no help from anybody else? He'd encouraged that idea, that he didn't give a damn about her. Now, both of them were paying. If only she'd stayed in camp, he would have had it all worked out by now.

He should have let her know his true feelings as soon as he admitted them to himself. Lord, what a mess he'd made!

In her place, he would also follow the river and keep it as a reference point knowing it would eventually lead to a town. Given her short hair and talent at deception, she would most likely keep on posing as a boy and pick up some kind of paying job.

Instead of staying where she belonged, with him.

The dark woods made for slow going, but he reckoned they'd progressed about a mile from the picket post. He shoved aside a bough and forced Baron through chest-high underbrush. Behind him, he heard

Dodd's ragged breathing in between swear words, the whip and crackle of leaves, and the thump of hooves. "Can't you find a better trail than this, Spencer?"

"You don't like it, you lead." Jeff lifted his lip as he added, "Sir."

"Just keep going," Dodds said.

Apparently Dodds didn't care to turn his back on him. Jeff hated exposing his own back to Dodds. He would be willing to lay down money that Dodds really did murder Willa's father.

A couple of weeks ago, whether he lived or died didn't seem to matter much. But things had changed, and he wanted to see Willa through.

He turned in the saddle to look at Dodds and see what he was up to.

Dodds lifted his revolver, a threat. "Mind the path ahead. I'll tell you when to stop."

The scoundrel did intend to kill him. He could smell it.

The path ahead was suddenly irresistible. He'd run for it and hope Dodds couldn't keep up in the dark. Then he'd find Willa and make things right.

He dug his heels into Baron's sides, leaned over the horse's neck, and yelled in its ear. Baron responded instantly, surging into a cantor.

Dodds shouted, swearing.

Jeff heard the blast and felt the blow to his head, an instant of pain, then blackness.

***

Edgar watched Spencer slide sideways out of the saddle and fall lifelessly to the ground. He hit heavy and rolled once, coming to rest with his shoulders jammed against a tree trunk. The moonlight revealed him lying mouth slack, eyes shut, the hair on the side of his head thickening with blood.

Spencer didn't look so formidable now.

A thrill of triumph prickled along Edgar's spine. One bullet, a lucky shot, and he'd cleared his only obstacle. Willa was still his. All he had left to do was to claim her.

Spencer's premature dash had forced Edgar into killing sooner than he would have chosen. He'd wanted to shoot him farther from camp. He listened to the receding hoof beats and reckoned Spencer's horse wasn't headed back to camp, not yet. If the sound of the shot had carried to the picket line, it would take the soldiers a little time to come this far and investigate. Even if they cared to stumble into the darkness chasing gunfire. He had time.

He laughed and spurred his mount forward to trample his dead foe. The horse balked and veered, refusing to step on the body. Edgar kicked and slashed at his mount with the riding crop. The horse danced about, sidestepped, and stubbornly fought Edgar's will.

Battling the animal was a waste of time and Edgar was in a hurry. He gave up taking that last shred of satisfaction, dealt the beast a final whack on the head and rode on past the crumpled heap that used to be Captain Jeff Spencer.

* * *

Willa heard the gunshot, loud, only a little way behind her. Probably it had nothing to do with her. Why did she feel that chill, a new stab of pain in her heart?

Just keep running. She kept her heels hard on Annie's flanks, forcing the mare forward. Branches slapped her face and scratched her cheeks.

Suddenly Annie lurched under her. Willa heard a crunch like a dry stick breaking, Annie's scream, and felt herself pitching from the saddle, hitting the ground so hard she lay paralyzed, breathless.

She heard Annie groaning in pain, trying to get up, thrashing.

Willa sucked in a lungful of air and lifted her head. In the brightness of the moonlight, she saw Annie struggle up on three legs, the fourth dangling.

"No," she whispered. "It can't be busted." She pushed to her feet and hobbled over to Annie, not feeling so sound herself. She ran her hand up the mare's drooping head, down her neck, shoulder, to the hurt leg.

She could make it out in the shimmer of moonlight. A jagged shard of white bone stuck out of the foreleg, just above the pastern.

"No, no, no," she sobbed. "You didn't do this!"

Annie's breath came out in a long moan. The mare raised her head, brushing her muzzle alongside Willa's arm, looking for comfort. Willa rubbed the velvety muzzle, mourning, knowing what she must do.

First Bobby, then Pa. Reynolds died right in front of her, and Captain Spencer didn't give a flip about her. Now the last friend left was leaving her for good. And she had to do it to her.

Maybe Captain Spencer was right. It didn't pay to care about anybody.

Willa took in a long choking breath and stroked Annie's neck one last time. She removed the saddlebags and let them drop. Then she pulled out her revolver.

"I can't," she whispered. She let her gun hand fall alongside her thigh. She didn't know how long she stood immobile before Annie staggered, shifting weight onto the broken leg. The mare squealed in pain and caught herself with the sound leg, blowing, sides heaving.

That was how it would be until she finally gave out, a slow, agonizing death.

Blind with tears, Willa pointed the weapon at the mare's skull and squeezed the trigger. The explosion lit up the woods and crashed in Willa's ears. Through a mist she saw Annie slump to earth, coming to rest on her side.

Sobbing, Willa holstered her revolver and bent over to pick up the saddlebags. As she straightened, she sensed something coming at her from behind. Before she could react, a heavy arm whipped around her throat and pulled her backwards. She felt the jerk of her revolver leaving the holster and the arm tightening on her neck. She struggled to get free, hearing the voice she hated rumble in her ear, "Settle down, Willa girl. I've got you now."

Chapter
Seventeen

Willa flailed in Edgar's grip, but the more she struggled, the tighter he clamped down on her throat. Her breath cut off so she couldn't scream, she continued to beat at him with her fists until her vision went blacker than the surrounding night.

When she came to, she was lying on her back, hands tied behind her with a rope, her throat aching. Edgar stood over her. "I haven't forgotten what a wildcat you can be." He licked his lips. "Wildcats can be tamed, but you aren't yet. It'll be fun getting there."

She cried out knowing she was too far away from camp for anyone to hear, but it didn't matter anyway, as her voice came out an ineffectual squeak.

"No use calling for help." He bent over and grabbed her arm. "Get up. We got to get moving before your shooting brings the Yankees." He pulled her to her feet, where she swayed, feeling numb and faint, staring at Annie's remains.

"Too bad about the mare," Edgar said. "I had plans for her too. This way." He shoved her forward, holding onto her arm. She lurched to one side, testing him, but she couldn't break free. "Stop that," he growled, and cuffed the side of her head.

She tried to yell again, but he jammed his arm under her chin, holding her jaws shut. He continued in a conversational tone. "I heard the mare make a fuss and figured it must be you. It wasn't hard to find you when you shot her."

He pulled her to the tree where his horse stood tethered. "Get on," he ordered. She had no choice but to mount, and it wasn't easy with her hands bound. He gave her a leg up and boosted her onto the horse's back. "Let's get out of here before somebody comes along. I'll get behind you so you can't pull any tricks," he told her as he mounted.

Behind her, Edgar urged the horse forward. "By the way, that captain can't marry you now. He's dead too. I'm the only friend you've got left." She absorbed his words, confused. Who said Captain Spencer was going to marry her? And he wasn't dead, anyway. Only a few minutes ago he was perfectly all right. Even after she lied, telling him she hated him.

145

"The Yankees got him," he continued. "I saw it happen. Didn't you hear the shot?"

The words pelted her like bullets. She recalled hearing a gunshot before Annie went down, but she hissed, "You're a damned liar!"

"Lesson one, girlie," Edgar growled. "Mind your manners or pay the price." She saw the flick of the riding crop from the corner of her eye and flinched as she felt the stinging blow on her cheek.

"I've got to teach you how it's going to be between us," he said, keeping the whip within her sight, "You be nice to me, and I'll be nice to you. That isn't so hard, is it?"

In a rage of grief she cried, "You killed Captain Spencer. Just like my Pa. Did you shoot him in the back?"

He smacked her across the face again with the riding crop. "Shut your mouth. The damn Yankees did it. Both times."

"Liar!" she twisted around and screamed in his face. "I'll see you burn in hell—"

"Shut up." He brought his fist around and punched her. Head buzzing, eyes watering, tasting blood, she saw him reach down and draw a knife from his boot. He grabbed her jacket collar, yanked up her head and pressed the blade against her cheek. "Listen here, girlie. You playing soldier didn't turn you into a big, strong man even if you do show more fight than you used to. I don't care if I have to cut you up. It'll be my own personal brand. Then the finest clothes won't make you look pretty enough for anybody else."

He gave her a shove and let go. "Got it?"

Willa faced forward, weeping silently, tears running from the corners of her eyes. Her hands clutched so tight the fingernails dug into her palms, not wanting him to see her despair. If only she'd seen him coming. If she'd known what he'd done to Captain Spencer, she would have shot him dead on sight. Now he had her gun, a knife, the riding crop, and her.

"After we get far enough away from the camps," Edgar said, "We'll go on to lesson two. We'll consummate our union, and you'll like it."

"I'd rather die." She choked back the tears and squared her shoulders. She'd do anything to ruin his sense of triumph. He'd probably punish her more, but she didn't care about that any more. "Anyway, you aren't the first. I've already been consummated."

Edgar didn't say anything right away. She took that to mean she'd caught him by surprise.

"You're too late. Captain Spencer got me first," she pushed on. "And you know what? He didn't have to use a knife or a riding crop to make me."

She braced herself for another wallop, but instead he breathed, "Whore. You can still redeem yourself by bearing me a strong son. But if it looks like a Spencer bastard, I swear I'll drown it."

Bile backed up from her stomach into her throat, sour and burning.

"By and by I'll get you home and make an honest woman out of you," he continued. "Don't give a thought to running again. I'll lock you up if I got to. They lock up crazy people, and I figure you have to be crazy to play soldier."

She set her jaw, thinking instead about Edgar Dodds dying. She'd never be free, not until he was dead and gone. Sooner or later, he'd have to sleep. Then she could avenge the lives of Captain Spencer and Pa.

Captain Spencer was gone, and she'd never felt so helpless and hopeless. She couldn't help loving him even if he couldn't love her back. Her heart ached with hurt and grief. Edgar might as well have killed her along with him. She felt dead inside, everything that mattered was gone, leaving a dark hole. Better the Yankees had killed her than this misery.

"See any sign of Yankees, let me know," he said. "Quiet, like. So you won't give them the alarm."

For once she didn't care about the Yankees. "It's dark and I can't see any better than you can."

"I'd hate to see them shoot a hole in that sweet breast of yours." His hand crept under her shirt, and grappled at her chest. "What's all this in the way?" he growled. He worked his hand underneath the bindings, kneading her flesh.

It was useless to fight him, trussed up like a calf waiting for slaughter. She shut her eyes and clamped her teeth, enduring the groping, listening to the labored breathing behind her.

"It would suit me to stop right here." His breath fanned hotly into her ear. "How'd you like that?" She shuddered, and he laughed. "Just keep on fighting me, girl. Keeps things interesting."

He let go of her breast and fiddled with his hands, taking something out of his pocket. She heard the scuff of a match and smelled the sulfur, then tobacco smoke. At least he had something to keep his hands busy besides pawing her.

She moaned and refilled her lungs though she'd just as soon not bother. She noticed a different scent mingled with his pipe fumes. Wood smoke, like a campfire.

Edgar didn't say anything about it. He probably couldn't smell anything with his nose full of pipe smoke.

Better say something. She didn't want the Yankees catching her.

But what if they did? One form of doom or another, and they'd have Edgar. She kept her mouth clamped shut. Would Yankees give a warning or kill them out of hand? In front, she'd take a bullet first.

With any luck, it would keep right on going and kill Edgar too.

Then again, the smoke might be coming from a farmer's chimney. Maybe a Confederate camp. Wheeler's forces, two thousand strong, occupied a lot of area. For the first time since Edgar had captured her, she felt a glow of hope.

Yankees might use her the same way he did if they knew she was a girl. But she'd still rather take her chances with them, even if the only good it did was to mess up Edgar's plans.

She focused her attention on the dark trail ahead and tried not to show Edgar she was alert to anything. She sat shoulders drooping, like he'd succeeded in breaking her spirit, then noticed a slight movement, a flutter of leaves in the woods ahead. Was it her imagination?

"What was that?" Edgar whispered.

"What?" She said it good and loud, her voice cracking the silence. "I didn't see anything."

"Shut up," he snapped. "Somebody'll hear you." He kept the horse moving, pipe set between his teeth, but she could feel him tense up behind her.

Good thing he couldn't see her face in the dark. The bitter grin hurt her battered lip, but she didn't care. They rode past the spot where she'd marked the movement. Nothing happened. Drat.

Here the wood smoke smelled stronger, mingled with frying bacon, just like a camp was nearby. Late night mist and still air held the scents close to the ground. The tired horse stumbled underneath her, then recovered.

"You better stop and rest this horse soon," she told Edgar. "He's loaded too heavy."

"Then maybe I ought to make you get off and walk."

"Fine. I'll walk."

She heard him puff his pipe, then say, "I'm thinking you're up to no good."

"I'd just rather walk for a while. I'm getting saddle galls."

"Can't be. You got to be used to it. All the riding you've been doing?"

Suddenly dark-uniformed men stepped out of the shadowy brush on either side of the trail, rifles held ready. "Halt, there!" one of them shouted. Another man grabbed the horse's bridle. "Put up your hands, you damned Rebs! We've got you!"

Willa stared down at the weapons pointed at her chest. She cried, "I can't!"

"Don't shoot me." Edgar's voice quavered. "Please don't."

"I said raise your hands!" the Yankee with the sergeant's stripes yelled.

"My hands are tied behind my back." She twisted around, trying to show him, but Edgar's bulk was in the way.

The Yankee took hold of her elbow and pulled it, nearly unseating her. She shifted her weight and managed to keep her balance.

"How come he's all trussed up?" the Yankee sergeant said to Edgar.

Edgar hesitated.

She held her breath. How much would he tell them? They wouldn't molest her if they thought she was a boy. She'd just be another prisoner of war.

"Deserter," Edgar finally said.

She sagged with relief. She didn't deny it even though Edgar had just heaped disgrace upon her. The Yankee sergeant shot her a wry look, then said to Edgar, "Dismount, you."

Edgar got down right away. Willa watched from atop the horse as they removed his gun belt.

"You Wheeler's men?" the sergeant said.

Edgar hesitated again, then nodded.

"You're behind our lines. That makes you a guerrilla. We hang guerrillas," one of the other Yankees said. His voice was flat with menace.

In the gathering light she could make out Edgar swallowing hard, looking worried. "I'm no goddamn guerrilla." His voice was a nervous squeak.

Despite the fix she was in, his situation was just as miserable as hers, maybe even worse. Seeing him disarmed and scared did her broken heart good.

"Check his boot. He's got a knife in it," she said to the Yankee sergeant.

Edgar glared at her. "Damn you, spiteful little,,,"

"Shut up, bushwhacker." The sergeant ran his hand into Edgar's boot and withdrew the knife. Then he turned to her, holding it ready in his hand.

She leaned away from him. Before she could swing one leg over the saddle and jump to avoid the blade, he seized her arm. She flinched as she felt the sawing, then realized the edge was just missing her flesh. The knots fell loose, freeing her hands.

"Dismount now," the sergeant said.

She obeyed, climbing down from the horse. She rubbed her rope-chaffed wrists. "Thanks," she mumbled to the sergeant.

One of the men laughed. "You should have left him tied up nice and neat."

The Yankee sergeant said, "No matter. Snyder, let's take these sorry looking graybacks to Captain Lucas for questioning. They try to escape, shoot to kill."

***

Edgar followed the colonel's aide into the tent and stood blinking in the yellow lamplight. Behind him shadowed the officer of the picket post and a guard. Willa remained outside with another guard.

149

The inside of the tent was furnished with a map-cluttered desk, a folding chair and a steamer trunk. A portly Yankee—the colonel, no doubt—sat on the edge of his cot, rumpled, stubbled and sleep-wrinkled, wrapped in a robe. His ill-humored gaze prowled from Edgar to the captain and back again. The aide took his place beside the colonel.

Edgar had heard all about Yankee prisons, stories of cold hell where he'd rot and starve. Bad enough, but all that talk of guerrillas and hanging worried him even more.

And what about Willa? Would she try to get him into even more trouble by telling them what she was and about his plans for her? Would any of that make any difference to them?

Hell. Presented with a ripe young female, they'd just want to do the same. She knew that, and wouldn't say a word to them. New confidence stiffened his back. He drew himself tall, showing them dignity befitting an officer.

The colonel glowered at him, then said to the captain, "This is Tennessee. What's a Georgia home guard major doing here?"

"Dodds, sir. Major Dodds. He rode into our lines, riding double with a Reb private. Said the private was a deserter." The captain's voice took on an apologetic, cowed tone. "I thought questioning a couple of Wheeler's men might be important enough to disturb you, if you please, sir."

"Where's the private?" the colonel said.

"Waiting outside. I assumed you'd rather see them individually."

The colonel nodded, then turned back to Edgar. "Major Dodds, is it? What do you have to say for yourself, out of place as you are?"

"Sir, I'm really a civilian. I resigned my commission a few days ago. I'm not even in the home guard any longer."

The colonel's frown deepened. "Poppycock! You are way out of your own territory. Why is that? You spying?"

Edgar shifted from one foot to the other. "I had to catch that deserter, sir."

"Are you telling me you took the trouble to cross the state line chasing after a worthless goddamned deserter?" The colonel snorted. "You've got to come up with a better lie than that."

Edgar felt his shoulders droop and pulled them back up. "Personal reasons, sir. He had something that belonged to me, a blooded mare. Unfortunately, he rode it to death."

"Your bad luck. You should have stayed in Georgia. I've a mind to treat you like a goddamned guerilla. Hang you from the nearest branch."

Edgar swallowed, feeling the choke around his neck already. The air cut off, his head light and dizzy, his knees loose and buttery. How could he be in such deep trouble? Just when he thought he was in the clear. He had to relieve himself, but dare not ask to be excused.

He dropped down on one knee, wringing his hands. "Sir, please. Have mercy. I'm not a guerilla. I'll even take your oath of allegiance." He unbuttoned his jacket. "Spare me, and I'll never wear this traitor's uniform again."

The colonel looked down at him like he was a bad smell. "I take it you'll cooperate?"

A reprieve? Edgar took a difficult breath, shucked off the jacket and threw it on the ground. "Anything, sir. Anything at all."

"Tell me everything you know about Wheeler's raiders. And you better be truthful, or it's the noose."

"Sir, I'm just the man you need." Edgar shoved to his feet and leaned close to the colonel, dropping his voice to a confidential whisper. "I know where there's a small detachment of Wheeler's cavalry, in a vulnerable situation, just waiting to be bagged."

"How's that?" The colonel looked suspicious. "And speak up this time."

"They've got the river to their backs, and they can't get across. You can take them." He snapped his fingers. "Easy. Then go to the next one. Gobble them up piecemeal."

"How big a detachment?"

"Only about a company. Two at the most. The main force is strung out along the river." He'd made that last part up, hoping he was close to right.

The aide spoke up. "Colonel, I don't know if we ought to trust him. It might be a trap."

The colonel ignored him and gestured to the map lying open on the desk. "Show me, Major Dodds."

Edgar leaned over the map, sweating, trying to make sense of the markings on it. Guiding them was his only chance to live, and he didn't even know where to start. He found the Tennessee River and traced it with his finger. "Isn't this where we are?"

The aide tapped another spot. "You're way off."

"Right. I just needed to get my bearings, sir." Edgar swallowed again past his dry throat.

The aide turned to the colonel. "He's useless. Can't even read a perishing map."

His throat closing with fear, Edgar stabbed at a point a couple of inches farther east. "I left them about there."

The colonel looked at the aide. "Well?"

The aide squinted down, studying. "I suppose it's possible. Still, there's no telling if they're still there."

"Never mind the map," the colonel said to Edgar. "You're taking my patrol for a look-see."

"But sir, all you have to do is follow the river and you'll run straight into them. You don't need me."

"I want you right there. Any lies, tricks, wrong turns, you're crow meat. Is that clear?"

Edgar started sweating again. "You put me at the head of the Federal column, the Confederates might shoot me down."

"You better pray they're poor shots," the colonel said.

"Sir, you can't use a prisoner of war this way." His voice came out feeble.

"I'll use you any goddamned way I like."

Edgar dropped his head so his chin rested on his chest. "Very well. I'll do whatever you say."

Could he really lead these Yankees straight back to Spencer's camp, no mistakes? He'd sure better try. It seemed easy enough. Like he'd told them, just follow the river.

The colonel said to the aide, "Mason, have all available men and horses ready without further delay. I mean to bag that rebel detachment. That'll make Washington sit up and take notice."

"Sir, do you wish to interview the rebel private now?" the captain said from the tent entrance.

"Of course." The colonel nodded toward Dodds and wrinkled his nose. "And by all means get this sniveling coward out of my tent."

***

Willa watched Edgar duck out of the tent, hating him. He avoided looking at her, as though he knew she'd heard every word through the thin canvas walls. The filthy murderer was willing to betray her friends to save his own skin. If only she could find a way to stop him.

"Hold him here," a Yankee staff officer told Edgar's guard. He turned to Willa's guard. "Now this one goes in for questioning."

The guard shoved her through the tent entrance. Inside, a man her father's age strapped a suspender over his shoulder and buttoned it. He looked at her, scowling.

"You the rebel deserter?"

"I'm Private Will Barber, 6th Georgia Cavalry, sir," she said softly. "I'm no deserter."

He picked up his coat. "That rebel major said you were."

"He's a liar. You can't believe anything he says."

"That so? He says he's going to lead us to a detachment of Wheeler's cavalry so we can bag them."

"I hope he does." She shuttered her eyes, hoping he wouldn't see through her own lie. "You're the ones who'll get bagged."

"I suspect both of you are full of humbug." He fingered the fabric of his coat, studying her face. "Was it Major Dodds that beat you up?"

She nodded.

"No love lost between you two, eh?"

She didn't reply.

"He said it was personal. You stole his mare."

"She was mine. Never was his. Anyway, she broke her leg and I had to shoot her." She said it matter-of-fact and dry-eyed through her grief.

"Is that detachment he's leading us to the same one you came from?"

She nodded. "Only it's not just a detachment. It's the main force you'll be running into."

"How many men?"

"Two thousand." She'd never tell him the two thousand men in General Wheeler's command had straggled over a wide area. "Armed to the teeth and ready to fight."

"I don't believe either one of you." The colonel shrugged on his coat. "I'm going to send both of you with the recon. Whichever one we find out is lying, we hang. While we're at it, I'd just as soon hold a double hanging. It's more efficient that way."

Chapter Eighteen

Willa sat watching the Yankees saddle up and load their weapons. She listened to them brag back and forth about how many of her friends they hoped to kill.

If only she could think of a way to warn the fellows. But here she was in the middle of the Yankee camp, the guards just itching for her to make a sudden move and give them an excuse to shoot her.

Not that she cared much. She was beginning to understand Captain Spencer's apathy about dying. He'd lost too much, and so had she.

Edgar hunched a few feet away from her, hugging his knees, curled up in a frightened ball, his face pale and sweaty. He seemed to have forgotten all about her, as though he was too busy worrying about himself.

He was pitiful. She would have felt sorry for him if she didn't hate him so much. "You scared, Edgar?"

He wouldn't look at her.

She touched her swollen cheek, wishing she could soothe her deeper hurts. "You're mighty brave when you've got a knife to cut somebody's throat. Where's that starch gone?"

"I'm just trying to save us both," he said.

"Ha. Turncoat. You'd betray anybody to save your own precious hide."

He whirled to her, fists ready. She scooted backwards on her bottom. One of the guards lowered his carbine, pointing it at Edgar. "Stop right there," he snapped.

Edgar cringed like a whipped dog, and Willa glared at him, wishing he hadn't stopped. "You should've shot him dead," she told the guard.

The other guard snickered. "Just when it was starting to get interesting. Why'd you stop him, Jack?"

"I wanted to shoot him. But I don't fancy wrecking the colonel's chance at a promotion. Then it'd be my neck."

The colonel's aide hustled up. "Take the prisoners to their mounts," he said. "We're ready to march."

***

Jeff observed his own crumpled body from a little above. He noted the bloody wound in his head, the awkward angle of his neck, piled up against a pine trunk. Yet, he didn't hurt a bit, felt free, superbly aware, even joyous.

Dodds tried to kill him. Did he succeed? Was this death? But he didn't have time to be dead. Willa needed him right now.

He stared at the ruin of himself. This was all wrong. He needed to go back and set things straight. Every fiber of whatever he had turned into cried out, "God, I need a second chance. I can't let him destroy her."

He heard a high-pitched buzzing, tingled all over and felt a rending pain. Suddenly he was lying on the solid ground, staring up at the daylight sky. His whole body ached, his head hurt sharply, and only one eye opened. He raised his hand to the wound and felt sticky clotted blood. His scalp was swollen around the deep slit where the bullet had creased his forehead. He eased his fingers lower, touching clots. Dried blood sealed his right eyelid shut. Thank God the eye felt intact underneath. He wiped the eyelid with his sleeve, rubbing the gore away until he could open the eye partly. He could see through the slit. Good. He had his full vision back. He carefully moved his legs, his shoulders and his head, finding bruises, nothing broken.

Only a graze had knocked him out and set him spinning into that strange dream. That was all, just a dream, no matter how real it seemed. The euphoria was gone now, and he felt broken, sick and weak.

That crack on the head had knocked him out all night long. The sun was already graying the sky. He dug into his pocket and found his watch. Dodds hadn't stopped to finish him off, or even rob him. The rotten bastard was in too big a hurry to find Willa.

Jeff popped the watch open. A little after six. His last recollection was late evening. He'd lost the entire night. Plenty could have happened to Willa in the past hours. He hated to count the possibilities.

He heaved to a sitting position, but dizziness flooded his brain. He shut his eyes and lowered his head until the faint spell cleared. Gathering his strength, he clenched his jaw, pushed to his feet and stood leaning against the tree, panting. Thick blood dribbled into his eye and he brushed it away. His head throbbed but he didn't faint this time.

The trail beside him was cut up with horse tracks, Dodds continuing to chase Willa. He must find her before Dodds did.

But what good could he do, unhorsed and unarmed? He'd never catch up with either one of them that way.

He must get help. He needed weapons, a mount, and reinforcements. He stepped away from the tree, weaving like a drunk, and headed toward camp.

After backtracking for a good half hour, he reckoned he was about to come upon the picket post he passed through the night before. He paused and called out in a low, carrying voice, "Hello! Friend!"

Nobody responded. Strange. Maybe his timing was off. He must not have walked far enough yet. A little way farther, and he knew he wasn't mistaken. He looked down at the well-churned ground and fresh manure where the trooper had sat on his horse all night.

What fool had ordered the picket withdrawn? Worse, what else had changed since he'd left camp?

He hurried to the horse picket, finding no horses, only corn trampled into the mud and more fresh manure. He wasn't going to get remounted and armed here. His men had left without him.

Colonel Crews must have passed down an order to pull out. Quinn would have expedited it in his captain's absence, assuming that he would catch up later, not realizing they'd left him stranded.

***

Willa swept along with the Yankees, whether she liked it or not. Her mount was no smooth-gaited Annie Laurie. A jarring trot was its favorite speed. No wonder they'd given it to her instead of enduring the beast's miserable gait themselves. The blue-coated trooper just ahead of her was holding onto her horse's reins, making sure she wasn't tempted to make any side trips.

She had given herself a headache trying to figure out how to keep the Yankees from finding the Confederate camp. She even told the colonel they were on the wrong track, but he clearly didn't believe her. He seemed to put more trust in Edgar's word. Edgar was riding up next to the colonel, talking to him, cozying up.

She couldn't misdirect the Yankees, and she couldn't escape. That left only one way to warn her friends. She might be throwing away her life like a handful of ashes, but what did she have left to live for anyway?

***

Jeff kicked at the still-smoking campfire residue. What in blazes was he supposed to do now? He came up with only two courses of action. He could go after Edgar and Willa on foot, or he could trail his men. Their path of cut-up earth was easy to read, headed east, away from the river. If he were lucky he would catch them after they stopped for tonight's bivouac.

By then Willa's trail would be colder than ever.

Better not waste any more time. He'd just have to find her any way he could. He turned, retracing his path. Then he heard a yell, off from a distance in the direction he faced. He stopped in mid-step, listening.

It sounded like somebody hollering "Yanks!" Excited, a little high. Wasn't it Willa's voice?

That part must be his imagination. Still, it was a warning, and he'd better take heed.

***

The big Yankee grabbed Willa in a chokehold just as Edgar had done. Again she struggled, but all it got her was a worse strangling on her already bruised throat. Realizing the futility of fighting him, she went limp.

"You shoulda plugged him," a sergeant said.

"Colonel said not to fire until he says to," the big Yankee said.

"Then I'll run him through and be done with it." The sergeant dragged his saber out of the scabbard and drew his arm back, leveling the weapon at her belly. "Cover his mouth so he don't squeal when I stick him."

The guard's solid grip kept her from moving away from the thrust.

"Here comes the colonel," the big Yankee said.

The sergeant paused and looked over his shoulder. He hesitated, lowering the blade.

Willa closed her eyes, shuddering. What would they do if they knew she was a woman? Surely they wouldn't be so quick to harm her then. Of course they would, but not with sabers. She'd rather take the blade. It would be quick and honorable.

The colonel rode up, his aide by his side, his face as red as his fancy saddle blanket. "What was all that commotion?" he raged. "You heard my orders! Silence in the ranks."

The sergeant spoke up. "Sir, this prisoner did all the yelling. Warning his friends." He lifted the saber. "With your permission, I'll silence him for good."

The colonel looked down at Willa, eyes furious. "You cost us our surprise, damn you."

"You would have done the same thing, sir." Her voice came out a whisper.

The colonel lifted his hat and smoothed his oiled hair. Then he whirled to the sergeant. "What's the matter with you? This one's been uncooperative all along. Should have gagged him from the start! See to it immediately." He wheeled his horse and hustled down the line toward the front of the column.

The sergeant sheathed his saber, chuckling. "Guess we get to save him for the hangings after all."

***

Jeff peered out from behind the screen of brush, watching two blue-coated vedettes ride cautiously through the deserted camp. Thank God

157

the warning shouts had given him time enough to go to ground. This would have been a hell of a time to get captured.

The vedettes cast about, looking left and right, then drew rein and consulted in low voices. One of them doubled back and cantered away. Must be going back to the main force to report. The other remained, sitting on his horse, facing Jeff's hiding place.

Jeff waited, hoping the Yankee would go away, needing to slip off before the rest of them arrived and the deserted camp was crawling with bluecoats. Instead, the pestilent fellow pulled a cigar out of his pocket, lit it, and sat puffing while his horse nibbled at the bushes. He gazed around the deserted campsite appraisingly, like he was planning to stake a homestead claim.

The bluecoat kept looking in his direction. *Sit tight, keep low.*

Then it was too late for him to move as the rest of them thundered up. He heard shouts of "Halt!" and pressed flat against the ground, listening.

"Bring up the prisoners."

Prisoners? Jeff raised a trifle to look. Edgar Dodds rode toward the head of the columns, a guard escorting him. His frightened eyes darted about.

Then Jeff spotted Willa trailing him, hands tied, a rag binding her mouth and tied behind her head. Even from where he lay, he saw the welts on her cheek and blood on the gag. The bastards beat her and tied her up, probably because she tried to warn her comrades. For that they were treating her worse than a common criminal.

He gathered to spring, then settled back down. Couldn't do her a bit of good by getting himself shot in a suicidal rush with nothing but his bare hands for fighting. He must figure out a smarter way to save her.

Willa sat straight, head erect, eyes forward, still game as Reynolds' little banty rooster.

That's the girl. Don't let the bastards break you.

He shifted his attention to Dodds and the pompous-looking Yankee officer who was saying to him, "Where are all those rebels you claimed we were going to trap?"

"Sir, I can't help it if they pulled out during the night." Edgar's voice was a scared whine. "They were here a few hours ago, all of them, and that's the God's honest truth. See the smoke? The campfires are still warm."

The colonel looked at an aide, who shrugged. "I hate to admit it, sir, but he's right. They didn't break camp but a few hours ago."

"Then we'll track them," the colonel said. "Send a courier back to headquarters for more men. As many as can be mounted." He smacked his fist into his palm. "By God, we'll hunt them down and exterminate them like rats! Make the political hacks in Washington City sit up and take notice. They'll hear about it all the way back to Peoria."

***

After the last Yankee horse trotted out of sight, Jeff quit his hiding place and jogged in pursuit, following the retrograde movement down a woodland trail, south along the river.

The image of Willa's battered face haunted him. If only she hadn't panicked and fled. If only he hadn't treated her so coldly. If only he'd earned her faith in his ability to protect her. If only . . .

He was a cavalryman, not a foot-racer, and injured besides. His boots were unsuited for running, heels turning on every bit of uneven, hoof-cut ground. Heart and drive weren't enough to make up for the blow to the head he had taken. He lagged farther behind, his lungs bursting and legs straining from the effort, muscle and wind no match for the Yankee horses. The wound reopened and blood clogged his eye. Dizzy, sweating, panting, head throbbing, he stumbled to a walk.

Slowing down was not acceptable. He straightened his spine and forced his aching body back into a shambling jog.

***

A vedette returned to the column and the Yankee colonel called a halt. Willa settled back in the saddle, glad for a rest from her horse's hard trot. Her spine ached and her buttocks were sore. She wanted a drink but couldn't speak up for water, not with this dirty yellow bandanna jammed between her jaws.

She squinted at the high sun signifying late morning. With any luck, her comrades had gone too far and too fast for the Yankees to catch them. On the move, they'd be hard to ambush.

Then the colonel turned from his conference with the vedette and faced his men, standing up in his stirrups. "Men, the rebel scum are just ahead." He drew his saber and lifted it, laying the flat atop his shoulder. "They don't suspect we are on their trail. We have the surprise and can whip them in detail."

He raised the saber over his head, striking a pose meant to be heroic. "Loyal Union men, we have the chance to make a name for ourselves on this day. Let us do our duty and put every last scoundrel to the sword."

His men responded with raised fists and a murmur of agreement, like they expected the Confederates to roll over and show their bellies.

Apparently the colonel wasn't waiting for reinforcements. He had come here with only about fifty men, so he must be counting on catching the fellows napping.

With a little warning given, that wouldn't happen. Then her friends would be up and ready to defend themselves. That Yankee colonel must be a greenhorn if he didn't expect a serious scrap from the Confederate cavalry, prepared or not.

"Sir," Willa's guard said, "What are we to do with these prisoners during the fight?"

"Let them take their risks along with the rest of us. Kill them if they try to escape." The colonel ordered the column forward again, bringing Willa and Edgar along.

She'd better do something in a hurry.

***

Edgar's gut looped into a scared knot. They expected him to ride into the fight with them unarmed, a helpless target.

He glanced at Willa. She was taking it all calmly as far as he could tell, eyes alert, shoulders high. She was a different girl than the one he'd planned to marry. Harder to scare. None of this was turning out right for him.

Could the tricky little tart be up to something? Whatever it was, it was likely to expose him to even more danger. But what harm could she do, tied and gagged? At least the Yankee bastards hadn't bothered to truss him up. Like they knew he wouldn't dare risk giving them any trouble.

***

Willa noticed a tree up ahead, in the middle of the path. Soldiers trotted their horses on one side or the other, and her guard veered to the left. She used her knees to guide her mount to the right.

The rope got hung up around the tree and slid out of the guard's unprepared hold. For the first time, her horse's head was unrestrained. She dug heels and shifted weight, guiding her mount off to the side. Then she kicked him into a quick-starting canter.

A Yankee grabbed for her and missed. Angry shouts of "Halt!" She leaned forward and kept flailing the horse's sides with her heels.

Next they would start shooting at her and ruin their own surprise. She drew her shoulder blades together, anticipating the hard blow of a bullet punching between them.

***

Edgar watched Willa make her run for it, not quite believing she would do something so foolish. The Yankees wouldn't stand for it. His own guard jammed a pistol to his head. "Goddamn you, don't get any ideas."

He shook his head so hard his jowls quivered. "I ain't running. Not me. No, no, no!"

Then one of the Yankees raised his carbine and fired. Willa slumped, then slid out of the saddle and landed in the ditch at the side of the road. Her horse kept going.

Edgar swallowed, staring at the girl where she landed, face in the mud, her hands still tied. Blood welled from her back. She moved, trying to get her legs under her, then sank again.

Edgar wanted to go to her, but the pistol in his face stopped him. The Yankee that had shot her started to dismount, but the colonel rode up, yelling, "Stay in that saddle and keep on marching, damn you! I'll have you bucked and gagged for breaking silence in the ranks!"

The trigger-happy bastard kept his seat, looking crestfallen, and the columns picked up speed again.

Edgar rode by Willa, heaped in the ditch. "You just going to leave him there?" he asked the colonel.

"He's not your concern," the colonel snapped. "Make a move, and you'll be on the ground too."

Given that choice, Edgar shut his mouth and turned away from her.

***

Jeff paused when he heard the single gun shot, listening for more firing.

It didn't come.

He sucked in a ragged breath and kept on going.

***

Edgar couldn't believe the foolishness of the Yankee colonel. Surely the Confederates would be aroused by the gunshot that dropped Willa. Why did the madman insist on leading his men blindly along the road through these thick woods, leading them straight into ambush, straight into disaster?

"This is insane," he told his guard. "They've been warned now, and they'll be waiting for us. They'll kill us all!"
The guard twisted around in the saddle and gave him an ugly grin. "If they don't kill you first, I will."

Edgar helplessly rode with the charge, his horse's lead rope tied to his guard's saddle. He saw the flashes through the trees and heard the crack, crack, crack of carbines and pistols. The high yipping of Rebel yells. A man next to him screamed and rolled out of the saddle, falling beneath the hooves. The colonel screamed "Return fire! Kill the bastards!"

Edgar's guard lifted his revolver and started blazing toward the gun-flashes. Heart pounding, breathing tight, Edgar lay over the neck of his horse to make himself smaller.

Still he was being carried forward, closer to that nest of gunfire. Bullets zipped past—one clipped off his hat, another tugged at his coat-sleeve.

He raised his head and looked toward the ambuscade, but couldn't make out any figures. The Confederates had made prompt use of the warning, hiding themselves Indian-style in the brush, leaving hardly anything visible for the Yankees to shoot at. Damn Willa's stupid escape try. Now, all because of her, he would die along with these Yankee fools.

A riderless horse bumped into his mount, the colonel's gray with the fancy red saddle blanket. Edgar's guard clutched his gut and fell back, crashing into him, smearing him with warm blood, clawing at him like a drowning man and fell away. Edgar clung to the saddle, shouting "Whoa, whoa, whoa." He dragged back on his horse's reins, and the lead horse, now riderless, slowed as well.

He was no longer toward the front, but toward the tail end of the Yankee column. None of the bluecoats seemed to be paying attention to him, too busy trying to stay alive. The smart ones were acting independently, dismounting and seeking cover. He caught a glimpse of the colonel, standing in the middle of the road, one bloody arm swinging useless, the other holding the saber upraised. His face was screwed up in rage as he yelled, "Rally! Rally, you damned cowards!"

Edgar tried to maneuver his horse toward the road's edge, but the guard's horse seemed determined to drag him along with the herd, toward the fighting. He fumbled with the lead rope, but couldn't untie the hard knot. The horses kept on edging the wrong way.

He gave it up, swung his leg around and jumped to the ground. He sprinted to the woods, dived behind the nearest tree, then crawled deeper into the brush and lay flat, shivering, weeping with terror, listening to the shouts and gunfire.

Chapter Nineteen

Jeff hurried toward the sound of fighting. He stayed close to the side of the road, next to the ditch, in case he must slip back into hiding.

The gunfire was loud, not far away. At least he'd kept from falling too far behind.

He spotted a rider coming, so he crossed the ditch and crouched behind a bush, watching. A bluecoat rode into view at a walk, hunched down in the saddle, face contracted with pain. The soldier supported his crippled forearm close to his body, his other hand covering the wound. Blood welled between his fingers.

Jeff let him draw alongside before he sprang from cover. He seized the Yankee's belt from behind and dragged him out of the saddle. The wretch hit the ground hard, letting out a string of swear words. Jeff dropped onto him, pinning his good arm with his knee. He snatched the revolver from the holster, cocked it and pointed at his enemy's head.

The bluecoat gagged out a choked sound. "I give," he whispered. "I give."

"That's right." Jeff snapped. "Give me your horse and your weapons, too." He unbuckled the wounded Yankee's gun belt and girded it around his own waist. Then he walked over to the horse, which had halted in favor of nibbling leaves next to the trail. He caught the reins and led the animal back to his prisoner.

The Yankee rolled onto his side and propped himself up on an elbow, eyes wide with dread. "What are you going to do with me?"

"One side or the other will pick you up in time." Jeff nodded toward the noise of the fight. "Who's getting the better of it?"

"The Rebs were waiting for us." The bluecoat settled back calmer, cradling his broken arm carefully. "We're getting all cut up. Just because they were warned."

"What warning?"

"A prisoner, some young kid, bolted and tried to escape. Brady shot him, all right, but he shouldn't a done it. That let them know we were coming."

Jeff felt the blood drain from his face. "Shot him?"

"Yeah. Damn fool kid is in the ditch up a ways."

"Dead?" Just saying the word felt like a punch in the gut.

"All I know is, he was still laying there when I came back by."

Jeff climbed into the saddle and urged the horse to a gallop. God, don't let him be too late.

***

Slowly Edgar's panic melted away. His breathing came easier and his shivering diminished. Although the fight was still going on he was safe in his hiding place, no bullets whizzing close. Nobody from either side could see him to shoot at him.

All he had to do was sit tight until the Yankees got whipped. He sure had seen that coming. The idiots had been stupid enough to ride into an ambush. Then he would present himself to the Confederates as a rescued prisoner. He would claim credit for causing that warning shot, be accepted as a hero, with no one left alive to tell them any different, except maybe a captured Yankee or two. Who was going to take their word over a Confederate major's?

Unless Willa betrayed him. After the shooting stopped, he'd go back to where she'd fallen. If she were still alive, he would have to decide what to do about her. Damn her, damn the Yankee that shot her, and damn Spencer for trespassing on what was rightfully Edgar's. After all his efforts, the girl had turned out to be nothing but trouble. She'd been nearly uncontrollable since he'd found her playing soldier boy. It infuriated him that she'd let Spencer have what she'd withheld from him. He was beginning to wonder whether he wanted her after all, tainted by coupling with another man. Maybe it would be better if he found her dead. Then she couldn't cause him any trouble telling people about his shooting Spencer and helping the Yankees. He could still take over her land. With her gone, who would object? And if she was still alive, well, that would be easy to fix. He'd just put his poor Willa out of her misery.

***

Jeff spotted her, a bloody gray heap lying face down in the mud. He jumped down, slapped the reins around a sapling and slid into the ditch, landing on his knees beside her.

Her face was pale, her eyes shut. He touched her mud-streaked, abused face. The memory of his dead wife knifed at the wound in his heart. Lord, don't let it happen again.

Her cheek was warm and her breath soft on the back of his hand. Still alive. Thank God for that much.

"Damn them, Willa. What did they do to you?" He loosened the knot on her gag and gently pulled it away from her mouth. She stirred and murmured and her eyes slit open, then closed again.

"Stay with me, Willa." He untied her wrists and let her hands fall free. Then he forced himself to look at the wound in her back.

The bullet hole was high, the ball having passed through the top part of her shoulder, across the blade. Thank God, it must have missed her vitals. The bleeding had stopped, but not before soaking her jacket to the waist. Willa's eyes popped open, and she stared at him wide-eyed, aware. She reached for his hand and held on, the strength of her grip encouraging him. He drew her hand to his mouth and kissed it.

"You're alive," she whispered. "Edgar said you were killed. I knew he was a liar."

He shook his head no, feeling a fresh wave of rage. "Who beat you? The Yankees? It wasn't enough they shot you?"

The muscle over her jaw tensed. "Edgar Dodds."

"That bastard." What else did he do to her? He wasn't sure he wanted to know. Bitterness backed up in his throat. "Where is he? I'm going to kill him, if it's the last thing I do."

A tear squeezed out the corner of her eye, and she shivered all over. He took her into his arms, careful not to disturb her wound, and cradled her to him. Clinging to him, she buried her face in his chest and sobbed quietly while his dark thoughts of vengeance chased each other back and forth in his mind like vicious little animals.

He listened to the continuous crack of guns. The fighting sounded louder, closer. If the shooting worked back this way he and Willa would be exposed. Now that he was rearmed, he could snipe at the Yankees. He wanted to punish them, but the urgent business was to protect Willa. He considered lifting her out of the ditch onto the horse, but his hands trembled from exhaustion and he doubted his strength.

"We need to get you away from the line of fire," he told her. "Can you walk if I help you?"

"I'll try," she whispered.

He left the horse tied, figuring on taking it out of sight after he'd made Willa safe. He carefully lifted the arm on her sound side and hoisted it around his shoulder. He stood, pulling her up with him. White-faced, her lips tight against her teeth, she leaned on him. He felt her effort to support herself upon her own legs and realized he was hardly stronger than she. The act of standing caused him to break out into new sweat. His ears buzzed and his vision narrowed. Ignoring the light-headedness, he climbed with her out of the ditch and staggered deeper into the woods, hauling her along. He started to let her down gently onto the earth when his knees gave way and his vision left him altogether.

***

Pain shot through Willa's shoulder as Captain Spencer collapsed and dropped her. She lay flat until the shock subsided enough to allow her to move, then she elbowed up. She reached to him with her free hand, despite the jolt to her injured shoulder, calling his name. What had gone wrong with him? He lay crumpled on his side, eyes closed. Although he didn't respond, she felt his chest rise and fall under her hand. He was breathing and alive. The bloody gash on his head marked Edgar's failed attempt on his life. She didn't see any other injuries and prayed there were none.

She touched his face, rejoicing in his presence.

The shock of seeing him gave her a new surge of vitality, after hearing Edgar crow over his supposed death. He was alive! Alive and with her, even though he had fallen into a dead faint. Certainly he'd gotten hurt trying to protect her, the same as he would have done for any of his troopers. She couldn't think clearly enough to guess how he had miraculously found her. Later, she could ask him. At the same time, she would take back the ugly thing she had said to him.

Riders thundered by as though Old Scratch was after them. The horse her captain had arrived on strained at the tether, but it held and the riders didn't stop. She couldn't see anything else from where she lay, so the soldiers probably couldn't see the two of them hiding behind the bushes either. Were they bluecoats on the run or had her friends gotten the worst of it? Broken as she was, it was still up to her to defend them both. She dragged the revolver out of his holster and set it down next to her. The effort cost her dearly. So weak and tired, she feared she would faint as well. Then she had no choice but to rest next to Captain Spencer on the damp earth and wait for him to awaken.

***

Edgar hid a long time before he dared move. From the sound of the fight the Confederates had driven the surviving Yankees back where they came from.

Was it safe to come out yet? He stuck his head up a little, then a little more. He stood up and picked his way among trees and underbrush toward the road.

The road was clear, except for a dead Yankee lying on his back right in front of him, dark blood still oozing from his chest, mouth and eyes sagging open. Edgar hurried around the body into the middle of the trail, looking in every direction. The path was narrow here, heavily wooded, and he couldn't see past a stone's throw. Much to his relief, the shooting had diminished. The fighting must be about over.

He returned to the corpse and confiscated the gun belt and saber. The dead man had a wallet in his pocket, which contained letters and a

166

few greenbacks. Edgar ignored the letters but stuffed the money into his own pocket. A quick search of the corpse brought him no other valuables. He found the pistol a few feet away, smelling of burnt powder, empty, shot out.

He hastily reloaded the pistol with the ammunition attached to the gun belt. Now he felt safer.

Suddenly he heard jingling hardware, approaching from the direction of the dying fight. He slipped behind a tree just before the riders arrived.

Bluecoats. He slumped lower, trying to make himself invisible.

Then he spotted two gray-clad men following the four Yankees closely, revolvers ready, guarding their batch of prisoners. He didn't see any sign of Willa.

He stepped away from the tree, hands held high. "Ho, friends," he called out.

"Halt!" the corporal in charge snapped. The little party shuffled to a stop, wary eyes and drawn weapons turning to Edgar.

"Who's in charge of this unit?" Edgar asked.

"Highest ranker on the field is Sergeant Quinn," the corporal said. "Captain Spencer's away."

"Sir. Call me sir, corporal." Edgar drew himself up and pointed to the star on his collar. "I am a major, and you shall address me as one. I didn't see a salute."

Without waiting to see if the corporal followed through, Edgar drew his pistol and strode up to one of the prisoners, the strapping rascal who had throttled Willa. "Dismount, you. I'm taking that horse. You can walk to prison for all I care, you damned Yankee."

The prisoner offered no argument, and Edgar swung up into the saddle. He turned the horse so he faced the insolent corporal, who was staring at him, I'll-be-damned all over his face.

"I'm in charge of this detail now, corporal."

"Sir?" The corporal cleared his throat. "Meaning no disrespect, where in the hell did you come from?"

"I was a prisoner, but now I'm free." Edgar puffed out his chest. "And, I might add, you owe whatever success you just now enjoyed to the reckless shot the Yankees took at me. Now I'm taking charge."

Armed, mounted and in power, Edgar figured things were starting to improve. "What's the status? Is the area secure?"

"Seems to be, sir." The noncom swiveled in the saddle and pointed behind him with his chin. "I believe we've about run them off."

"They may call up reinforcements and counterattack." Edgar said. "Get the troop ready to pull out. Carry on."

Edgar left them to their own devices and hustled up the road, scanning the ditches for any sign of Willa. In his situation, anyone would have done what he had done. That Yankee colonel was going to murder him if he didn't cooperate. But if Willa could talk she would spin quite a tale, he was sure of it.

When Willa bolted and got shot for her impulsiveness, he was so shaken he'd hardly noticed where she fell. It hadn't seemed to matter much at the time, because he was convinced he'd be next. Now that it did matter, he tried to recall anything distinctive about the path, but one tree looked like the next and the ditch was just a red trench in the dirt.

Until he spotted a horse tethered to one of those nondescript trees dead ahead. The fully equipped cavalry horse lifted its head and looked at him, ears pricked. It carried a U S brand on its deep bay flank. One of the Yankee horses, staked here with no rider in sight.

Now edgy, Edgar looked around but didn't see anybody. The brush was thick enough to hide anybody who didn't want to be seen. He drew his revolver and walked his mount closer. This might have been the same place Willa went down, but where was she? He didn't see her in the road nor in the ditch.

Edgar dismounted and tied his own horse. He walked over to the bay and examined it, but found no clue as to why it was tethered and waiting. If the rider had been shot off, the animal would be running loose. Someone left it here deliberately, planning to return.

Edgar studied the ditch and noticed it was trampled and disturbed in one area. Was that where Willa lay? Did she leave on her own power, or did somebody drag her body out?

Whoever it was didn't ride away on the horse. Maybe Willa was still about. Upon closer examination he saw deep boot prints leading out of the ditch. Comforted by the weight of his revolver in his hand, he warily followed the tracks.

***

Despite Willa's determination not to faint, she passed in and out of consciousness. During a moment of awareness she heard a horse walk up and stop. Then someone dismounted and tramped about, but she couldn't see a thing through the bushes. She tried to raise herself for a better look, but pain, weakness and the threat of another faint forced her back down. She clutched the heavy revolver and waited. She didn't dare call out. The rider might be a friend coming to help, or he might be a Yankee. Worse yet, he could be Edgar.

She glanced over at Captain Spencer, who was still unconscious but stirring, and might awaken soon. It couldn't be soon enough for her. The intruder was coming on at a stealthy walk, right towards her, as though following their trail. When he hove into view above the underbrush, she recognized Edgar. She should have shot him down, but the gun wavered in her grip, her vision blurred and she dared not shoot and miss. She

168

cried out, "Stop!" It sounded like a whimper in her throat. She tried to keep the revolver aimed at him and saw that he held a pistol as well, pointed at her. He swung it toward Captain Spencer, then back to her, shock and confusion on his mean face. "Stop!" she warned again. "No closer!"

"What's he doing here?" Edgar growled. "I saw him get killed miles back. Is he dead now?"

"Leave us alone." Her heartbeats pounded in her ears. If she dropped the gun both of them would be helpless and Edgar could do whatever he pleased. "Go away and leave us alone."

Edgar's expression went sly and he aimed at the unconscious man. "I ought to finish off your boyfriend. He don't look so healthy as it is. But I might not. Do whatever I tell you, and I'll think about letting him go."

"Don't," she heard Captain Spencer whisper, not so unconscious after all. "He's lying." She didn't dare look at him because she would have to take her eyes off Edgar, but she felt a rush of hope knowing he was awake and with her.

Edgar glared at him, pure hatred. "She ought to know if she tries to shoot me, I'll still get you."

"She'll shoot to kill, and you'll still be dead," Captain Spencer told him. "Take her advice and walk away."

"We could still be a team, Willa." Edgar said, shifting his features to give her what he must have thought was a pleasant smile. "You and me, and the captain gets to live." His mouth twisted. "Or I'll kill you both here and now."

Before she could think of an answer, she caught a quick movement from the corner of her eye and heard Captain Spencer yell, "Shoot him!" Reacting as much from reflex as thought, she squeezed the trigger and the gun jumped in her hand. At the same time, she saw fire spit from Edgar's gun and heard the thunderclaps of the two pistols discharging as one. The captain sprang to his feet and leaped toward Edgar, forcing Willa to hold her fire so she wouldn't hit him by accident. He piled into her tormenter low, cutting him down at the knees and toppling the bigger man. The pistol flew from Edgar's grip. Captain Spencer broke away from Edgar and pounced on the weapon, rising to his knees, holding it in both hands pointed straight at Edgar, who was still lying on his side where he fell.

"You got him." Captain Spencer seemed to relax a bit.

Willa felt tears start again. "Is he dead?" Her voice came out shaky. She stared at Edgar, expecting him to rise up and overcome them. Instead, her tormenter answered by moving his head and locking his eyes onto hers. He let out a gurgle and a groan. Blood spread over his chest and dribbled from his slack mouth.

She watched her captain sway to his feet, approach him warily and stand over him, revolver ready. "Dying," he told her.

Relief washed through her. Maybe she ought to feel bad about killing a man, but she'd done it before to save her beloved, and she'd done it again. God save her, she would do it a third time if she had to. "He was going to kill us both," she said.

Captain Spencer nodded, not taking his eyes off Edgar.

She forced herself up onto her elbows, hardly noticing the tears running down her own cheeks. "Edgar, you killed Pa, didn't you?"

The dying man just stared at her, struggling for breath, eyes glazing over. "He objected to what you'd done, and you killed him for it. He finally tried to do the right thing by me and it got him killed." She could have sworn she saw feeble assent in Edgar's dimming eyes before the last shuddering breath escaped from his blood-drenched chest. He jerked once, as though his vicious soul gave the ruined body a final kick before it departed.

***

Jeff stared at the dead man. "It's over. He can't ever hurt you any more." It had taken every drop of will in him to gather the strength to leap violently to one side and rush Edgar. Thank God it had worked, spoiling Edgar's aim while Willa's traced true as though directed by Providence. He let his gun hand fall and drooped, bracing himself against a tree with his free hand.

Willa. He whirled, rushing back to where she lay struggling to sit up. He sank to his knees next to her, still sick and light-headed.

He slipped his arm around her back. Her gaze fixed on his face. Her worried look convinced him she was lucid.

"He didn't shoot you, did he?" she said.

He shook his head. "You did fine. That bastard talked some nonsense about you two being a team, but he didn't reckon on such teamwork from us."

She buried her tear-streaked face in his chest, shivering, and he drew her to him. He checked her back wound, found no fresh blood, thank God. He took out his handkerchief and wiped the damp clay from her bruised face, his heart full of tenderness.

"Give me a minute to collect myself, and I'll get you out of here," he he said softly. He must gather himself emotionally as well as physically. He feared he would break down, overcome by reaction. "Everything is going to be all right."

She managed a smile. In his opinion she was beautiful, even blood-streaked and battered. How was it he justified turning away from her? He could hardly recall his rationale. Whatever reason he had given

170

himself, he now realized it was nothing but blindness and stupidity. He deserved the back of her hand, and could hardly hope for better.

Jeff heard a single horse chuffing up the trail and jerked his head up, listening. He glanced at Willa and raised a silencing finger to his lips. Revolver ready, he pushed himself up, peering through the brush. Recognition brought a flood of relief. "Corporal Harris! Over here," he called out.

The noncom reined in, mouth slack with surprise. "Jefferson! We damn near gave up on you."

"Will's here, too," Jeff said. "He's wounded and we've got to move him."

Harris approached them and took in the full scene. He stared at Edgar's body. "What happened to Major Whatshisname?"

"There was a skirmish, you know," Jeff told him. "Guess he took a stray bullet."

"Sure he did." Harris shrugged. "That must be what happened." Minutes later, with Harris' help, Jeff sat astride the captured horse, holding Willa in front of him. He held the horse to a slow walk, the least jarring gait.

"I didn't trust that major," Harris told him. "After I got those prisoners under guard I went hunting. Simpson told me what he pulled at that horse picket last night. Nobody saw you or Will after that. Quinn and I figured he was bad business, but didn't know what to do about it. What did that so-called major have against you?"

"It's a long story. Yankees took them both prisoner. It appeared the major saw fit to guide them to our camp. Why did you break camp in the middle of the night?"

"Colonel Crews ordered us to pull out," Harris said. "I guess that was a good thing."

Jeff slouched in the saddle. He shifted Willa's weight, centering her better, resting his numb arm. Soon he could let down, but not until after he saw to his troop. "I see you whipped them pretty fair. Did we have many losses?"

Harris shook his head again. "Don't think so, but I haven't taken roll call yet. They came in real noisy. We took cover and set up an ambush."

"What you heard was Private Barber getting shot. He tried to escape just as they were coming up on you. Planned it that way, I guess." He dropped his gaze down to Willa. "Hear that, soldier? Your sacrifice worked. You spoiled their surprise."

Her eyes were shut, but he figured she could understand what he said.

"We would've whipped them even without the warning," Harris said. "But our noses would've been bloodied."

"I overheard that the Yankee colonel had already sent for reinforcements," Jeff told him. He ignored the odd look Harris gave him. "Might be another attack coming, and we don't want to be scattered all up and down the road when they hit. Tell Sergeant Quinn to prepare to pull out. Then find us drinking water. There must be a farmhouse nearby that can provide wagons for our wounded."

He glanced down at the valiant woman in his arms. "This one deserves the best care we can offer," he said.

Chapter Twenty

Willa curled up on the horse blanket that served as a pallet, waiting for the troop to get under way. The worst of her fears had subsided, leaving her feeling safe and protected even in her new vulnerability. Although Captain Spencer was busy attending his command duties, he was close by. Hurt as he was, he refused to let the bullet wound in his head be an excuse to take it easy.

Willa sat in the canvas-covered wagon, staring unfocused at the stack of weapons the men had captured. Her friends had survived the fight, capturing much-needed equipment and horses. Captain Spencer told her they gave her the credit for warning them. She didn't bother to tell him that her actions were less from bravery than from despair, and their admiration didn't make getting shot hurt any less. The pain, centered high in her shoulder, spread outward and racked her whole body. She wanted to blank it out by falling asleep, but the stabbing and throbbing wouldn't allow it.

No longer did she fear that the men would turn on her if they found out she was a girl. She now knew that Captain Spencer wouldn't let anybody touch her. He had personally washed and dressed her wound, settled her in this wagon, then left her alone to rest after assuring her she was going to survive. He knew about things like that, so it must be true no matter how wretched she felt.

She recalled her grief and rage when Edgar had told her Captain Spencer was dead, and the surge of joy when she'd seen his living face. Even if she couldn't make him love her, he was the best friend she had left, and she trusted him. He wouldn't let anything else bad happen to her.

He'd told her he was going to send her to his home as soon as he was able, and she'd stay there long enough to recover. It sounded like heaven, and she didn't even have to die to enjoy it. But what then? She couldn't live on his charity forever. And it was a sure bet her own farm wouldn't support a rabbit, in the state Edgar had left it.

What was it Edgar said—could it really be Captain Spencer had spoken of marrying her? What sort of nonsense was that? Surely it was just another one of Edgar's lies. It wasn't worth a moment's thought.

***

Jeff ordered the troop into motion, then he rode down the column to check on Willa. He'd hated leaving her alone, but he'd needed to get them all out of harm's way before he let down. And let down he must for the weariness was catching up with him again and the fainting spells threatened to drop him from the saddle. He'd ride in the wagon with Willa, see to her comfort and try to mend the wrongness between them, provided she would tolerate him. His stiff-necked denial of his own feelings had made a mess of things. He couldn't blame her if she really did hate him.

Then he'd taken a stand, saying he would marry her, though telling himself it was only to protect her from Dodds. He'd lied to himself about that, too. Now he could own up to the truth, admit he loved her and wanted her for himself. Most likely he'd ruined things between them completely by acting like an imbecile. If she wouldn't have him, it was his own fault.

He met the wagon, returning the driver's salute. Then he moved around to the rear so he could look inside the open back. Huddled on the floor, Willa gave him her broken-lipped smile, not at all grudging or hateful. Seeing her hurt like that stabbed him in the gut. If only he'd done a better job of protecting her. She wouldn't have been so scared of Edgar if she'd known how far he would have gone to keep the bastard away from her. She wouldn't have fled, and she wouldn't have gotten hurt. If only she would give him a chance to win back her faith.

***

Willa watched Captain Spencer climb into the wagon. He settled beside her, resting his back against the wall of the wagon-bed. His lined, haggard face and the bloodstained bandanna tied around his head gave him a disreputable appearance, but he was still the handsomest man she'd ever seen. She figured she was an even sorrier mess, bunged up and half dead.

His softening gaze fixed on her, his face etched with concern. Or maybe pity.

The driver clicked up the team and the wagon jolted to a start. She held her lips together, trying not to show the pain.

"How are you doing?" Captain Spencer asked.

"Tolerable." She wasn't about to admit how bad she hurt. "You all right?"

He nodded. "I've got just the thing for what ails you." He pulled a flask out of his pocket and uncorked it. "Found it in that Yankee colonel's saddlebag."

She wrinkled her nose and shook her head. "I don't drink that stuff."

"It'll help the pain."

"That's for sure. Pa never felt any pain, far as I could tell." Her words sounded bitter, harder than she intended.

Frowning, he examined the flask as though seeing it for the first time. Then he re-stopped it and slipped it back into his pocket. "All right, I respect that you don't want any whiskey. We don't have any laudanum on hand. What else can I do for you?"

"I'm fine, Captain Spencer." Just then a hard bump sent a stab of pain through her back, and she bit the inside of her cheek to keep from crying out.

He laid his hand on her arm, and the sympathetic touch seemed to take away some of the hurt. Even if pity was all he could give her, she would settle for that.

"Never mind me, Captain Spencer." She turned her face away, hoping he didn't see the tears in her eyes. "I'm just fine. You can go about your business."

"You are my only business, right now. I'm staying." He paused. "But only if you want me to."

"I would like that," she whispered. "Truly I would."

He sat unmoving for a time, a quiet vigil. Nothing strained, just the two of them jolting along in the hard-riding wagon. She pillowed her head on his arm, listening to his breathing, loving the sound of it. She drew courage from his presence and the warmth of his hand on hers. She was unspeakably grateful that Edgar mistook him for dead and failed to finish him.

After an interval he spoke. "I'm going to mention you in my report, referring to the fact that you almost got yourself killed by spoiling the surprise attack."

"I couldn't let those Yankees slaughter my friends," she told him.

"Private Barber's wound, valiantly incurred in the line of duty, ended his loyal service. That's how I'm going to state it. You'll get an honorable discharge."

Her cheeks warmed. Even he couldn't deny her achievements, keeping up with the men, performing as well as any of them.

"Edgar brought them," she said. "He would've been glad to get you all killed to save his own neck."

"He can't do any more damage now. I wish I'd shot him on sight."

She felt a fresh surge of relief, knowing Edgar couldn't get to her and brutalize her ever again. What he'd done to her was bad enough, but what he'd planned to do was unbearable.

"Captain Langston knows about you," Captain Spencer continued, "And I doubt he's kept such an interesting piece of gossip to himself. But none of the officers will want this affair to turn into a public scandal. I'm sure we can get you discharged without any official fuss."

Then her secret was out, or would be soon, but Captain Spencer was of a mind to shield her. It mattered less anyway, now that she didn't have to hide from Edgar any more. She turned her face to look at him. "I'm sorry I said I hated you. It was a lie. I was mad, that's all."

The corners of his mouth tensed into a frown. "Even so, you have every right to feel that way. I was a perfect jackass."

She managed a smile. "You sure were."

"I deserved that." Tenderly he stroked a lock of hair away from her forehead. His touch smoothed her tension and the pain receded a trifle more.

"I told Dodds I was going to marry you," he said. "Even sent for the chaplain."

So Edgar didn't lie about that. "You would have gone that far to protect me? That was... gallant."

"I'll send for that chaplain again. Right now, if you say the word."

"That's good of you, but Edgar's gone," she told him. "I don't need that kind of help any more."

"Protecting you was only part of it." He paused as though ordering his thoughts. "After Jeannie died I didn't want to ever love anybody again. Didn't want to leave myself open to another chance of loss. And somehow I thought it would be disloyal to her memory, even though she probably wouldn't have agreed. I knew it was happening, that I cared for you, and I tried to deny it because I didn't want to let myself get hurt again. I hurt you instead, and I'm sorry. It was supremely selfish of me to behave that way."

"I thought it was because you found me lacking," she whispered.

He groaned. "Great God! No! Never!"

She didn't believe him. He was just being kind. What could he possibly see in her?
"Willa, listen. I want you to marry me. Not because of Edgar, but because of you. I love you, sweetheart."
Sweetheart.

She swallowed past the tightness in her throat, hardly believing what he said. She stared at him, searching for any touch of insincerity in his expression. His gaze met hers, and what she saw there made her want to cry again, this time for happiness. "I've always loved you," she told him. "From the very first time I saw you."

"Then marry me."

He hadn't even asked whether Edgar had ruined her for him. Surely he'd thought of that, but he hadn't made it a condition, and she loved him all the more for it. "I want you to know something. Edgar wanted to have his way with me." She lifted her hand to her hurt lip. "He beat me, but he never got to do anything else to me. You're the only man I've ever been with."

Captain Spencer brushed her cheek with his fingertips and said softly, "For both our sakes I'm glad. I feared he forced you even though you fought him like a wildcat."

"If he had, would you still be asking me to marry you?" she asked.

"It wouldn't have made any difference." He bent down and kissed her lightly on her bruised lips.

She grinned so hard it hurt. "Aren't you afraid the men will see us?"

He smiled and shrugged. "They'll have to know sooner or later. Can't wait to see their faces when we tell them. Let's get this settled before you take another notion to run away. Say yes and I'll send for the chaplain."

It was still too much to grasp. "Captain Spencer! Do you really mean it? Or did that head wound addle your brains?"

He laughed out loud and his lips brushed hers again, softly, careful of her hurts. "More than life itself. And I wish you would start calling me Jeff. A wife ought to call her husband by his given name."

Epilogue

September, 1865

The buggy crested a little hill and Willa sat tall, looking out over her land, the first time she'd laid eyes on it for a whole year. Travel through Georgia was finally safe enough to chance. The Yankee brand of law and order was better than the anarchy that had ruled during the first months of uneasy peace. Jeff had brought along a loaded revolver just in case anybody was still bushwhacking for a living.

To Willa's surprise, ripe white cotton bloomed in the same field where last year's corn crop was plundered. Her kitchen garden spot flourished as though she'd planted the beans, tomatoes, corn and squash herself. Someone had pieced together a tiny cabin a little way from the heap of ashes that marked her old house.

"Somebody has squatted on our land," Jeff said.

Willa nodded. "Squatted and laid eggs, it appears. I didn't expect to see anything but pokeweed and dog fennel. I wonder who—"

"I hope I don't have to evict them." He frowned. "Times are hard, the whole country's gone up in flames. Whoever it is probably doesn't have anywhere else to go."

She dropped her hand on his denim-clad thigh and stroked it, loving his compassion. "Whoever they are they've been earning their keep. We can't maintain the land ourselves anyhow, not with us living in Augusta. You said yourself we needed tenants."

"Let's see about this." Jeff drove the buggy closer and stopped the livery horse just short of the new cabin.

Willa stepped down from the buggy without waiting for a helping hand. The traveling skirt swirled around her legs, a sensation she was getting used to, even liking.

Jeff caught her arm, shaking his head, exasperated. "Next time let me help you get down. If you fell, in your condition . . ."

"Drat. Did it again." She laughed out loud. "I'm still learning how to act. Until I met Mother Spencer and your sisters, nobody taught me hardly anything about being a lady. Anyway, my balance is still pretty good."

"Just be careful, sweetheart." He reached his hand all the way around her thickened waist and gave her a gentle squeeze. She felt a flutter in her belly, as though the baby responded to its father's touch, or its mother's happiness.

All those months of healing from her wounds and waiting, learning not to feel like a mere guest after he'd left her in his astonished mother's care at their Augusta home. Coping with corsets, hoop skirts and feminine underthings, fearing Jeff would not live through the war's final death-throes.

Then that bright, warm day when he finally rode into the yard after the North Carolina surrender. Hungry, thin, exhausted, so dirty he'd refused to enter the house until he'd stripped off his rotting uniform, buried it, and soaked himself in a tub. But he was whole. And nothing need ever separate them again.

She squinted at the two dark figures walking toward them from the cotton field, then laughed out loud, delighted. "Josh!"

"Friend of yours?" Jeff asked.

"It's Josh! He came back! I told you about him. He took a beating because he wouldn't tell Edgar Dodds on me. He ran away from Edgar too. And look! He's got a woman with him."

Josh said something to the woman, who hesitated, then hung back, watching, while he came on forward.

***

Jeff took Willa's arm and strode forward. "Let's meet him halfway." He studied the black man, noting the set features and the impassive expression. Josh stopped in front of him, standing firm, as though determined to block his way. The young black man scraped off his hat, showed grudging respect. He glanced at Willa, his eyes widening in recognition. Disappointment, too? Then he dropped his gaze diffidently. "Master. Miz Willa," he mumbled.

"Josh, this is my husband, Mr. Spencer," Willa said.

Jeff extended a hand to Josh, who seemed surprised by the civil gesture. He grasped Josh's hand firmly, then let go. Josh let his arm drop to his side, nodding his head. "Master Spencer." His features went impassive again.

"You the people responsible for all that planting?" Jeff swept his hand toward the cotton field. "And you built the cabin?"

Josh nodded, a glint in his eyes betraying defiance. "Yessuh. The Yankees say freedmen can take over abandoned land. I took a notion to

179

claim part of Major Dodds' place, but it wasn't big enough for that Gabe rascal and me both. Nobody knew where Miz Willa gone, and that land was just goin' beggin'.'" He glanced at her again, then stared at the ground. "Now she be here in the very flesh." He shifted his hat in his hands. "Good seein' you back, Miz Willa."

"She didn't abandon the land," Jeff said. "I just got through paying the taxes."

Josh squared his shoulders as though bracing against a heavy burden. "Yessuh. I be tellin' Lucy to start packin' her things."

Jeff knew the backbreaking hours that these people put into that red earth, the hopes and dreams planted there along with the seed and sweat. Still, Josh wasn't whining or begging, but manfully accepting the hard justice he expected. Kicking him off would serve no purpose, and confiscating the cotton would be sheer robbery. "Don't see any reason you can't stay and harvest that fine-looking crop. Set aside enough of the profit to pay us back for your tenancy, and we'll be square."

A different light appeared in Josh's eyes. Hope. He nodded vigorously. "I can do that. Thank you, sah," he whispered.

***

Willa wandered over to the family cemetery while the men talked sharecropping. She left it to Jeff to work out an agreement that would be fair to everyone.

She stopped in front of Bobby's grave marker, feeling a deep peace, the sense of homecoming she'd been longing for.

"I'm all right now, Bobby," she said. "Ma, you hear me too?" She glanced at the marker next to Bobby's. "I've got a new family. You'd like Jeff, both of you. And Bobby, you're going to have a nephew, or maybe a niece. If it's a boy, we're naming him after you. Jeff already said we could."

The wind picked up. Was that her brother's presence she felt? She cupped her hand over her belly. "Things were hard for a while, with Edgar after me. I didn't mind joining the army, even if it was hard and even if I did get shot. But Jeff was wonderful once he sorted out his feelings about me. He sent me to his house, but he was gone till after the war finished. He's back now for good, and I'm the happiest girl in the world."

She smiled and hugged herself. "Now look at me! People even think I'm pretty! Of course, we don't tell just anybody I used to be a soldier. Kind of a family secret. The men in our troop knew in the end, but they're family, too. And I found out I needn't be afraid of them."

Then she walked past Bobby's and her mother's grave, over to Pa's. The rude wooden marker was still in place, most likely due to Josh's care. "Look, Pa, I'm finally the kind of woman you wanted. It suits me fine.

"Edgar killed you, didn't he, Pa? Even if he never did own up to it. I tried to figure out why, and the only thing I can come up with, must be you changed your mind about letting him marry me after you found out what he tried to do."

She wiped a cleansing tear from underneath her eye. "Maybe you weren't the best pa, but I guess you tried to do right by me in the end."

***

Jeff shook hands with Josh again, sealing their agreement. He was satisfied to claim enough crops to pay the taxes and hold the land for the future. In the meantime, the newly freed Negroes would harvest the fruits of their hard work.

He excused himself and strode toward his wife. Jeff grinned, savoring the improvement in her appearance since she had decided to take up womanhood again. Her short amber hair had grown to shoulder length, framing her face. The gaunt lines of cheek and chin filled and softened into their promised womanliness. The skirt and blouse revealed the curves she'd managed to hide in a man's clothes. Some of those curves were thickening, another sign of blossoming fertility.

He'd gotten her pregnant right after coming home from the war, not what he'd planned, after what happened to his first wife and child.

It would be different this time, he told himself. Nothing could drag him away from Willa's side when she needed him. Not ever again.

Lord, it was liberating to let himself love again and to be loved in return. He felt truly alive, sharing his renewed passion for life with this extraordinary woman.

She was so engrossed in paying homage to her family's graves that she didn't even look around. He took off his hat to pay his respect and stood behind her, waiting.

Finally aware of him, Willa turned and gave him a warm smile. "It's all right," she said. "Josh and his wife will take care of this land better than I was ever able to without any help from Pa."

"We'll get a better marker for your father," Jeff said. "An engraved stone that will last."

Willa gazed over her shoulder at the little cemetery plot. "I'll always miss them, but you've given me back so much of what I lost."

He embraced her, gathering her in his arms, feeling her tight belly against him. His wife, his child. "It works both way, sweetheart. You've given my very soul back to me."

She melted against him, then lifted her head and looked at the expanse of her childhood home. "I'm satisfied everything is all right here," Willa said. "Now I'm ready to go back to Augusta. It will be good to get home again."

About the Author:

Lydia Hawke is a native Floridian born in St. Augustine who has always been avidly interested in Southern history. She graduated Summa Cum Laude with a BA in Communications from the University of North Florida.

Lydia's fiction work has finaled in several literary contests and she has published nonfiction articles in Civil War magazines and other publications. She is a correspondent for Civil War Courier and Clay Today Newspaper.

She breeds and shows champion Collies and competes with them in agility. She owns an electrical contracting business with her husband Larry, and they have one married daughter.

Lydia enjoys horseback riding, scuba diving, training her dogs, and is a licensed amateur radio operator. An officer in the Greater Orange Park Dog Club, the Greater Jacksonville Collie Club, she is also a member of the Collie Club of America, Pals and Paws Dog Agility Club, Orange Park Amateur Radio Club, Orange Park Community Theatre, First Coast Romance Writers, EPIC— Electronic Published Authors Connection and Romance Writers of America.

You can find out more about Lydia at www.lydiahawke.us.

She would love to hear from you at lydiafilzen@comcast.net.

FIRETRAIL
Now available

Blake Winberry ran his gaze from the woman's pale, strained face to the weapon in her hand, hoping to God his meddling was not a huge blunder.

He had acted on his best instincts honed by his experience at war. He had expected thieves to cut and run at the first sign of a threat, but this man had chosen to stand and resist. Had he misinterpreted the situation, which had seemed clear cut before? Did he kill the woman's husband, for God's sake?

"People warned me of bushwhackers in the area, and it appeared... I saw them abusing you, and I..." Blake nodded toward the dead man, fearing to ask. "Did you know him?"

"Not until he accosted me." She let out a shaky breath. "I believe you saved my life. Thank you, Captain—"

Relief flooded through him. "Winberry. Blake Winberry."

"I'm Mrs. Rogers." She swayed on her feet.

"Better sit down." He stepped forward to take her arm but she backed up a step. She moved without his assistance to a grassy spot at the road's shoulder, where she folded to the ground.

"Why don't you give me that revolver?" he asked. "You might set it off by accident."

She stared at him and gripped it even tighter, if that was possible. "What if they come back?"

"Mind where you point it. Please."

The trace of a smile crossed her face. Now that he had the situation in hand, he took notice that she was the loveliest vagabond he had ever seen. Her heavy dark hair, undone, framed her upturned face. Her plain widow's weeds did not entirely obscure her fine figure. "Are you afraid I will shoot you, Captain Winberry?" she asked.

"Should I be?"

SILENT WITNESS
Coming soon

Mark's glance leveled on the front of the Halloween-colored tee shirt, Kevin, the groomer at her boarding kennel, had given her as a joke. What a day to snatch up this horrid shirt that read, "Vicious, Power-hungry Bitch" emblazoned across the bust line. The jacket would have concealed it, but oh, no. She just had to pick that moment to take it off.

He raised one of his neat dark eyebrows. "That's not how I remember you, Dani."

"Uh, I'm not really vicious. I only bite when provoked." She gave him a wry smile. "Don't risk it."

"Good to know you haven't changed after all. I liked you the way you were." His gaze returned to her face, and he appeared to suppress a smile. *Such a bashful guy. Yeah. Right.*

Printed in the United States
42158LVS00007B/154-186